HAROLD Q. MASUR is the author of twelve Scott Jordan mysteries and countless short stories. Like his hero, he began as a practicing lawyer, but started writing short stories just before World War II. In 1952 he won the Storyteller's Award from the Mutual Broadcasting System for achievement in the field of popular fiction, and his books have been translated into French, German, Italian, Spanish, and Japanese. At Bennett Cerf's suggestion, the Pentagon brought him to Washington to participate in war games with the general staff. Mr. Masur has served as a president of the Mystery Writers of America (1973–1974) and, beginning in 1974, as council to the organization. *Bury Me Deep* is the first of his Scott Jordan novels.

OTTO PENZLER, series editor of Quill Mysterious Classics, owns The Mysterious Bookshop in New York City. He is the publisher of The Mysterious Press and *The Armchair Detective* magazine. Mr. Penzler co-authored, with Chris Steinbrunner, the *Encyclopedia of Mystery and Detection*, for which he received the Edgar Allan Poe Award from the Mystery Writers of America.

BURY ME DEEP

BURY ME DEEP

HAROLD Q. MASUR

A Quill Mysterious Classic

Series Editor:
OTTO PENZLER

Quill
New York • 1984

Library of Congress Catalog Card Number: 84-60105

ISBN: 0-688-03154-4

Printed in the United States of America

First Morrow Edition

1 2 3 4 5 6 7 8 9 10

BOOK DESIGN BY RICHARD ORIOLO

· 1 ·

It was a cold Thursday evening when I first saw the blonde.
I had just come home from Penn Station and I opened the
door to my apartment and found her there. She was curled
up on my sofa, listening to my radio, and sipping her own
brandy. At least I assumed it was her own because I dislike
brandy and never buy it.

I stood there, rooted. Her costume had me floored. She
was wearing black panties and a black bra and that was all.
She sat with one long leg folded comfortably under her and
she smiled at me. I had never seen her before in my life,
and I stood just inside the foyer, gaping at her in slack-
jawed astonishment and still hanging onto my Gladstone
bag, completely unaware at the moment of its fifty-pound
load.

She was a leggy, bosomy number, flamboyantly con-
structed, with bright jonquil-yellow hair and a pearly skin
that contrasted startlingly against the black underthings. She
looked up at me, and the alcoholic glassiness in her eyes
didn't keep her from making them warm and cordial. Women
have looked at me like that before, but never in church.

"Jordan?" she asked, almost in a whisper.

I nodded, still dazed.

"You're a little late," she said.

I put my bag down and came warily into the room. "On the contrary," I said. "I'm early."

Which I was. I had arrived at Penn Station aboard the *Sun Queen* only twenty minutes ago, about a week ahead of schedule. One week of Miami glutted me. The frenzied pace, the flash gambling, the top-heavy women bulging out of undersized bathing suits and flashing with oversized diamonds—all had begun to pall. The quest for pleasure down there is almost grim in its intensity, and so on a sudden impulse I had left the Magic City without a word to anyone in New York.

And here, completely at home, and about as embarrassed as a trapeze artist, was this undraped blonde.

I moved toward her. I saw her clothes piled carelessly on a leather hassock in the corner. A moss-green dress and coat, and on top of that a matching hat with a Nile-green feather angled rakishly out of its brim.

I stood in front of her, flat-footed, ransacking my memory and finding it as blank as the expression on a blind man's face. Even at that range my nostrils clogged. The odor of jasmine wrestled with alcohol fumes and pulled a draw. Her eyes were half closed and her mouth was half smiling. The almost vacant expression on her face told me that she was already drunk or fast getting there.

"Park yourself," she said, fingering the sofa at her side with claret-tipped fingers.

The inner man whispered, *Don't be a chump, Jordan. Go ahead. Never look a gift horse in the mouth.* But the lawyer in me was suspicious. *Easy, old boy, step lightly. All that glitters is not gold. The effluvium here reaches all the way to Denmark.* I gave it some fast thought. She was not in the wrong apartment, for she knew and had spoken my name. Nor had she been planted here by some friend with a bright sense of humor, because no one could possibly have anticipated my arrival.

I shook my head. "Look, sister," I said. "This is all very nice. I'm deeply complimented. You have a swell body, and some other time I'd be glad to compare birthmarks. But I've just traveled thirteen hundred miles and I'm tired, gritty, and in no mood for games. I need a bath and a ten-hour sleep. In short, I need privacy. And I want to know how you got into this place and what the gag is.''

"Gag?" The smile wavered, but hung on. She looked confused. She struggled up, peering at me. She said, "Aw, you're kidding.''

"I am in a pig's neck," I told her.

The smile lost its grip. She looked as if she had just discovered half a worm in an apple she'd been munching.

"Say," she demanded sharply, "isn't this the Drummond?"

"It is.''

"Apartment 7E?"

"Right.''

"You're Jordan?"

"According to my birth certificate I am.''

She squirmed comfortably back and was smiling again. "Then take it easy and leave everything to li'l Verna. Verna knows just what to do.''

"And just what," I asked, "is Verna going to do?"

"You'll see," she snickered. "Any minute now. Come here and relax.''

She worried me. She picked up the glass and took a sip of brandy. I scowled down at her.

"Put your clothes on," I said.

"Oh, no." She shook her head. "You don't understand. It's much better with my clothes off because——''

The doorbell rang and cut her short. She reacted as if someone had suddenly electrified the sofa. Her chin jumped up, her teeth clicked, her face came alive, and she bounced off the sofa like a bolt of silk uncoiling on a dry-goods counter. She came surging into me, knocking me back and down into a club chair two paces behind me. Then she twisted and tumbled adroitly into my lap. Her head tilted sideways, her arms went around my neck. "Pay no attention," she whispered hoarsely. And then she was kissing me. Hard. I sat there, stunned, not moving, rigid as a department-store dummy.

She was good, very good, an expert technician, even without my co-operation, and I felt myself sliding into a mildly pleasant tail spin.

Then, quite abruptly, we had company.

A man stepped softly into the room and stopped dead. It was George, the colored doorman, and he was armed with the two bottles of ginger ale I had asked him to bring me on the way up. His bottom lip hung pendulously and he gave us a quick double take. Then his glance met mine and his right eye winked. He placed the bottles quietly on the floor and backed out.

That was that. But the blonde was still in my lap and still glued to my mouth and I'd had more than enough. I got a hand under her chin and pried her loose.

"Who was it?" she muttered.

"My conscience," I said. "Get up."

Her fingers clung to my neck. Her eyes were flecked and her mouth, shapeless now, the lacquer veneer smeared, reached up hungrily. "Gimme," she breathed.

"Jesus," I said, screwing my head away. "You're a pip."

Suddenly and overpoweringly I wanted her away from me. I wanted her out of my apartment and out of my life, beautiful body, brandy fumes, libido, and all.

Her face was crumpled. "Don't you like me?" she asked in a sullen voice.

"You're all right," I said. "It's the perfume."

I broke her grip on my neck and stood up. She went sliding out of my lap and down my legs and thumped solidly against the broadloom carpet. She sat there, propped against her hands, blinking up at me stupidly, her face blank. A glimmer of doubt crept up inside her and peeked out from behind the glazed eyes. Her lips quivered.

She said inanely, "You're crazy. My perfume comes from Paris. Ten dollars an ounce. It's called 'Disaster.' "

"I don't care if it's called 'Catastrophe,' " I said. "Get up and get dressed."

Her mouth broke open. She was bewildered. "Hey! I don't get this."

"Then I'll make it plain," I said. I picked up her clothes and tossed them at her feet. "Put these on and start talking. If you're not dressed in five minutes I'll throw you out into the hall naked. I mean it. I don't even care what the neighbors think. I'm in an ugly mood and it's getting worse. Now hop on it."

Her eyes widened. They seemed to hang out like green-gage plums. She looked at me, incredulous. Suddenly her face changed, twisted like a cruller, grew hard and tight, and for a moment it held a touch of pure jungle. She began to curse, harshly and with competence.

I bent down and jerked her off the floor. I gripped her shoulders and shook her. Not gently. The yellow hair tumbled loosely around her face. Her teeth were chattering.

"Save the language," I growled, "for somebody who appreciates it. Answer me, what are you doing here?"

"Ouch!" she whimpered. "You're hurting me."

Under the lip rouge, her mouth was bloodless. Her tongue licked out. I let her go and stepped back. She swayed unsteadily.

"I wanna drink," she muttered.

"Talk first."

Her mouth tightened stubbornly.

I sighed. "All right. Go ahead. Just one. And you can take the bottle with you."

She lurched for the bottle and poured herself a drink that would float the Staten Island ferry. She put it down in one long pull like a shot of medicine. It was something to see.

I said, "I hope it loosens your tongue, sweetheart. Now, let's hear your story."

She slopped down the glass and bent forward. "I'll talk," she squawked. "I'll talk plenty. Nobody can pull a stunt like this on Verna and get away with it. Somebody's going to pay. You wait and see."

"I'm waiting," I said. "Let's hear it."

Her face was stiff, and strain pinched her nostrils. She

took a long, shivering breath and trembled the full length of her body. There was a moist shine on her temples. A yellowish pallor drew at her cheeks, and she teetered back, clutching at the sofa for support.

She said, "You know who sent me . . . because . . . because . . ." The words broke off and trailed into a ragged whisper that became harsh breathing.

She stood in front of me, trying to speak. Her mouth was working crookedly but no sounds came out. I saw the greenish irises of her eyes rise up very slowly and vanish under the heavy lids, leaving nothing but two balls of mottled white.

Then she slid around in a half circle, very deliberately, exactly as if she hadn't a bone or a muscle in her body, and she oozed liquidly to the floor like a lump of melting wax.

• 2 •

She lay there with her hair splayed out and glistening brightly under the lamp, snoring like a pipe fitter with asthma.

Her eyes were squeezed tightly shut. Her breathing was harsh and irregular. She was drunker than two sailors on a week-end leave.

I muttered an oath and looked down at her, considering the alternatives. I could permit her to sleep it off and then question her some more. Or I could carry her to the street, dump her into a cab, and let the driver take her home. The first got a fast rejection. She seemed good for about fifteen hours. The second called for an investigation.

I emptied the contents of her purse onto the sofa. It contained surprisingly little. A latchkey, a *flacon* of perfume which I handled with great care. If it broke I might have to move out of the building. A hundred-dollar bill, crisp and brand-new. Some assorted currency, and that was about all. No address. No marks of identification. Nothing except thirty-three cents in a small change purse and a piece of stiff white bond paper, bearing my name and address written in ink: Scott Jordan, Apt. 7E, The Drummond.

That was the lot.

Everything went back into the purse except the piece of paper. I frowned down at her. Without an address I could not send her home. But one thing was certain. She was not going to stay here. I could put her into a cab and let the driver roll her around the park until she got sober. The crisp air might hasten the job.

Getting her dressed was a tough assignment. She was no help at all. I propped her up against a leg of the sofa and lifted her arms and managed to get the dress down over her head. She was as limp as a caterpillar playing dead. Twice she slipped forward into my arms and I caught a double lungful of jasmine and alcohol. I finally got her dress zippered down the side.

I slid the moss-green coat over her shoulders and fastened the top button under her chin, capelike. I located a pair of slippers, wedged them on her bare feet—no stockings were visible—and was all set to go.

Her breathing worried me. It was difficult and labored. She kept sucking air in through her mouth raggedly. Her face was very wet, the rouge caked in the hollows under her cheekbones. I didn't like it, but alcohol often had that reaction.

I crossed to the bedroom for a swift survey. Conditions were normal. Bed tight, drawers shut, everything under control. I didn't really know what I was looking for, but with a blonde in the living room there might be a brunette or an albino in the bedroom. There wasn't.

I went down to the street and flagged a cab and stood on the running board, directing it to the service entrance.

"What's up?" asked the driver.

He was a sharp-jawed specimen with pointed ears that kept his tweed cap from falling into his eyes. I folded a ten-dollar bill and hung it under his nose. He sniffed at it like a bird dog.

"Want this?" I asked.

He gave me a lopsided grin. "Who do you want killed?"

"Got any scruples?"

"Yeah. Like an alley cat."

"Good. I have a lady friend upstairs who has exceeded her alcoholic capacity."

"Stuccoed?"

"Completely. I'm going to bring her down and put her in your cab. I want you to drive her around until she's sober."

"And then?"

"Dump her at the nearest subway. Run her to Los Angeles. Take her home. Anything she wants."

He eyed me carefully. "What if she sleeps all night?"

"The air will bring her around. I'm not asking for a refund if she wakes up in ten minutes."

He sucked speculatively on a tooth. "Where does this dame live?"

I shrugged. "I don't know. You get another sawbuck if you take her home and bring me the address. The name is Jordan."

He was still cagey. "What if she lives up in White Plains?"

"The lady is well heeled. She can pay for anything she gets. The ten dollars is a bonus."

He cut the ignition and ducked his chin.

"You got a deal, Jack. Haul her down."

I left him. When I got back to the apartment I found the blonde sprawled out on the floor again. Her mouth was open, showing the edge of her teeth. She was paler than before, her face drained and a little pasty. I cocked the feathered hat on her head. I put her purse into my pocket and was just hoisting her off the floor when the doorbell rang again.

I let her go and she slipped to the floor like a bundle of laundry. I stood motionless, my back rigid, head cocked to one side, ears tuned. Nobody knew I was home and I was not expecting visitors. For a moment there was silence, then the vibrator rattled against the bell with the urgency of a fire alarm.

A determined finger was pushing the buzzer. I let it ring. After a while it stopped and as the silence lengthened I let out a slow breath.

I was beginning to smile when the bell suddenly got convulsions again.

Under my breath I muttered oaths in Arabic, Hindu, and Chinese, all mementos of the last war. I stopped as the bell's shrill insistence faded. It did not ring again.

Instead a heavy fist hammered against the door. I bent forward a little, the back of my neck bristling like a cat's back. I inhaled sharply and strode out of the living room and into the foyer and grabbed the knob and yanked the door open.

Three people stood in the corridor.

Two men and a girl. The man who was knocking had his fist upraised for another try and almost fell into the room. Glasses, thicker than the palm of your hand, were braced against the bridge of a clublike nose. It was enormous. It was a shapeless monstrosity pasted against his face by a make-up man with a macabre sense of humor. A black derby stood on his skull. A long-skirted trench coat flapped against his knees.

At his side was a nervous young man with an unhealthy face wearing a blank grin. I turned and the girl held my gaze like a rivet. She stared at me the same way. She had a slender, graceful figure, hair like burnished copper, animated blue eyes. Her mouth was slightly parted as she watched me. For a moment I felt weak. It was as though I had met her a long time ago. Her smooth brow was puckering into a frown.

The man with the derby spoke in a sharp nasal voice. "Okay, step aside."

Behind the heavy lenses his eyes were hugely magnified. His bony hand fell on my shoulder.

I said softly, "Easy. Where do you think you're going?"

"Inside."

I shook my head. "Think again."

He seemed surprised. His eyes glinted. "What is this—
a rib?"

"Hardly. What do you want?"

"I want in," he said.

"Not today, brother."

The girl's eyes widened. She gave her head a puzzled
toss. "That—that's not Bob," she said.

The man scowled at her. Black brows contracted over his
nose as he turned on me with a deepening frown. His eyes
were the kind of eyes that had peered through many keyholes
and seen many things, few of them pleasant. He emptied
his lungs and said, "Let's have a look anyway."

I planted my feet solidly. "Get your paw off me," I said.

He took the hand off my shoulder and put it against my
chest. He should not have done it. No one will ever make
me like being shoved around.

"You're asking for it," I said.

I gave it to him. It was a very fine shot. His nose made
a target that was hard to miss. I put my weight behind it.
I shot my fist out like an engine piston and his head jolted
back with an ugly wrench. He bounced against the opposite
wall. The black derby fell and rolled along the carpet. For
a brief moment nothing happened and then, suddenly, his
nose squirted like a crushed tomato.

The young man was white. The blemishes on his face
stood out like a rash. He moved sideways, his chin drawn
in, gulping.

The girl did not scream. She goggled at me. There was
an eager look in her eyes, as if she was excited. Her full
bottom lip was caught between her teeth.

The tall man produced a large gray handkerchief. He
dammed up his nose with it and threw his head back, letting
the flood congeal. After a moment he lowered his chin and
his eyes focused on me sharply.

"Still anxious to come in?" I asked pleasantly.

"Somebody's going to pay for this," he said.

"Not me," I told him. "A man's home is his castle and he can defend it unto death. I can quote precedents."

Between narrowed lids his eyes were venomous. He stooped, retrieved the derby, and stalked toward the elevator. The young man trotted after him. The girl held her ground. I smiled at her. She smiled back and it was like getting hit with a battery of klieg lamps.

"You're Scott Jordan," she said.

"My birth certificate says so. But I was beginning to doubt it."

"May I come in?"

I thought of the blonde lying on the floor. She saw my hesitation and added, "I'd like very much to talk with you."

I shook my head. "Some other time."

She looked at me oddly. "Where . . . we were looking for Bob Cambreau."

"He's not here. When I find him I'm going to kill him."

"I—I don't understand."

"I'll explain it all at his funeral."

The elevator door clanged open. The operator called out, "Going down."

She gave me a fleeting, somewhat tentative smile, whirled abruptly, and sprinted for the car. She moved like a fawn at the crack of a rifle.

I closed the door and stood still, thinking about Bob Cambreau with mixed emotions. Originally, I had made the trip south to handle the sale of his Palm Beach shack, a small item of fifteen rooms, landscaped gardens, swimming pool, and tennis court. Bob was a client of mine, a good one—for several reasons. We had gone to school together, he had more money than he could spend, and he was always getting into trouble. On leaving New York I had given him a key to my apartment. I remembered that now and it almost explained the presence of the blonde.

I went into the living room and frowned down at her. Bob was a notorious chaser. A *bon vivant*. An easy spender. Perhaps she was one of his more amorous escapades. He

collected women like some men collect stamps or jade. They
were his hobby. He was married, but had recently separated
from his wife.

The blonde was still out, her breathing still ragged and
uneven. I picked her up and carried her through the hall to
the freight elevator. The old man who ran it swung open
the door and admitted us with an unblinking, dead-pan
expression. Another drunk would not ruin the building's
reputation. It was not his building anyway.

In the street the cab driver hopped out and held the door
open. I deposited the blonde on the rear seat. She tumbled
sideways, her skirt climbing high over a length of round
white thigh. The cab driver whistled.

"Boy! That's what I call a bun!"

He speared the ten-dollar bill almost before I had it out
of my pocket.

"You know what to do," I said.

"Don't worry, Jack. I always know what to do."

"Keep the windows closed," I said. "She's sweating.
Don't give her too much breeze."

"Sure." He was in a hurry to be off. I tossed her purse
into her lap. The engine throbbed. The cab spurted away
from the curb. I watched it turn the corner out of my sight
and then I exhaled a long sigh of relief.

Back in the apartment I mixed a highball, brought it to
the bathroom, ran a tubful of steaming water, stripped,
climbed in, closed my eyes, and relaxed. A calm, comforting lethargy stole through me like a footpad at night. I
reached for the glass and had a drink. I was beginning to
feel almost normal. Drowsiness hung onto my eyelids like
a pair of sandbags. I saw the copper-haired girl in a mist
and wondered if she too was one of Bob Cambreau's girl
friends. I did not like the thought.

The doorbell got hysterical again.

I struggled up with a groan. I did not want much. Only
peace and quiet. I decided to stuff a wad of paper in the
bell before retiring. The bell rang itself out.

I was relaxing again when I heard a noise. The creaking

of footsteps. *Inside the apartment*. I sat erect. Someone was moving around.

I yelled, "Hey!"

No answer. The steps advanced with a heavy tread through the bedroom. I had my eyes glued to the bathroom door when he materialized. He was a solid, dark man. He had a square, hard-muscled face, dark as polished cordovan, shining black hair over a flat skull. He wore the blue-gray uniform of a merchant marine officer. He was barrel thick through the chest and the seams of his coat looked ready to burst apart. He squinted at me along eyes that were gray, cold, and steady.

I sat in the tub and stared back at him.

"Where is she?" he asked out of clenched jaws.

"Who?"

A vein throbbed in a blue diagonal across his temple. "Cute, eh? Listen, Jordan. I want Verna. I'm going to find her if I have to tear this place apart. Where is she?"

I shook my head. "Listen, I don't have the vaguest notion who you are, or what you're talking about. And what's more, I don't give a damn. This is my apartment and I want you to get the hell out of it."

He flexed his right hand and made it into a fist and looked at it. It was a good hand for uprooting trees if you couldn't find an ax. His voice rumbled. "She was here. I saw her come up."

"Nobody's here," I said angrily. "I was alone—till you walked in."

His eyes met mine solidly. They were chilled. He backed up into the bedroom. I heard him moving around, searching. After a moment he reappeared and spread pylon-thick legs in the doorway. He gave me a bleak, hard stare.

"She's gone now," he said. "But she was here. I can smell her perfume. Here's a tip, Jordan. Stay away from her. If I ever catch you putting your hands on Verna I'll kill you."

With that he turned and was gone. The building seemed to shudder as he slammed the door.

I was now as sore as an open wound. Looked at from any angle it was crazy. A guy I don't know from Adam barges in and threatens to kill me if I touch a strange girl I never want to see.

I got up and toweled briskly and padded out to the door and found it off the latch. I closed and locked it. Then I wadded some paper against the bell. I opened the windows wide and flushed out the smell of jasmine.

I went to bed. I started to read a mystery story by an aged English lady that opened at a garden party in a country vicarage and had all the vigorous action of an exhausted turtle. Experience had long proved it a better sedative than phenobarbital.

On page three I was fast asleep.

I was dreaming. I dreamed that I was running after an undraped blonde and that a man in a gray-blue uniform was trying to stop me. He had a hand on my shoulder and was dragging me back.

· 3 ·

I awakened. Consciousness crept back reluctantly. There *was* a hand on my shoulder. It was a hard hand and it kept shaking me.

A voice from far away said, "He must be alive. He's too warm to be dead."

I don't think I had been sleeping for more than two hours. I struggled up. My head felt thick, my eyes grated, and my muscles numb and wooden. My tongue was swollen and tasted like a piece of dry flannel.

"Wassamatter?" I mumbled in a furry voice.

A lean face with dark, brooding eyes swam vaguely into focus. I didn't know it then but I was going to get to know that face very well.

"Jordan?" the face asked.

"Yeah." I blinked at him.

"Okay, boy, get up. Get outa bed." There was no compromising with that tone.

I swung my feet to the floor and held my head and groaned. I was completely bushed. I felt terrible. I felt worse than if I'd had no sleep at all. Then I looked up and saw two other men in the room. One of them had rusty hair and cold eyes and about as much expression in his face as you'll find in a bag of walnuts. He wasn't wearing a uniform but everything about him said cop. Beside him stood the old man who ran the freight elevator.

Looking at him, the lean-faced man said, jerking a thumb at me, "This the bird?"

The old man ducked his head. "Yes, sir. That's him, all right. I guess his name is Jordan. I don't know tenants by their names, but he's the one who brung the lady down in my car. He was carrying her and I figured she was drunk. She musta been. She was breathin' like she was. I didn't say nuthin'. It wasn't none of my business. I just run the car and——"

"What did she look like?"

"Yaller hair. You never saw hair so yaller. Nice lookin' too. She hadn't oughta drunk so much."

I was wide awake now.

"Hey!" I said. "What is this? What's going on?"

The lean-faced man flashed a leather folder with a badge pinned to it. "Lieutenant John Nola," he said quietly. "Homicide Bureau."

"Homicide!"

"Take it easy, boy. Don't blow off. We got a lot to talk about."

A cold vacuum sucked at the pit of my stomach.

"Talk?" I said. "About what?"

He didn't answer me. He turned to the rusty-haired dick and said, "Get that hackie in here, Wienick."

Wienick stepped out and Lieutenant Nola stood there, watching me speculatively. There was intelligence in his dark eyes. The set of his jaw was determined, but not ag-

gressive or arrogant. Wienick came back into the bedroom.
The knife-faced taxi driver was with him.

He was jittery. His fingers were pulling nervously at his
collar. His ferrety eyes spotted me and he jabbed out a
finger, quivering with anger.

"That's him!" he bleated. "That's the sonovabitch who
dumped the broad on me. He said she was drunk. He said
to run her around until she got sober. But she didn't. She
never got sober. When I turned to look at her, there she
was on the floor of the cab—stone dead."

I jumped up. For a moment I couldn't talk. My throat
was constricted. I guess I had almost been expecting it, but
now it jarred me. My lungs emptied and I stared at him.

"You!" he yelped. "Dumping a dead broad in my cab
and giving me a lousy ten bucks to get rid of her."

I swallowed. "How much did you want—fifteen?" And
I wasn't trying to be funny. I just couldn't think of anything
to say.

He chopped jerkily at the air with his hand. "You see,
he admits it. He knew she was going to conk out. The dirty
sonova——"

"Okay," Nola cut in. "Take him out, Wienick."

Wienick steered him forcibly from the room.

I looked at the lieutenant. "I don't get it. Is she really
dead?"

"They don't come any deader." His eyes were unwavering.

"But how—when——"

"You don't know?" he asked, eying me obliquely.

I spread my hands. "How should I know? She was alive
when I took her down to the cab. I figured she was drunk.
What killed her?"

"Poison. Probably in the liquor she swallowed. We're
getting a post-mortem on her tonight. What had she been
drinking?"

"Brandy," I said.

"This it?" He pulled a bottle out of his pocket.

I nodded slowly. "I guess so."

"Yours?"

"No. I don't like brandy and never buy it."

He looked skeptical. "How did it get here?"

"I don't know. She must have brought it herself."

Wienick came back into the room and stood watching me with his hands in his pockets.

Nola asked, "What was her name?"

"Verna," I told him.

"Verna what?"

"I don't know. I never saw her before in my life. It sounds crazy as hell, I know, but I can't help it. I just got home from a business trip this evening and there she was—sitting in my living room with that bottle of brandy. She had made herself at home. I swear I don't know who she was or how she got in."

Wienick snorted.

I glared at him. "How about her purse?"

Nola shook his head. "Nothing there. So you found her here. What happened?"

"She had been drinking," I said. "She folded on me. She passed out before I had a chance to question her."

"So you took her downstairs and dumped her into a taxi."

"Sure. I didn't want her here. I figured she'd sober up and tell the driver where to take her."

Nola turned. "Get the doorman, Wienick."

The plain-clothes dick went to the door and came back a moment later with George. George looked unhappy. He stood there, swallowing hard, his face glistening with moisture.

Nola said, "You remember what you told us, George?"

"Yes, suh."

"Tell it again."

George ran a tongue around the rim of his mouth. "Well, suh, when Mistuh Jordan here got outa the cab with his bag he ask me to get him some ginger ale. I brought some from the drugstore like he said, but when I rung the bell nobody answered, so I think maybe he's in the bathroom and I tries the door and it was open. I just come right on in." He stopped.

"What did you see?" Nola prodded.

George flicked me with harried eyes. "I'm powerful sorry, Mistuh Jordan," he said.

I shrugged. "That's all right, George."

"What did you see?" repeated Nola.

"Mistuh Jordan was sittin' in a chair with this girl, the blonde girl, the one they said is daid, and she was sittin' in his lap."

"What were they doing, George?"

He swallowed hugely. "They was kissin', suh."

Wienick tilted his head. "I got to hand it to you, buddy. Pretty good for a guy who never saw the dame before in his life. Christ, I'd like to see what would happen if you knew her for a week!" His lip curled. "That's what I call a fatal charm. One look and they're in your lap. Two looks and they're dead."

Nola nodded. "Okay, Jordan. Get dressed. We're taking you downtown."

I looked at him blankly. "You don't think I had anything to do——"

"Just get your clothes on, son."

I dressed automatically, trying to think, but it was no use. My brain seemed to be sloshing around loosely, as if it wasn't properly anchored to my skull.

We filed into the living room. Nola paused and his keen eyes swept over the furniture. Then he got down on his knees and looked under the furniture. He reached under the sofa and when he straightened, a cloth glove dangled from his fingers. It was a lilac-colored woman's glove.

"This hers?" he asked.

"I guess so," I said. "I never saw it before."

Wienick made a disgusted noise. We went down to the street. A squad car with a uniformed cop behind the wheel was waiting at the curb. I sat in the rear between Nola and Wienick. Casual-like, no handcuffs. But I didn't feel casual. I was as nervous as a canary in a swinging cage. My mind was spinning. I was thinking, What is this? What's happening? Me, a lawyer, about to be charged with a murder I did not commit of a girl I didn't even know.

The streets flicked by. A signal light winked red, but the cop sent his siren into a shriek that parted two cars and we careened through them against the traffic tide. He was good.

I leaned back and closed my eyes. I was thinking about a girl. A girl with bright yellow hair, hard, a bit gaudy perhaps, but alive and breathing. A girl addicted to brandy and too much make-up. A girl who doused herself with too much perfume called "Disaster."

What a name for a perfume!

• 4 •

Inspector Elmo Boyce was a heavy-jowled, thick-necked man with a horsehide complexion. He sat behind his battered desk in the drafty old building on Centre Street and eyed me with the suspicious eyes of a man who has dealt with the seamy aspects of a great city for more years than he likes to remember. I had just finished telling him my story. He snorted skeptically.

"Right out of Andersen's *Fairy Tales*. I'd get indigestion swallowing a yarn like that."

"It's true," I said doggedly. "Every word of it."

Lieutenant John Nola was sitting in a hard straight chair, tilted back against the wall, a cigarette hanging from the corner of his mouth, his eyes squinted against the upward curl of smoke.

Boyce said, "You could have wired her that you were coming home and she was there, waiting for you."

"I could have. But I didn't. You'd have a hell of a time proving it. The fact is, I came home a week ahead of time and nobody was expecting me."

"What made you cut your vacation short?"

"I didn't like Miami."

"Why?"

"It's a long story. For one thing I don't like sand in my trunks."

His chin thrust out. "Sense of humor, too."

I said, "Look, Inspector, don't get the idea I'm a smart aleck. There are some questions a man can't answer without sounding silly."

He massaged his jaw. "You heard the doorman's story?"

"I did."

"And you admit the girl was in your lap?"

"Yes."

"Yet you insist you hardly knew her."

"I didn't know her at all."

He said with exasperation, "But she started kissing you."

"That's right. I know it sounds screwy. It is screwy."

"And to prove you were a man with a man's normal instincts, you got a hammer lock on this girl you didn't know and started kissing her right back."

I shook my head. "Not at all."

Nola's chair settled solidly on all four legs. He looked at me hard. "Are you saying the doorman lied?"

"Not lied," I said. "Just mistaken."

"How?"

"It's simple," I said. "You know how inaccurate the testimony of an eyewitness can be. No two people ever see an accident in the same way. How often will you find witnesses giving the same description of a holdup man? George simply told you what he thought he saw. Actually he saw a woman in my lap and he thought *we* were making love. Because that is what two people in our position are supposed to be doing. So that is the way he told it. But love is a reciprocal enterprise, it needs two performers. The fact is, I was not kissing the girl, but trying to break loose."

Boyce sighed irritably. "The guy talks like a lawyer."

Nola glanced at him. "He is. I thought you knew." He tapped ash off his cigarette. "Before the war Jordan was a postal inspector, studied law at night. Got admitted to the

bar a couple of years before he enlisted.'' Nola saw my
surprise and added dryly, ''We learn things fast around here.
For example, you were in North Africa, India, China; one
of Donovon's bright lads in the cloak-and-dagger
department.''

Boyce looked disgusted. ''That's fine. That's just dandy.
Our number one suspect turns out to be a lawyer, a smart
young mouthpiece who knows all the answers. He knows
about the fallibility of witnesses and what they see or what
they don't see but think they see.''

I felt myself getting warm under the collar. I leaned forward.

''What the hell do you want?'' I demanded tightly. ''You
want me to tell you that I knew the girl, that we were living
together in sin, that I got sick of her perfume and killed
her. That I poisoned her in my own apartment and dumped
her into a cab downstairs where everybody and his uncle
could identify me. Do you imagine I'd think for a single
instant I could get away with that kind of stuff? Give me
credit for a little brains, Inspector. Maybe I'm not the smart-
est guy in the world, but if I was making this story up, I
could certainly do a lot better than that. Only the story I
told you happens to be the truth.''

Nola said mildly. ''Okay, boy, don't fly off.'' He gave
me a long, level stare. ''All right, suppose we believe your
story up to that point. There's something that's harder to
swallow. Her clothes. According to the doorman she was
dressed only in her underwear.''

''Precisely,'' snapped Boyce. ''Why would a strange girl
be in your apartment, half naked?''

''Maybe you can tell me,'' I said. ''I'm damned if I can
explain it. She was undressed when I came home. Why
would I ask her to take off her clothes?''

He leered. ''You really want me to tell you?''

Nola sighed. ''I never find girls waiting for me like that
in my room.''

''You got to surprise them,'' advised Boyce elaborately.
''You got to come home unexpectedly.''

''Very funny,'' I said. ''Ha, ha.''

Nola held up his cigarette and inspected it. "What did you take out of her purse?"

I looked at him. His eyes met mine through narrowed lids. I didn't say anything. He was a very smart apple and he would smell a lie from way off.

"Come now," he said coaxingly, "you wouldn't ask us to believe that you never fished through her purse while she was stretched out to learn her identity."

I nodded. "All right. I did go through her purse. But the only thing I removed was a piece of paper with my name and address on it."

"Ah, and what else did you find?"

"A latchkey, a *flacon* of perfume, a hundred-dollar bill, and some odd cash."

Nola sat up. His jaw hardened. "A hundred-dollar bill? Are you sure?"

"Positive."

"Wienick!" he growled sharply. It was the first time I'd heard him raise his voice. The muscles were bunched along the corners of his suddenly grim mouth. Wienick's blunt face came through the door. "Pick up that cabby," Nola snapped. "And don't be too gentle." Wienick disappeared. Nola sat there, rubbing his knuckles.

He shook his head morosely. "Goddam ghoul! Stealing from a dead girl."

I looked at him, surprised. A homicide dick, a man who had seen every conceivable kind of murder, with enough feeling still left in him to be outraged by the simple act of larceny. A cop with sensibilities. At the moment we stood on opposite sides of the fence, but there was something about this man that I liked.

"How about her clothes?" I asked. "Laundry or dry-cleaning marks—anything to give you a lead?"

He shook his head dourly. "Everything was brand-new. Every stitch. All bought in big department stores. You'd never get those clerks to make an identification."

"Somebody," I said, "is bound to miss her and show up at the morgue."

"We can't wait for that," Boyce growled. "Clues in a murder case freeze up too fast. Things grow cold. Memories are short."

"People don't just happen," I said. "She must have some relatives."

Nola shook his head. "Do you know how many stiffs we plant in potter's field each year? How many we give away to medical schools? Bodies no one ever claims. No family, no friends, no nothing. You might think they grew out of the ground like potatoes."

The phone rang and Boyce picked it up. He spoke his name and listened awhile. Then he hung up and his eyes settled steadily on mine.

"Where did you get the brandy?"

"For the tenth time," I said wearily, "I never saw it before. I hate brandy. It makes me sick. I never buy it."

Nola glanced at him. "The lab?"

"Yeah," said Boyce. "There was enough chloral hydrate in it to knock off a regiment of Cossacks."

"Chloral hydrate," Nola mused half to himself. "Knock-out drops. Commonly known as a Mickey Finn."

"Deadly stuff, eh?"

"Very. Unless carefully administered. An overdose will put you away for the good long sleep."

Boyce flung his head back and gazed at the ceiling. "Oh, this is a pip!" he growled. "The guy comes home and finds an undressed girl in his apartment. He doesn't know her. He never saw her before. She is swilling brandy laced with a lethal poison. She jumps into his lap and makes love to him. But he'll have none of it. He chases her off. He is not a guy who gets familiar with strange ladies. This is the story he tells and we can take it or leave it."

His huge palm made a sharp report against his forehead. "Three more years before I can retire," he said. "Three long, hard years, if I keep my sanity. Nola, ask him some questions."

Nola rose slowly and wandered over to the window. He peered into the street. After a while he turned. His dark

eyes were brooding and distant. "The brandy was bought
in Heron's. We found a piece of their wrapping paper. I
have a man working on it." He shrugged resignedly. "Probably won't do any good. Enough liquor goes out of Heron's
every day to burst the dikes in Holland." He plucked a
shred of tobacco from his lip and looked at me. "Let's shoot
it from another angle. Perhaps the girl was waiting for somebody else."

I nodded. "No doubt. Right after Verna passed out, my
bell rang. I went to the door and found two men standing
in the hall."

I deliberately omitted any mention of the girl. At the
moment I did not know why.

Boyce placed his palms flat against the desk, watching
me fiercely. Nola leaned forward on the balls of his feet,
his eyes alert.

"Men?" Boyce said. "Who were they?"

"I don't know. I had never seen them before. They tried
to force their way into the apartment."

"Go ahead. Keep talking, dammit! Must we yank it out
of you with forceps? What happened then?"

"A very one-sided fight," I said indifferently. "I pasted
one of the men in the nose. They got discouraged and went
away. If you look carefully you'll probably find a little blood
on the carpet outside my door."

"Describe them," said Nola. There was a small notebook
in his hand.

"The head man," I said, "was tall, over six feet, very
thin. Black derby, long dark trench coat, seedy looking. He
wore heavy glasses on the biggest and lumpiest nose I ever
saw. The other was in his early twenties, slight, pimpled,
and scared green."

Nola wrote swiftly. He put the notebook away. He raised
his eyes and focused them on me sharply. His face was
set hard.

"All right, Jordan. Let's have it."

I looked at him. "What do you mean?"

"Who else came to the apartment?" he demanded.

I swallowed and looked down at my hands. They were a little moist. He was good. He was very good. I began to be a little afraid of him.

"Yes," I said slowly. "I did have another visitor, but he came after the blonde was gone. I had come back and was taking a bath when he walked in on me."

"Another stranger?" asked Boyce sarcastically.

I nodded. "Another stranger."

"Don't you have friends?"

"Yes, but I was not due back in New York for another week, remember?"

"Let's get on," Nola muttered impatiently. "What did this bird want?"

"The girl. He was very emphatic about it. He came in and searched for her and then warned me that he'd kill me if I ever laid a hand on her again."

"Is that why you stuffed the doorbell with paper?"

"Partly. I had to get some sleep. I had to stop people from tramping through the place as if it was Huber's Museum."

He moved his head to one side and rubbed the back of his neck, without removing his gaze from my face. His eyes were flat and searching. He said abruptly, "All right, Jordan. Let's have the rest of it."

I blinked at him.

"What do you want?" I asked warily.

"The rest of it. The part you're holding back."

I shook my head. "You have the whole story."

He said stonily, "No. You're covering up. You're keeping something or somebody under wraps. Let me tell you something, Jordan. I don't need much sleep. I can stay up all night and all tomorrow and tomorrow night. I can hammer at you until you crack. I can hold you on suspicion of murder or as a material witness. You know that, you're a lawyer. Use your head and open up. Because sure as hell you're going to talk to me—sooner or later. You may as well cut the sparring and do it now."

I was silent. I sat there and considered it. He was right.

You can travel a long way to protect a client, and a longer to protect a friend, and beyond that you come to the end of the road and it's no use trying.

I inhaled and let it out slowly.

Then I said, "You're right. One of the men who came to the apartment looked at me and said, 'That isn't Bob.' I believe I know who he meant. Bob Cambreau. Cambreau is a client of mine, a broker. The name is probably familiar to you. I made the trip south to sell some property of his in Palm Beach."

"Why would they expect to find him in your apartment?" Nola asked.

"Because I gave him a key."

The two men exchanged glances. Boyce nodded. He said shortly, "Now we're moving. You'll have to pick up Cambreau and——" He broke off to answer the phone. An odious expression twisted his mouth. His face was wooden. He said, "No, not yet. No results. We'll let you know."

He slammed the handset into its cradle and turned to Nola. His face was flushed and disgust sharpened his voice. "The Honorable Philip Lohman, District Attorney of New York County. Out looking for publicity so he can boot himself up to Albany. Aagh!" He made a noise in his throat.

I knew how he felt. Lohman, a former corporation counsel with the right connections, had got himself nominated and then elected as prosecutor. But by no stretch of anyone's imagination, except perhaps his own, would he ever be considered another Tom Dewey or William Travers Jerome. I had seen him in action. I did not like his arrogant tactics. Fortunately, however, he had retained some capable men from the last administration.

Nola nodded sympathetically. "God help us if we're going to be saddled with Lohman in this case!" He switched back to me and said, "So Cambreau sent you to Florida and took a key to your apartment."

"Forget it." I was disturbed. "There's nothing in that angle. If you think he deliberately got me out of town just to use my apartment for some off-color business, you're barking up the wrong tree. That Palm Beach deal had been hanging fire for a long time.''

"Why *did* you give him the key?''

"Because he had just separated from his wife. He was staying at his club and I thought he might like a change. I told him he could use my apartment until I came back.''

"Where can we find this Cambreau?''

I shrugged. "At some bar probably.''

Nola picked up his hat. "Okay, Jordan. You know his haunts. Let's go.''

· 5 ·

It was quite a safari.

Broadway had pulsed into neon-glaring night life. Swollen throngs milled restlessly with a rapacious appetite for pleasure. Box-office windows spawned long queues, and the traffic din was a steady roar in your ears. Electric signs flickered nervously against countless faces, and on Fifty-second Street the taxicabs were disgorging a steady stream of patrons into the plushy night clubs that were little more than overdressed clip joints.

Nola sighed. "Everybody seems to have money except cops.''

"Except honest cops,'' I corrected him.

We had been searching for Bob Cambreau without success. The headwaiter at the Copa told us he had been there and left. We tried some of the seedier gin mills on Sixth Avenue, the Greek's and O'Malley's, and a couple of the quiet *bistros* along the river that he sometimes frequented for some really serious drinking, but we did not find him. So we climbed into the squad car and cruised down to the Village.

And struck pay dirt at our first stop.

I put the question to the heavy-breasted, swart-faced woman

behind the counter at Mama Lucia's, a bar and spaghetti house in the basement of an old building. She nodded dolorously and flung her hand toward the back room.

It was a small booth partitioned by a frayed green curtain. It held four hard chairs and a square table covered with a red-checkered cloth. Flung across the table, beside an empty bottle of Napoleon, were two thick arms, and cradled in the arms was Bob Cambreau's big sandy head.

He looked terrible. His face was darkly flushed and livid, his open eyes were red veined and sightless and as empty as the bottle of Napoleon. A two-day beard stubble darkened his jaws. He was drunk to the point of paralysis, but that was nothing new with Bob.

I shook his shoulder and called, "Bob . . . Bob . . ."

I called to him but I couldn't reach him. I pulled his head back and slapped him across the face. There was no reaction at all. He never batted an eyelash.

Nola said, "Let's get some black coffee into him."

We worked on him for an hour. Black coffee, and then a walk through the streets, around the block several times, dragging him between us. After a while he began to moan and then he went over to the curb and was sick. After that he was just weak. We supported him back to Mama Lucia's and sat him down in the small booth.

He recognized me with a rueful grin.

"Hiya, Scott, old boy," he said thickly. "What's up?"

"Plenty," I told him grimly. "Are you clear now, Bob? Can you hear me? Can you think straight?"

He missed the urgency in my voice. He blinked at the table. "Where is it? Who swiped my Napoleon?"

"Nobody," I told him. "You drank it."

"By myself?" He looked pleased. "They haven't stopped distilling the stuff. Let's order some more."

"Later," I said. "First we talk."

"Talk?" He glanced curiously at the lieutenant, seeming to notice him for the first time.

"Meet a friend of mine," I said. "John Nola."

Bob extended a clumsy paw which Nola accepted gravely.

"Any friend of Scott's," he said, "is a friend of Bob Cambreau. What do you drink?" He rapped on the table. "Let's get a waiter in here. Hey——" He caught himself, his fist upraised, and now he was gaping at me, goggle-eyed, his face as stiff as a board.

"I'm a monkey's uncle!" he whispered. "I must be drunk. I'm seeing things. You're not here, Scott. You're a mirage. You're in Florida. I oughta go on the wagon."

I said grimly, "It's me, Bob. I'm here all right. Got back this evening."

"Why? You were supposed to stay down there until——"

"I know," I said, "but I didn't like it."

He blinked stupidly, then his brow got striated with lines of concentration. It was coming back to him. Suddenly his face was harshly strained and he sat up.

"Jesus! What day is today?"

"Thursday."

His chair skidded back and tumbled over as he bounced abruptly to his feet. "I—I have a date," he said urgently. "You stay here, Scott. You just stay here."

I gripped his arm. "It's no use, Bob. It's too late."

He stood motionless, staring at me, his mouth working. "You—you've been home already."

I nodded.

"She was there?"

"She was there," I said quietly, "but she's gone now."

He picked up the chair and sank slowly into it. He looked beaten. He put his large red face in his hands and sucked in a long rasping breath.

In spite of the huge fortune he had inherited and somehow kept intact, I felt a little sorry for Bob. Back in school he had been a big, good-natured, hard-muscled athlete, but too much liquor and too many women and too much money had turned him into a soft, sybaritic, good-time Charlie, a *bon vivant*, a fellow who was digging his grave with his appetites. He started to shake, and I stared at him curiously. Then he took his hand away and I saw that he was rocking

with laughter. When he caught his breath, he asked, "Good
Lord! You didn't walk in on her, did you, Scott?"

Nola was leaning forward, sharply intent.

"Yes," I said. "I walked in on her." And then, without
warning, I was furious. I saw red. "Damn it, Bob! I gave
you a key to my apartment so you could sleep there, not to
use as a parlor house for every chippy you picked up off
the streets. It may not be much, but it's my home, not a
cheap riding academy."

He stopped smiling. He looked subdued. "You're wrong,
Scott. I admit I was going to use your place but not for
what you think. Hell, I don't even know who that girl was.
I never even saw her."

I was flabbergasted. I said, gaping at him, "But you had
a date with her."

"Well," he admitted, "you might call it a date,
but——" He stopped and his glance shifted uncertainly to
Nola.

"You can talk," I prompted. "He's all right."

Bob shrugged. "I guess it's no secret. You know that
Vivian and I haven't been getting along, that we split up a
couple of weeks ago. God knows I'm no prize, but then
Vivian is no angel either. Maybe we should never have been
married. Anyway, after you went south, things came to a
boil. We both wanted a divorce. Her lawyer got in touch
with me and . . . well, you know the only grounds for
divorce in New York."

"Infidelity," I said.

"Yes. We talked it over and——"

"I can guess the rest," I broke in caustically. "He put
it up to you. This legal paragon suggested that you do the
gallant thing. Allow yourself to be compromised. Let Vivian
find you in a hotel room with a strange young lady, con-
veniently undressed."

Bob grinned weakly and nodded.

"Naturally," I said. "And then Vivian would file suit
and her witnesses would testify to your perfidy and the judge
would grant a decree. In due time it would become final.

Everything cut and dried and neatly packaged. And how much, may I ask, was your bank account to be nicked this time?"

"Plenty. Vivian's no piker."

"And the young lady obliging enough to risk her reputation, you know nothing about her?"

"Not a thing. My contribution was the hotel room. Vivian's lawyer offered to supply the corespondent and the witnesses."

"Your contribution," I said bitterly, "was my apartment."

"Oh, come off it, Scott. I was trapped. The raid was set for this evening. I couldn't find a room anywhere. What was I to do? After all, there was nothing wrong."

I said, "If I know you there would have been plenty wrong."

"For Pete's sake! Let's not go into that," he said irritably. "No lecture on morals or my lack of them, please." He rubbed his face and when he took his hand away he was grinning. "And anyway, if anything happened it would depend on what the girl looked like. What *did* she look like, Scott?"

"Not bad," I said. "But you'd never get to first base with her."

"Why not? Every woman has her price, ranging all the way from because she likes you up to a pair of diamond earrings."

I shook my head sadly. "You're jaded. We're getting off the track. How did the girl get into my apartment?"

"I put the door off the latch this morning."

"But she mentioned my name."

He had a quiet chuckle. "She probably thought you were the guy. The lawyer simply told her to go up to Jordan's apartment, 7E, at the Drummond."

I turned to Nola.

"There you are," I said. "That's why the girl was waiting in her panties. When I marched in she thought I was the prospective defendant. And when the doorman rang the bell, she was certain the witnesses had arrived. So she followed instructions and jumped into my lap and started kissing me. Catching us in an embrace like that would clinch a divorce action.''

Bob Cambreau was sitting up eagerly. ''What's your beef? An undressed broad sits in your lap and starts to kiss you. Would I complain? Not at all. But I had to be sitting here, getting drunk.''

Nola abandoned his spectator role. He looked at Bob. ''Who was your wife's lawyer, Cambreau?''

''Chap by the name of Floyd Dillon.''

Nola glanced at me. ''Know him?''

''Slightly,'' I said. ''Near as I can recall he doesn't run a divorce mill. He has a mixed practice, mostly civil, but he'll handle anything that pays.''

''I think we'd better have a talk with Dillon.''

''Just a minute,'' Bob said. ''Where's the girl now?''

''Forget it,'' I told him. ''This is one dame won't even look at you.''

''Nonsense. I have references from the best debutantes in town.''

''No doubt. But it still wouldn't make a single iota of difference to her.''

He reached for my arm. ''Come on, son, give out. Don't be selfish. Dressed in panties and jumped in your lap, hey? How do you like that? Tell me, where can I find her?''

''In the morgue,'' I said bluntly.

He dropped my arm and looked at me queerly.

''That's right,'' I said. ''In the morgue. She's dead.''

He coughed and turned pale. ''You're kidding.''

''Like hell,'' I said roughly. ''Maybe I didn't make myself clear. This is Lieutenant John Nola of the Homicide Bureau.''

It dawned on him slowly and he began to believe. He faced Nola, aghast.

''How—how did it happen?''

''Poison,'' I said. ''In a bottle of brandy. Did you leave a bottle of brandy in my apartment, Bob?''

His mouth hung open. He moved his fingers stiffly across

the table and his tongue came out and passed slowly over his dry lips. He said in a hoarse whisper, "Christ, no! I hadn't been near your apartment until this morning. Sweet Jesus! Is this going to make a stink!"

He looked at me, the muscles in his face flaccid, and I thought if he was lying he was doing a better piece of acting than anybody in Hollywood.

· 6 ·

The first step, obviously, was to locate Floyd Dillon and learn the girl's identity. Bob's story had practically cleared me, but Nola asked me along; he wanted the answers to some questions. We left Bob, chastened and temporarily sober, and headed uptown in the squad car.

Nola was quietly introspective. He said in a thin voice, "This divorce racket stinks."

"It does," I agreed. "It's collusion and it's dishonest, but it happens to be the general practice in this state. The court knows damn well what's going on, but the judge will blink his eyes unless the case is too flagrant."

Nola frowned. "I suppose it has to be that way."

"Naturally. The only ground for divorce here is infidelity. You make a hard and fast rule about a thing like that and people will find ways to break it. In other states you can shed a mate for any number of reasons—impotence, fraud, desertion, cruelty, or even drunkenness. But not here. In a way that's preposterous. Just look at it. People are not infallible. They make mistakes. Suppose a woman gets to hate her husband so much the very sight of him is repulsive. Must she be saddled with the guy for life? Or can she call it quits and try again?"

"Why not separate?" asked Nola.

"A highly unsatisfactory status," I said. "You're married but you sleep alone. You have obligations but no privileges.

And then one day you fall in love again and you want to get married. But you already have one spouse. Which is all the law allows you. You're hanging off a limb. It's either a divorce, or bigamy, or sin—take your choice.''

He shifted in his seat. ''There's always Reno.''

''Yes, my friend,'' I said, laughing briefly, ''there's always Reno. Reno may grind them out like sausages and often they're not worth the paper they're written on. It's a hell of a note and sometimes a sad one, but a guy armed with a Reno divorce may later find himself guilty of bigamy in Connecticut.''

Nola frowned. ''Play that again slowly.''

''It's this way. To get a divorce in any state you have to be a resident of that state. So a woman goes to Reno for six weeks and fulfills their residence requirements, gets her decree and comes home. She thinks she's divorced. Then New York steps in and says, 'Sorry, nothing doing. You can't fool us, sister. You were never a bona fide resident of Nevada. You just went there to get a divorce, and as soon as you got it you left. You never intended to make Nevada your home. Tough luck, ma'am, we cannot recognize the divorce.' ''

Nola flicked his cigarette out of the window. His lips were pursed. He said, ''It's a rotten situation and something ought to be done about it.'' He coughed and looked at me. ''But not all Reno divorces are bad.''

I spread my hands and said, ''No, not all. A husband can have some local lawyer out there make an appearance for him. Or he can consent to the entry of a decree. That would stop him from later setting it aside.''

The car swung left on Fifty-ninth Street. On our right Central Park was dark and barren with the naked tree branches silhouetted like crippled limbs, while on the other side lights glittered brightly in the chrome and polished mahogany *bistros* of the sleek luxury hotels.

Nola said abruptly, ''They ought to relax the laws in this state.''

''That,'' I said, ''is a job for the legislature, a body highly sensitive to lobbying and powerful influences. Certain potent organizations are against making it too easy to get a divorce."

For a moment Nola made no comment, then he murmured softly, "Who knows? Maybe they're right."

The car pulled up before a huge monolith of a building and we climbed down and went into an impressive glass-fronted lobby, heavily carpeted, gleaming and modern, and patrolled by a couple of stalwart ancients in gaudy uniforms. A blond-wood elevator scaled us up to the twentieth floor as smoothly as mercury in a thermometer. We found Floyd Dillon's door and Nola touched the button. Inside a gong chimed twice, deeply and sonorously, like a cathedral bell.

A man in evening clothes opened the door. He inspected us briefly, frowning. He said, "Yes, gentlemen?"

Nola stepped forward. "Mr. Dillon?"

That got us another yes, and deepened the frown over the long, bridgeless nose. He was in his late thirties and wore it well, except for a slight bulge around the middle. Dark, well groomed, handsome in a ponderous Roman senator way, he had the general appearance of a man who often took stock of himself and was invariably pleased with the result.

Nola introduced himself, flashing his buzzer. "Headquarters," he added. "Homicide Bureau. We have some questions to ask."

Only the creases on his brow deepened. On the surface, Dillon remained suave and fairly calm. "I don't think I understand." He tossed a glance over his shoulder, back into the apartment. "I'm entertaining. I trust you'll be brief."

Nola said politely but firmly, "I think we'd better go inside."

For an instant Dillon hesitated, then he stepped aside and waved us in. We marched into the living room and I stopped short, surprised.

A woman sat on the chesterfield with a cigarette in one hand and a glass in the other. She was striking. A brunette with sable-black hair and a firm figure, too much of which was visible under the molded orchid-colored gown. Her eyes met mine in a wide, dark stare that ended in a welcoming smile.

"Scott Jordan!" she exclaimed. "Hello. This *is* a surprise. I thought you were out of town. When did you get back?"

"Hello, Vivian. This evening."

It was Bob's estranged wife, Vivian Cambreau. I introduced her to Nola, emphasizing the name and watching his face. It showed no more reaction than the side of a wall.

She laughed musically. "Well, Scott, you look surprised—finding me here. I'm rather surprised myself. I had no idea you knew Floyd."

"He doesn't," Dillon said brusquely. "This appears to be a professional visit."

She arched her brows. "At this hour?"

"Lawyers are like doctors," I said, smiling. "Sickness and crime work around the clock."

Concern flitted across her eyes. "Is—is something wrong, Floyd?"

"I hardly think so," he said. He smiled reassuringly at her. "Nothing that need trouble you."

I looked at him and behind that cool and supercilious façade I thought I saw the seeds of apprehension sprouting. We tossed a couple of embarrassed looks around at each other, like a small bomb with a short fuse that everybody was trying to get rid of, and then Vivian, sensing our reluctance to talk in front of her, rose with a slow, languid grace. Seeing her in that strapless gown with her smooth olive shoulders, it was not hard to understand why an old lecher like Bob had married her.

She said, "Perhaps I'd better leave. No, don't bother, Floyd. I'll be all right. I'll take a cab. Phone me later, darling."

She flung a mauve-colored cape over her shoulders, murmured politely to Nola, hoped that she would see me again soon, though there wasn't much conviction in it, and glided into the foyer with Dillon at her silver heels.

He came back and struck a pose, arms folded across his starched white shirt, chin upthrust. He was regarding us along his nose. It was very dignified and I thought that it would certainly impress a municipal court jury of shipping clerks.

He rumbled oratorically, "Now, gentlemen, what is this all about?"

Nola said bluntly, "I understand Mrs. Cambreau is getting a divorce."

"I beg your pardon." Dillon scowled. "How does that concern you?"

"You'd be surprised," Nola said shortly. "Answer my questions, please. Without the sparring. You're her lawyer?"

Dillon dropped his arms and became watchful. "I am, yes."

"A divorce on what grounds?"

"See here," Dillon said vehemently, "by what authority——"

"Answer the question," Nola cracked. His voice was hard and his mouth was as thin as a blade.

Dillon cleared his throat. "There is only one cause for divorce in this state. Infidelity."

"Exactly. Let's get down to facts, Counselor. You were making all the arrangements. You laid the scene for a raid this evening at Jordan's apartment. Please, don't interrupt! I happen to know that it's true. I know, too, that you were going to supply the corespondent and had dispatched witnesses to catch this girl and Mr. Cambreau in an indiscretion. Listen to me, I don't give a damn about the legal ethics involved, that's between you and your conscience and it's none of my business, but I do mean to find out the name of that girl. Who was she, Dillon?"

Floyd Dillon stood rigidly, flame fanning his face. He kept his teeth shut when he spoke. "What—did—you—say?"

"There he goes," I sighed. "He'll deny it until he's blue. He's scared stiff, afraid of what the Grievance Committee will say if this thing gets too much publicity."

The muscles in his neck thickened and he swung toward me, his voice harsh with anger. "Let me understand this. Are you accusing me of attempting to suborn perjury?"

"In fancy language, yes."

For a moment, as he glared at me, I thought his control was going to crack.

"Easy," snapped Nola. "To hell with the legal chicanery involved! I'm working on a murder. I want the name of that girl."

Dillon straightened and cleared his throat.

I said, "Look at him, Lieutenant. He's thinking up a lie."

Dillon turned on me furiously, but Nola nailed him with a terse command.

"Hold it! We'll have no cockfight here." His eyes were level and hard. "Now hear me, Dillon, your little play for this evening laid an egg. It flopped. You set the scene but Cambreau never made his entrance. He was down in the Village, dead drunk. Instead, Jordan came home unexpectedly and found the girl in his apartment. This girl you had sent there. She's dead. She was poisoned in Jordan's place and you're the only link we have to establish her identity. I want to know her name."

Floyd Dillon paled. He stared at Nola, his nostrils pinched, his eyes incredulous. Then he gave a small, strained laugh. "That's not very funny."

"Murder never is," Nola said.

Dillon wet his lips and looked at me. "I can't believe it. In your apartment?"

"That's where she drank the poison. She died in a taxi."

He swallowed, taking a long breath and regaining his composure slowly. His eyes grew sharp and a little foxy. Finally he shrugged and said, "Sorry. I don't think I can help you. The girl I hired for the job called me at the last moment and said she was too ill to go."

"Neat," I said sarcastically, "but hardly good enough. How about the witnesses? They showed up all right."

"I couldn't locate them in time," he said.

"That's easy to check," Nola said pointedly.

"Certainly. If I gave you the girl's name."

Nola's mouth tightened and he shifted his feet. His eyes, narrowed and brittle, settled squarely on Dillon. "Let me get this straight. Are you refusing to co-operate?"

"I didn't say that, Lieutenant. I know my duties as a citizen. I also know my obligations and privileges as a lawyer. I'll do whatever I can—within reason."

Nola brooded at him. "I want you to come down to the morgue for a look at the girl."

He didn't like it. The prospect was not a pleasant one. But he lifted his shoulders resignedly and nodded.

· 7 ·

Death was old stuff to me. A few years ago the war had shown me death in wholesale quantities. I had seen a single bomb flatten a whole village. In the Orient I had seen cholera and the plague snuff out lives with the remorseless efficiency of a giant roller grinding an anthill. I had seen them drop like flies and the bodies left rotting for days because of old customs and primitive fears. All this I had seen, but I had never got used to it.

And now as we entered the county morgue a cold, damp chill lay flat against my back.

The attendant, a small shriveled specimen with a hairless skull, greeted Nola. "Hiya, Lieutenant. Who you looking for?"

"You checked in a blonde earlier this evening?"

"Couple of hours ago."

"The medical examiner posted her yet?"

"Yeah." His grin was moist and toothless and his monologue strange. "Shouldn't have let him touch her," he said dolefully. "Shame to cut up a squab like that. What a looker!" He shook his head. "Some shape! Me, I never have no luck. Stuck overnight with a piece like that and she colder'n a mackerel.''

"Let's have a look at her," Nola said.

"Sure thing."

He piloted the way into a cold, dank room, one wall looking like a monster filing cabinet, its grisly contents pegged neatly away, murder victims, accident victims, and those unclaimed bodies and homeless dregs that cling to the fringe of every great city.

The attendant grabbed a handle and one of the drawers came sliding out.

"Here she is, gents."

Despite his outward aplomb, Dillon was shaken. Maybe it was due to our surroundings, which were depressing, or maybe it was due to what he was likely to see.

Verna's face was exposed. She looked terrible. Her face was starkly white and taut. No high-priced mortician had applied his gruesome art here. No rouge to conceal the ugly stricture of death. No soft satin sheets for Verna, only a bare metal tray—and later perhaps nothing more than a plain pine box. That was all she would ever get.

Floyd Dillon cast her a single look and his face turned the color and consistency of suet. He had the look of a man who awakens suddenly from a nightmare to turn on a light and find a ghost sitting in bed with him. He emitted a low, sick noise and turned away and stumbled gropingly into the corridor.

We followed him.

Nola regarded him curiously. "I gather you don't like corpses, Dillon. Or is it this one in particular?"

Dillon stood there, stunned, his mouth slack. He seemed unable to answer.

Nola said briskly, "Well, do you recognize her?"

He nodded slowly and lifted his eyes. "Yes," he said in a low voice.

"She the girl you sent up to Jordan's apartment?"

He pulled himself together and blinked at us. "No," he said. "She is not."

It was our turn to be stunned.

"But you recognize her?" Nola asked.

"Yes, I do."

"Follow me." Nola got the assistant medical examiner on duty to put an office at our disposal. It held a scarred oak desk, a couple of straight-backed chairs, and a print of Washington at Valley Forge that looked no colder than Nola's eyes. Floyd Dillon deposited himself in one of the chairs and went about the business of collecting his wits.

Nola hung one of his hips on an edge of the desk. "About the girl," he said. "Let's have it."

Dillon said, "She is—or rather was—a witness in a case I'm handling."

"Her name?"

"Verna Ford."

That was it. She *was* the girl he'd sent up to my apartment. But he was being cagey about it. He still did not want to admit the fact.

"Where did she live?"

Dillon gave him an address in Queens, adding, "She was a dancer in some club on East Fifty-eighth Street. The Magic Lamp, I think it was."

Nola got a cigarette burning. He blew a twin stream of smoke from his nostrils, watched it hang in the air motionless for a moment, then flatten and dissolve against the ceiling. He looked down at Dillon.

"Let me make myself clear. The divorce angle can stay under wraps. I'm not out to smear you. But I want this story and I want it straight, understand? No legal double talk, no cards close to the vest, no red herrings. Do I make myself plain?"

Dillon nodded.

"All right, go ahead."

Dillon said, "Verna Ford was the key witness in a simple survival case. About two weeks ago, several people were killed in an accident. They had just returned from Miami in a Southern Airways plane and had landed at the Municipal Airport. It was about 2:00 A.M. and three of the passengers got into one of those special Cadillacs for a lift back to Manhattan. It had been snowing and raining. The road was icy. The car skidded, turned over, and crashed against a pole. The driver and two of the passengers were killed. They were an elderly man and his young bride, James and Ivy Pernot.

"Verna Ford was the first person to reach the scene of the accident. The driver of the Cadillac and James Pernot were already dead. Ivy was still alive and in considerable pain. There was not much Verna could do. She went to call for help. When the ambulance arrived, Ivy was also dead."

I turned to Nola. "May I ask a question?"

He nodded.

I said to Dillon, "Verna Ford was the sole witness that Ivy Pernot survived her husband?"

"Precisely."

"And both James and Ivy have relatives who are now claiming his estate?"

He nodded. "Correct."

I said, "That would make our friend Verna damn valuable alive to one of the claimants and damn valuable dead to the other."

Dillon inclined his head and said nothing.

Nola pursed his lips and his gaze swiveled around to me.

"This isn't new," I said. "It's happened before. Here are two married people in a common accident. It's a question of survival. Suppose the wife died first. A dead person cannot inherit. Hence she could not take her husband's estate and her heirs would be out in the cold. But if she survived him by one single instant, his estate goes to her, and on her death to her relatives instead of his."

Nola switched his gaze to Dillon.

"Ivy Pernot had a brother," Dillon said.

"His name?"

"Eric Quimby." Dillon gave some additional facts which Nola scribbled into his notebook.

"On the other hand," I continued, "if the husband died after his wife, then the husband's relatives get the estate."

Dillon shifted in his chair and his voice was acid. "James Pernot had a niece. Karen Alithea Pernot. She's fighting this case tooth and nail."

"Ah," Nola commented softly, "so the vultures gather."

"They always do," I said.

He looked down at Dillon. "I take it you represent the wife's brother."

Dillon nodded shortly. "Yes. I happen to be Quimby's lawyer."

"Did Pernot leave much money?"

"In the neighborhood of a hundred thousand dollars."

"That's a good neighborhood," I said. "And a nice fashionable number. And it makes a pretty good motive for murder."

Nola said morosely, "A guy was knocked off in Brooklyn last year for thirty-six cents." He walked over to the window and looked out. After a moment he turned and his eyes were thoughtful. "Seems like the niece could be tailored for this kill. The Ford girl's testimony would knock any chance she had of getting her uncle's dough into a cocked hat."

Dillon's nod was emphatic. "Exactly the way I see it."

He was pushing it too hard.

I said, "That would make it too easy. The niece isn't the only one."

Nola stared at me and waited.

"Look at it this way," I said. "Dillon here is no dewy-eyed law clerk. He'd make Verna put her testimony in writing. Affidavits and depositions, all properly attested and in good order. But Verna was a very smart little girl. Suppose she suddenly realized her value. A pile of money depended on her story. So she got an idea and wanted a cut. Maybe she threatened to change her testimony. With her story down in black and white it might not be a bad idea to eliminate her from the picture. Send her up to my apartment with a bottle of poisoned brandy and let her——"

Dillon came up, his face suddenly charged with blood, his throat snarling. He advanced and I popped up and bent a little, ready to meet him.

Nola wedged himself between us.

"Goddam it!" he snapped. "Stop acting like a pair of prima donnas—both of you."

"You heard him," Dillon fumed in a strangled voice. "He practically accused me of killing the girl."

"Don't be so sensitive. Sit down."

Dillon remained upright. He said, ranting, "Verna Ford was my star witness. I wanted her alive. I needed her testimony. I will not stand here and listen to these scurrilous and unwarranted attacks."

"Boy!" I said admiringly. "You really get action out of this bird."

"Quiet," growled Nola. "Take it easy, Dillon. Ignore him. The man's irrational and grabbing at straws. He came home dead tired and had this thing dropped in his lap. I have another question. You said only two passengers were killed. How about the third? Why isn't he a witness?"

"Because," grumbled Dillon, still boiling, "we can't find him."

"What do you mean?"

"Just that. The third passenger in that Cadillac is gone. Vanished. Disappeared into thin air. Verna Ford claimed that he was thrown clear of the car and looked unconscious, but when she returned with help he was gone."

"And you tried to find him?"

"Naturally. I put a private detective on it. I ran ads in the papers. But he never showed up. He's gone, I tell you, no trace at all, just as if he'd melted down a drain."

Nola chewed on his lips, his expression remote.

"Amnesia," I suggested. "A blow on the head would cause it. Maybe he's lost and wandering around."

"Impossible," said Dillon flatly. "Missing Persons have no report. We checked every hospital in town. Nor have there been any out-of-town inquiries."

I leered at him. "Did you check the morgue?"

Dillon looked blank.

"What are you driving at?" demanded Nola.

"Look at it," I said swiftly. "Just look at it. A fortune

is at stake and a witness is strangely missing. A guy injured in an accident and nobody can find him. Nuts! Suppose Dillon found him and his testimony contradicted Verna Ford's story. *Pouf!* A fortune goes up in smoke. Put yourself in Dillon's shoes. Remember all the money that's at stake. How could you make sure of keeping it? Knock off this new witness. Hide his body, drop it in a lime pit, a cement block dumped in the East River. Maybe that's the real reason he can't be found——''

The idea grew and I was carried away with it. I did not see Dillon move in.

His fist caught me over the left ear and I fell backward across a chair. It was a fine blow. He weighed over two hundred pounds and put it all behind his fist. His face was apoplectic, the cords bulging in his neck. He'd lost all control. I saw his foot coming and rolled over.

It was Nola who surprised me. He exhibited more strength than I believed he had. He was on Dillon swiftly, pinning and locking the big man's arms behind his back.

"Let go," Dillon breathed fiercely.

I stood up.

Nola said, "Stand still, Jordan. You had it coming. You've been priming him all night. Behave, or I'll toss you both behind bars for disturbing the peace."

I grinned affably. "You're better than I thought, Dillon. Let's try this again sometime, when I'm looking."

His mouth was twisted. "Any time."

"Right now," I said. "Lock the door, Lieutenant. This would cost you a couple of bucks at any arena in town."

"Quiet," Nola grunted. "I got half a mind to let him take you. There are dead people next door trying to. get some rest. Give them some peace." He released Dillon. "Go ahead," he said. "Keep that date with your lady friend. I'll talk with you tomorrow, and don't be taking any sudden business trips. I want you on tap."

Dillon glared murderously at me and strode through the door.

Nola regarded me gloomily. He said softly, "I like the way your mind works, Jordan, but you'd better learn to control that tongue. Keep spouting your theories all over the place and

I'll have another murder on my hands." Concentration made deep folds in his brow. "Well, what do you make of it?"

I said, "He's lying, of course. The dead girl is the same one he sent up to my apartment. She said her name was Verna. It's not a common name and anyway it would be too much of a coincidence. She was undressed and she acted exactly as a lawyer would instruct a corespondent in a divorce case to act."

"You think he's lying?"

"Certainly. He's a stuffed shirt and he's afraid the bright light of publicity would show up the collusive and unethical nature of the action and the part he played in it. He's scared that the Grievance Committee would be forced to take action."

"Did you know that he was friendly with Mrs. Cambreau?"

"I did not. I was surprised to find her there."

Nola's eyes were half closed. "They seemed mighty close friends. Perhaps that was why he didn't want to connect the divorce with the Ford killing. Maybe he was trying to keep Mrs. Cambreau's name clear."

I nodded reluctantly. That was one way to look at it.

"Where did he say Verna Ford worked?" I asked.

"The Magic Lamp. Ever hear of it?"

"No. I'm not much of a night-club habitué."

"It's the usual sort of a dive," he said. "Floor show, fair liquor, fancy prices. It's owned by Leo Arnim." He paused and watched me and saw that the name made no impression. He went on. "Arnim is an ex-con who just got out of the can. Some years back he got into a fight. A small-time gambler made some crack about Arnim's wife and Arnim clipped the guy. He fell and broke his skull against the edge of a table. He died and the D.A. took a man-slaughter plea and Arnim was sent up the river. A couple of months ago he was released on parole and bought into the Magic Lamp. A couple of old henchmen with clean records fronted in the sale for him, but he's the real owner."

I didn't say anything. Arnim sounded like the proper playmate for a girl like Verna. We batted it around for a while and then I began to realize again how bushed I was and I said, "How about it, Lieutenant? Where do I stand?

You going to book me, or let me go home and get some sleep?''

He sighed and tugged at his under lip and let it snap back. Then he looked at me and smiled. "Go on home," he said. "Beat it."

I left him and went out to the street and woke a cab driver who was sleeping behind his wheel. On the way uptown I sank back, exhausted, but my spinning brain would not let me relax.

I thought of many things. I thought about an old man and his young bride who had been killed in an automobile accident. And I thought about the bride's brother, Eric Quimby, a lad who was after the old man's dough and had hired Floyd Dillon to get it for him. I thought, too, about the old man's niece, a girl named Karen Pernot, who also wanted the old man's money. And I wondered whether Verna Ford had stirred that cauldron into a porridge of murder for herself.

I could see her lying on the floor, a very torrid blonde, not so torrid now, who had danced in a joint called the Magic Lamp for an ex-con named Leo Arnim. And then I thought of some carefully laid divorce plans that had ended in the blonde's death and dropped me headlong into this cauldron.

I got out of the cab at the Drummond and went into the elevator. It was late and there were no stops and it shot me up to the seventh floor as if it was running away from the Collector of Internal Revenue. I opened the door and snapped on the light and took four paces into the living room, and then I saw the girl and reared back on my heels.

She was curled up on the sofa, sleeping.

My stomach got into a game of leapfrog with itself and I thought, "God help me. This is where I came in."

• 8 •

I recognized her at once. She was the same girl who had stood outside my door with the club-nosed man and his companion earlier in the evening.

I looked down at her and caught my breath. She was lovely. She lay curled on the sofa like a kitten, lashes smudged across olive cheekbones, her copper hair shining like a polished penny. A couple of freckles dotted her nose. She had a good chin and a mouth you wanted to nibble. She was wearing a tweed suit over a figure that was not large but was put together very neatly.

Any other girl I would have picked up and dumped into the hall.

I reached out a finger to touch her shoulder, almost reverently, and a voice breathed softly and alcoholically against the back of my neck, "Careful, old sock, you'll wake her."

I whirled around. Bob Cambreau grinned toothily at me. His eyes were still red, but his face was shaved and he looked better.

"Who is the girl?" I asked, whispering.

"Dulcy," he said briefly, as if that explained everything.

"And who," I asked, "is Dulcy?"

He told me and I vaguely remembered. She was a half cousin of Bob's who had visited his family years ago when I was there, a slim-hipped, sparkling kid. She was in now from Chicago and staying with Vivian because it was impossible to find accommodations of her own.

"What brought her here?" I asked.

"She phoned," Bob said. "I was here and took the call. Incidentally, I'm sleeping here tonight. Anyway, Vivian was out and Dulcy was lonely so I told her to come on over."

I remembered her earlier mission. "And what bird brain had the idea of sending her here this evening with those two sleazy characters to witness your moral turpitude?"

"Floyd Dillon," said Bob. "He insisted that one of the witnesses know the defendant personally. Accurate identification, you know, assure the judge no error has been made. And Dulcy, fresh from the Windy City, was called in for an assist."

"But she's so young," I said.

"She's twenty-two."

"Well, she looks innocent——"

Dulcy sat up without warning. "I'm not at all innocent." Her eyes were blue or violet or maybe both.

"You witch!" grinned Bob. "You were awake all the time."

"Sure." She smiled at me, frankly and openly. Her manner was easy and direct. She said boldly, "Hello, Scott. We meet again."

"Hello." I couldn't take my eyes off her.

"I guess you didn't expect to see me again so soon."

"Certainly not tonight," I admitted.

She laughed nicely. "Sleep is for babies and old men. Life is too short to spend in bed."

"Oh," said Bob, leering, "I wouldn't say that."

"You have an evil mind, Robert," she told him mildly, "and you'll come to no good end."

"Seriously," I said, "I'm tired, completely knocked out, but I'm glad you're here."

"Thank you, Scott. No punching noses?"

I grinned at her. "Not yours, at any rate."

Bob rubbed his hands. "This calls for a small celebration. What have we in the way of refreshments?" He rummaged in the liquor cabinet and came up with a bottle and his voice held reverend awe. "A magnum of champagne! Veuve Cliquot, no less! Well, well, well."

"I was saving it for a special occasion," I said, and looked gravely at Dulcy. "I guess this is it."

She smiled without speaking.

"A rare vintage like this," said Bob, "must be properly chilled." He disappeared into the pantry.

She sat down, looking solemn. I sat down beside her and she took my arm and said, "Bob told me about the murder. It must have been dreadful for you. I'm sorry, Scott."

"It could have been worse—if she'd died here."

"Did the police hound you much?"

"They were all right. I did some fast talking."

She looked at me. "I wondered why you wouldn't let me in when I asked. Now I understand."

"She was here then," I said. "Not dead yet, unconscious. I was worried. And I'll tell you something else." I smiled at her. "I hated like the devil to send you away."

She nodded soberly. "I knew something was wrong when we found you here instead of Bob. I confess, I was a little jealous."

That puzzled me.

She said, "It was strange. I guessed who you were immediately. And I thought you had that girl here with you and wanted to be alone with her."

"You're wonderful," I said. "Completely artless. And I'm delighted you felt that way, but you hardly knew me."

"Don't laugh," she said earnestly. "You lit the torch when I was only fourteen and Bob sometimes wrote about you to keep it burning. I've been around. I've met a lot of men and I don't have to be hit with a bat."

"If I wasn't a coward," I said, "I'd kiss you."

She moved toward me, her eyes dark. "Be courageous, Scott."

I was reaching for her shoulders when the phone rang. I picked it up.

"Jordan?" a man's voice said, hard and rasping.

I said yes and for a moment only the sound of static electricity crackled along the wires.

"If Verna talked," the voice said, "you'll have to watch your step, Jordan."

I held my breath. "Who is this?"

"Never mind. She always did talk too much. See what it bought her. You're dumb, Jordan, see? Learn and live. You don't know a thing. One peep and you end up on a slab beside her."

He hung up. The line went deader than the Holy Roman Empire. I stood there, looking stiffly at the handset. Then I put it down slowly and the idea struck me and it was not a pleasant thought. Somebody had a motive for killing Verna and if he thought she had told me anything . . . I sucked in a long breath.

"Who was it?" asked Dulcy, her eyes concerned. "You look as if you'd had a nightmare."

I adjusted a careful smile on my mouth. Bob came back with champagne and broke the tension.

"Here we are," he announced. "A small libation will brighten the spirit." He found some glasses and poured.

Dulcy sipped her drink and watched me over the rim of her glass. "I've never been mixed up in a murder before," she said. "It gives me a lurid feeling. I hear murder is old stuff to you. Bob says you killed seven Japs in the last war."

"Bob was kidding," I said. "They weren't Japs at all. They were Koreans and they died from dysentery."

She wrinkled her nose. "Was the girl pretty, Scott?"

"Verna Ford? Yes, she was beautiful in an indecent sort of way."

"Any clues?" asked Bob.

"Several. A bottle of brandy, a seafaring gent, and a law case involving a large sum of money in which Verna was the principal witness."

I had to answer a barrage of questions about Floyd Dillon and the two claimants and the strangely missing witness who had disappeared from the scene of the accident.

Dulcy said seriously, "The niece, Karen Pernot, must be guilty. She had the greatest motive—to eliminate Verna as a witness."

"The Homicide men are considering it," I said dryly.

"Don't be too hasty," she added. "Perhaps somebody who wanted her to get the money did it."

"The killer," I said, "was smart—taking advantage of the divorce setup to confuse the issue."

Dulcy shook her head emphatically. "Murderers are never smart. He's bound to be caught. With toxicologists, moulage, comparison microscopes, and truth serums like scopolamine, the average criminal hasn't got a chance."

We gaped at her and Bob muttered blankly, "I'll be damned!"

She laughed. "Don't look so bewildered. It's not strange. I took a criminology course once and I like mysteries, especially where I can match my brains against the criminal. It's very stimulating." She sat back, adding blandly, "There's really only one way to commit a successful murder."

"Yes?" I said. "What is it?"

A small mischievous smile played around her mouth. "It's quite simple and it doesn't need organization. The murderer must play a lone hand. First you find a discarded gun, preferably in an ash can, then you wait at night in a dark alley for an utter stranger to come along. You shoot him, carefully wipe off your fingerprints, drop the gun into the river, then take a leisurely trip to South America. No fingerprints, no clues, no murder weapon, and most important of all—no motive."

Bob blinked rapidly. I said, "You're right, of course. But lots of murders go unsolved."

She shrugged gracefully. "Luck. Blundering on somebody's part."

"We could go on like this until dawn," I said, "but my brain feels shriveled. Get your bonnet and I'll take you home."

She sighed a soft, resigned sigh. "Too bad this is a bachelor establishment. Well, there's always tomorrow."

We left Bob stretched out on the sofa with the dead magnum in his arms, already snoring, and went out and down into the street. It was a fine night, crisp and clear, with the navy-blue sky a dark and theatrical backdrop against the building towers.

Dulcy lifted her eyes. "So many stars," she said. "Shall we walk, Scott?"

"I couldn't make it, not tonight."

A lone cab drifted up and slowed hopefully and I flagged it and we climbed in. We drove through the park. Occasional lights flickered across her face, glinting on the copper hair. I felt her hand in mine and we were oddly silent. I felt tongue-tied, and I wanted to grab her, but I sat motionless. That's the way it is sometimes when a girl really jars you.

She turned toward me and said quickly, "I think you'd better kiss me, Scott."

The suddenness of it rattled me. She was facing me, her lips parted and her eyes so dark and large I almost fell into them. I felt shaky. And then she was in my arms and we were kissing. There was nothing casual about it. I'd skated around in my time, but this was different.

After a while we broke. She gave a small, breathless laugh. "Stop those bells," she said. "How do you feel, Scott?"

"Weak," I said. "Weak, but much better. It was like being caught in the propeller of a B-29. Where have you been hiding all my life?"

"The Middle West, Chicago."

"How long are you staying?"

"I may never go back."

"Can I see you tomorrow?"

"Yes."

"And the day after?"

"Yes."

I swallowed hard. "Listen, Dulcy, I guess it's crazy, my being hit like this. I always thought when it happened I'd have so much to say, such big words, and now I can't talk. I want to stand on a roof and yell. I'm dead tired yet I feel like high-jumping over the moon."

She leaned against me comfortably. "You've said it all, darling. I understand."

We lapsed into silence then. When the cab reached Vivian's apartment on Park Avenue I took her to the door, kissed her, then said good night.

"Till tomorrow," she said. "Good night, darling."

It happened just like that. I had a girl. I floated out of there and went home and fell asleep on a cumulus cloud.

· 9 ·

It was almost noon when I showed up at the office. Cassidy greeted me, indicating a pile of newsprint on her desk.

Cassidy is plump, forty, and highly efficient. She can draw from memory any legal document from a summons to a writ of mandamus.

"So you're back," she said. "Welcome home. We're getting notorious if not exactly famous."

I had to tell her the whole story.

"I had quite a time here myself," she complained. "Reporters. Hundreds of 'em. They wouldn't leave." She smiled broadly. "An odd thing happened. Manna from heaven. An angel came along, sized up the situation, and lured them all to a bar downstairs, promising some sensational revelations."

"A bewitching creature," I said, grinning, "with bronze hair and violet eyes. That would be Dulcy. What else happened?"

"Two phone calls. Lieutenant John Nola wants you to ring him. Also a Miss Karen Pernot. I think she's mentioned in the papers this morning. The dead girl was a witness in a case Miss Pernot is involved in."

I pursed my lips. "She leave a number?"

"It's on your desk."

I took the papers into my office. The story had made headlines. GIRL MYSTERIOUSLY POISONED. FOUND DEAD IN CAB. There was no mention of Bob's divorce and we could thank Nola for that. But Verna's part in the automobile deaths of James and Ivy Pernot was highlighted, with bizarre speculations about the missing witness. Reprinted photos showed the Southern Airways Cadillac crushed like a folded accordion. Floyd Dillon had declined to make any statement on behalf of his client, Eric Quimby. The old man's niece, Karen Pernot, had refused to see reporters, though it was understood she had been questioned by the police. Verna Ford was placed in my apartment immediately prior to her death with speculations on the purpose of her visit. Attorney Scott Jordan appeared to be working in close collaboration with the police.

I found the slip of paper with Karen Pernot's number and dialed it. A woman's voice answered the phone, clearly the voice of a domestic, cold, impersonal, diffident, and after some preliminary sparring I heard a nice contralto, low and highly polished to a cultured gloss.

"Are you the Scott Jordan involved in last night's unpleasantness?"

I said I was.

"There is a matter of importance I wish to discuss. Would you call on me this afternoon?"

"What time?" I inquired.

"At your own convenience." The voice was sirup smooth.

"Fair enough," I agreed. "And the address?"

She mentioned a number on East Seventy-fifth. We thanked each other politely, like two diplomats negotiating a loan, and hung up. After a moment I dialed Headquarters.

"Jordan speaking," I said when Nola's voice was in my ear.

"You're a late sleeper," he accused. "Are you busy at the moment?"

"Not so I need a battery of extra stenographers. Why do you ask?"

"Can you come down here?"

I recognized that tone. He was wound up.

"What for?" I asked.

"We found something in Verna Ford's room. A man. The D.A. is going to charge him with the murder."

"Congratulations," I said. "You chaps are on the ball. Who is he?"

"Verna Ford's boy friend. Merchant marine officer, second mate on the S.S. *Jacob Block*, a tramp tied up in Staten Island."

"Square-jawed chap?" I asked, excited. "Wearing a uniform too tight for a beer-keg chest?"

"The same."

"He's our man," I said. "The guy who broke in on me while I was bathing. What's his name?"

"Walther—Frank Walther. Gallop down here, Jordan."

I hung up. I reached for a large volume of Shakespeare's *Collected Plays* that stood on the phone cabinet. It contained no plays because it had a hollow interior designed to hold a fifth of bourbon. It had been a gift from Bob and I used it because I didn't like to have a bottle lying around the office exposed. I am not a drinking man, but I found that an occasional pull helped me to square off against life.

I champed impatiently all the way to Centre Street. Things were happening, the case was not static, and that was a good sign.

At Headquarters I found Nola with Inspector Boyce and a tall slate-haired man whom I instantly recognized as District Attorney Philip Lohman. He had blinking eyes behind rimless pince-nez clamped to a sharp nose that hung over a thin, humorless mouth. His manner was as stiff and as starched as the snow-white shirt on his lean torso.

He measured me deliberately while Nola introduced us, rubbing his thumb along a rolled lapel, and looking highly pleased with himself. I disliked the man instinctively.

Boyce said, "I'm not sure we can hang it on this bird. But Lohman thinks he can build a case."

I turned to Nola. "You found him in Verna's room?"

He nodded. "We went over to case the joint and there he was. We found a key to the room in his pocket. He didn't want to come along for questioning. Wienick was with me and we had to drum his skull some, but we brought him in and when he learned the girl was dead he flew off. He went wild. We slapped him into a cell and he almost tore the bars loose."

"He's our man, all right," Lohman said smugly.

"Where is he now?" I asked Nola.

"Downstairs."

I glanced at the District Attorney. "What makes you think he killed the girl?"

Lohman gave me a patronizing smile. "I'll tell you, Jordan, because you're a lawyer involved in this case and I expect to call you as a witness for the state. This Walther had a thousand dollars in his pocket."

"How does that make him guilty?"

"We found the girl's bankbook. She withdrew that sum from her account yesterday."

I eyed him obliquely. "Go ahead. There must be more."

He chuckled quietly. He was feeling fine. "There is, considerably more. We found in his possession a diamond stickpin, fully two carats and highly valuable. Sailors seldom wear ornaments of that nature and we checked on it. The pin was designed by Lantier's." He took off his glasses and pointed them at me. "It was sold to James Pernot, the elderly gentleman concerning whose demise the girl was a witness."

I was jolted. "What do you make of it?" I asked Nola.

He shrugged. "This is Lohman's play. He feels Walther stole the money and the pin from the girl."

"What's Walther's story?"

"He claims he found the pin in her room and was going to confront her with it."

I swung back to Lohman. "What else? There must be more."

He acted like a man laying down a royal flush. "There certainly is. The man admits he was in love with the girl. We can show that he recently learned a lot of things about her, unpleasant things. That she was a liar and a cheat and worse. She used to work in a dance studio where you could buy more than dancing lessons. He knew the girl was going to your apartment and his imagination ran away with him. He was furious with jealousy. It was his grotesque notion of justice to give her a bottle of poisoned brandy when she went to visit her lover."

"Meaning me?" I asked.

"That is the way Walther saw it."

I turned grimly to Boyce. "Any objection to my talking with Walther?"

Boyce shot a glance at Lohman, then shrugged massively. "Why not?" He flipped a switch and spoke into the box on his desk. "Bring up Frank Walther."

We sat back. The door opened and a cop ushered him

in. He looked like hell. He looked like the end of a ten-round bout with Joe Louis. One eye was closed and swollen, congealed blood hung from his nose, his mouth was puffed, his jaw discolored. He wore a bandage across his forehead. He saw me and his back stiffened like a saber. His eyes grew sullen and bitter. The corners of his mouth curved down.

I said, "I hear they're charging you with murder."

His eyes were hot. He said nothing.

"Listen," I told him brusquely, "this is no time for the big silent act. Use your skull for something else besides a target for a night stick."

His jaw clamped. "I want a lawyer."

"I'm a lawyer," I said.

"You!" he sneered. "I'd rot in hell first."

"You may have to at that," I said dryly, "because you have a stubborn one-track mind. If you think there was anything between Verna and me, you're wrong. I never saw her before last night. She came to see me on a professional matter. There was nothing between us. I have no idea where she got the brandy. Did you give it to her?"

He jerked his head at Lohman. "He thinks so."

"I don't," I said.

Lohman lunged forward, scowling. "See here, Jordan, we didn't bring Walther up here so you could——"

"Baloney!" I growled. "The man is entitled to counsel. I'll represent him if he lets me."

Walther watched us, narrow-eyed and frowning. He absorbed the animosity between us. Perhaps he disliked me, but he hated Lohman.

"Okay, Jordan," he said suddenly. "You're my lawyer."

Lohman was livid. "That's enough. Put this man back in his cell."

"Hold it!" I barked. "If you do I'll be back here with a habeas corpus inside an hour. This is perfectly legal. Take him away now and we'll air your brilliant deductions in open court this afternoon."

He almost choked. The pince-nez dropped the full length

of its ribbon. His mouth was tight and bloodless. He controlled himself with a visible effort. "I can't figure you,
Jordan. In your position I should think you'd want this case
cleared up as soon as possible."

"Not at the expense of an innocent man," I told him
contemptuously. "Go ahead. Haul him off. Thirty minutes
won't make a hell of a lot of difference."

Fuming, Lohman jabbed a shaking finger at Walther.
"Do what you like. Retain him. That's your privilege. But
let me give you some advice. He's not clear himself, not
by a long shot. This wouldn't be the first time a lawyer
railroaded a client to clear his own record."

Walther's lips were tight against his teeth. "I'll take a
chance on Jordan."

"Good," I said. "Now let's have your story."

Boiled down it sounded logical enough. His ship, thirty-
two days at sea, out of Calcutta, had docked yesterday
morning. He supervised unloading until midafternoon and
then he called on Verna. She acted strangely. She would
not make a date with him, or tell him where she was going.
His questions produced a temper. When she went into the
bathroom, he spied a piece of paper with my name and
address on it. When she left he trailed her to the Drummond.
He hung around the lobby for some time, and then, prodded
by jealousy, he came upstairs to find her. I was in the
tub at the time. But Verna was already gone and he went
back to her room to wait for her, and that was when Nola
found him.

I asked about the diamond tiepin.

"I found that in Verna's drawer," he said. "I figured
she was in a jam and I wanted to ask her about it."

"And the thousand dollars?"

"My own. The company paid me off yesterday."

"That can be checked," I said.

Nola said, "We didn't look very hard after we found
Walther. I'll send a man back to Verna's room." He went
to the door and spoke to someone in the hall.

There was no expression on Boyce's rawhide face. Philip

Lohman had his feet planted squarely on the floor. He was seething.

"How about Verna's private life?" I asked Walther.

He stared fixedly at his hands. "She used to work in a dance studio. That's where I met her. Then she got this job in the Magic Lamp. She boasted about it and when I asked how come, she blew up again. She yelled, 'I can dance, can't I? And I got the juiciest figure you ever saw, haven't I?' " He lifted his bruised face. His eyes were distant and hurt and full of remembering. "Yeah," he breathed softly. "She had a figure all right. Christ, she was beautiful!" His lips twisted, he held up his paws. "I'd like to get my hands on the bastard who did it."

I waited till he calmed. "Anything else?"

He looked at me. "She promised to buy me a ship of my own. I thought she was kidding."

I swiveled and said to Boyce, "What's the score? Do you want to release him?"

"Ask Lohman. This is his baby."

The District Attorney spoke between stiff lips. "We're holding him. My own investigators are still working on it."

I snorted. "Listen, Walther, if they ask any more questions, just stick to your story. If they get rough, clam up altogether. Keep your mouth shut. Don't sign anything. I'll try to get you released tomorrow. They'll have to haul you before a committing magistrate or ask for a Grand Jury indictment and they haven't enough evidence to make anything stick. Do what I tell you, understand?"

He nodded. Boyce spoke into his box again. A cop entered and led Walther away.

Lohman's breath whistled through his pinched nostrils. Anger rouged his cheekbones. "Keep acting in this high-handed manner, Jordan, and you'll find yourself in one sweet jam."

"Nuts!" I said. "Of all the blundering incompetence— charging a guy with murder on such flimsy evidence—this takes the prize. You didn't have a shred of honest evidence. How about the brandy? Why didn't you trace that to Walther?

Or proof that he had possession of chloral hydrate. When a man commits murder in the heat of passion because of jealousy, he doesn't use poison. More likely his bare hands. Perhaps he was in love with a tramp, that can happen to anybody, but he wasn't an imbecile. He wouldn't kill her and then sit in her room, knowing that would be the first place the cops would search. Not with a stolen tiepin and a thousand bucks in his kick.''

I spun on my heel and stalked out of the room.

Nola fell into step with me when I was halfway down the hall. He said quietly, ''Watch your step. Lohman's on fire. He's back there making threats.''

''To hell with him,'' I said. ''He's a windbag.''

He touched my arm. ''Let's stop off at my office.''

We went in and sat down. He glanced at some reports, then his eyes came level with mine.

''Heron's couldn't help us on the brandy,'' he said. ''Too many people in and out all day. How much of the stuff did she drink?''

''Not much before I got there—from the looks of the bottle. Before she keeled over she took a pull like a thirsty stevedore.''

He nodded. ''According to Tolnay, our toxicologist, chloral hydrate works fairly quick in alcohol. Fatal dose is about forty grains. An overdose brings on swift coma, hard breathing, and then all at once the victim is gone.''

''That's how it hit her,'' I said. ''I thought she was drunk, but she must have been in a coma.''

He looked moodily at his desk. ''We never found the mate to that glove. But we found the century note on that taxi driver.'' His lip curled. ''We had to twist him a bit. He claimed he looked into her purse to find her address and spotted the bill. He didn't think she'd miss it.''

''Dishonest,'' I said, ''but logical.''

Nola mused thoughtfully. ''I wonder how she got the tiepin.''

''Two guesses,'' I said. ''Either she stole it or somebody gave it to her. She could have lifted it from James Pernot

after the accident. From his corpse. I wouldn't put it past
her. She was a girl who'd empty a blind man's tin cup. On
the other hand, this chap, Eric Quimby, may have given it
to her." Nola sat immobile, waiting for me to explain. "As
a binder," I said. "To tie up a bargain. To keep her tes-
tifying on his side of the case. She was the kind of girl
who'd want some payment in advance. And Quimby may
have found it among his sister's effects."

Nola stroked his chin. "Her bank account shows some
fancy deposits the last week or so." A knock sounded on
the door and he said, "Come in."

Wienick entered and placed a small pink bundle on
the desk.

"Look at it, Lieutenant."

Nola shook out a pair of silk panties and a thin sheaf of
currency fluttered to the desk. They were hundred-dollar
bills. He riffled through them.

"We found them in her bottom drawer," Wienick explained. "Rolled up like that."

I grinned smugly. "That dents Lohman's case. The rest
of his motives will dissolve the same way."

Nola sniffed distastefully at the bills.

"Jasmine," I said. "Verna's perfume."

"Perfumed money!" He shuddered.

"Probably comes from the panties," I said.

"They put perfume on those things?"

"Some of them do."

He opened his eyes wide. "I been missing a lot."

Wienick snickered. Nola glared darkly. The plain-clothes
man backed out hastily.

Nola picked up his pen and rolled it round and around in
his fingers aimlessly and then put it down. He said, "We
traced Verna's movements yesterday. Where do you think
she went?"

"To solicit business at the Brooklyn Navy Yard."

It didn't make him smile. He said slowly, "She went to
an address on East Seventy-fifth Street and visited Miss
Karen Pernot."

I sat up and blinked hard. "Did you ask her about it?"

He squirmed uncomfortably. "We talked to her. You can learn as much by questioning that wall." He shrugged heavily. "What the hell can a guy do when there's a lot of expensive legal talent around, threatening to see the mayor?" He grimaced.

I sat back. "She rang me this morning."

His eyes widened. "What for?"

"She wants to see me."

He ran his hand through his dark hair. "About what?"

"I'll tell you after I've been there. Matter of fact, I'm on my way now."

He leaned back and tugged gently at the lobe of his right ear. He said slowly, "Well, watch your step. The guy who killed Verna killed her because she knew something. Maybe he thinks she told you."

That was a nice thought. I got up and left him. His last words kept ringing in my ears.

I felt like an accident going someplace to happen.

· 10 ·

The limestone front may have been white at the time Crocker was bossing Tammany Hall. Shaded pewter now, it stood pinched off between two new towering apartment buildings, a sort of bulwark of a passing era. I climbed the steps and peered through the iron grillwork and saw nothing.

The woman who answered my ring wore a stiff black alpaca dress and the long spiritless face of an old draft horse. She looked down her nose at my card and held it gingerly between two fingers like the tail of a dead mouse. She opened the door wide and admitted me into a somber, gloomy hall and put me into a curved teakwood chair as comfortable as a camel's back. Then she broke through a pair of ponderous red drapes into a room from which emerged the sound of a piano.

Against the tones of the piano a woman was singing in a deep, not unpleasant contralto. I listened for a moment, thinking that the melody was familiar but unable to place it. Then the voice slid up the scale, got a little out of range, wavered uncertainly, and suddenly cracked like an eggshell in a fist. A man's voice, with a trace of an accent, said, "No, no, no, Karen. Theenk the tone in your head. Get a picture of it and then project. Come, we try again."

His fingers ran up the keys and the voice ran up the scale. This time it struck the note on pitch and held, not bad, but certainly not extraordinary. I'd heard better on macaroni programs.

"Good," the man said enthusiastically. "Good. Bring it forward. Fine, Karen, fine."

He was really oiling her. As the note died he flourished a cadenza, ending the passage.

I sat there with my hat on my knees and waited. On the wall in front of me, in an ornate gilt frame, an old boy in a ruffled collar peered out of a pair of vacant eyes at nobody in particular. I wondered if he was one of the early Pernots or just something the family had picked up at an auction.

The man inside was speaking again.

"You must hold the notes in your diaphragm, Karen. Watch your phrasing and relax." He emitted a trembling sigh. "You will be a great star in my operetta. All you need is the start."

He started to play again and she sang an odd, lilting melody that haunted my memory. Her voice was fluid here, and full, and in the middle register quite good. She held a long note and I held my breath. She beat me by three counts.

The man said, "Make it round and let it flow. Bravo," he added, "bravo." The song ended. There was a bit of polite applause, no louder than the flutter of a sparrow's wings.

Old horse-face came out. "This way, please."

I followed her through the drapes into a semicircular room

illuminated by a spangled chandelier that went out of style
with bustles. At the piano sat a dark man with a long, curved
nose, long sideburns, a thin mustache, and a split chin, oily
hair, heavy eyelids, and the general appearance of a lad
who makes his living dancing with lonely wives. He sat
there and looked at me with no particular expression on his
carefully tended face.

A slim old gent hoisted himself out of a chair and moved
toward me on wobbling legs, his arm extended, offering a
dry and shriveled claw. I took it and squeezed it gently for
fear of having it come apart in my hand like a stale cracker.

He was dressed in a wing collar, an Oxford-gray morning
coat, and striped trousers. He had the sunken, caved-in face
of a very old and very tired man who knows his time has
run out but doesn't like to think about it. His skin had the
almost transparent quality of thin parchment and was stretched
tightly across his face. Wrinkled folds hung like a rooster's
wattles from his throat. The ashes in his rheumy eyes had
died and long since cooled, and a few strands of silken hair,
the color of tarnished silver, clung with quiet desperation
to the bony structure of a narrow skull.

"Come in, sir." His voice was a senile squeak. "Sorry
to have kept you waiting, but Mr. Cassini permits nothing
to interfere with Karen's lessons." He smiled mechanically,
exposing an excellent set of porcelain dentures. "I am Paynter, Miss Pernot's attorney." His hand swung in a small
arc. "Miss Pernot—Mr. Jordan."

I looked at her. She was standing elegantly in the curve
of a Steinway concert grand and she was well worth a look.
Dark eyes gleamed at me and the smooth, low voice said,
"So nice of you to come. What do you drink, Mr. Jordan?"

"Bourbon," I told her, as long as she was inquiring.

She ducked her head toward the dark man on the piano
stool. "Rudy, please—some drinks."

He fondled her with his eyes, rose smoothly, and went
out. I thought he was walking on his toes.

She smiled at me. A cool smile out of warm eyes. Her
face was carved alabaster with a small, vivid mouth and a

pair of dark, feline eyes. Lampblack hair was parted in the middle and pulled into a tight knot at the back of her small, neat head. A black velvet dinner dress was sucked in tightly around her slim waist by a thick violet belt studded with brass nailheads. A violet bag about the size of a dispatch case rested on the Steinway.

"We read all about you in the papers, Mr. Jordan," she said. "I suppose you're wondering why I asked you to come here."

"Uh-huh."

She put her left elbow into her right palm and showed me a delicate frown. "I'll come to the point. We had a caller this morning, a certain Lieutenant Nola. A policeman," she added in a half whisper like a young girl saying her first dirty word. "I believe you know him."

I nodded.

She sighed softly. "It was very awkward. So embarrassing. So many questions."

"Ugh!" I said. "Nasty fellows, policemen."

She glanced sharply to see if I was kidding her and then smiled again. She said, "Yes. Unpleasant but necessary, I suppose. But they must know their place. We put him in his. I must confess, I did not like his tone, or his implications."

"That ought to teach him a lesson."

"Won't you sit down, Mr. Jordan?"

I got lodged in a leather chair and crossed my knees.

She said, "He had the temerity to imply that I might know something about that unfortunate affair last night. The death of that girl."

"Do you?" I kept a bland face.

"Naturally not."

"Absurd," Cassini said, coming in with a tray.

"Where could he have got such an idea?" Paynter said querulously.

I shrugged. "It's like this. Murders get committed and people have to be questioned. They've got to find the guilty person in order to discourage that sort of thing. Being a homicide detective, it's Nola's job to interrogate anybody who might be interested in the girl's death."

Karen Pernot arched an eyebrow. "But why me?"

I smiled at her. "You probably know the answer, but I'll tell you anyway. Just in case you're being cagey and trying to find out how much I know. Verna Ford's testimony in your uncle's survival case was going to cost you a lot of money and that wasn't calculated to make you very fond of her. In fact, she would be a lot more valuable to you dead than alive."

"Nonsense," she said, looking piqued.

"Ridiculous," echoed Cassini.

Paynter trotted forward three paces. "But Karen, this detective was simply doing his duty and——"

"You!" Her dark eyes withered him. "You've done nothing but make excuses, Rowland. I'm quite tired of it. That girl was poisoned and she's dead and I shan't weep about it. I am not sorry and I shall not be harassed or bullied. By anyone. And I will not sit idly by and let Ivy's brother collect Uncle Jim's money. It's preposterous, utterly preposterous. A total stranger!" Her voice scaled up one full octave. "I won't have it, I tell you. I will not have it."

Paynter made a feeble gesture. "You don't understand, Karen. These problems are covered by specific laws. Uncle Jim did not leave a will and——"

Her hands flew to her ears. "Please! I don't want to hear any more. You know how important this is to me—and to Rudy. And you're scarcely putting up a fight."

He slumped helplessly. "It takes time, Karen. We filed our claim."

"Time—time——" Her eyes simmered like water in a kettle. She turned towards me. "What do *you* think, Mr. Jordan?"

"About what?"

"The money. Who should get it?"

I shrugged. "Courts and juries make the decisions."

"Your opinion," she insisted. "Surely you can give me that. Does Eric Quimby deserve the money simply because his sister was married to Uncle Jim for a few days?"

I said, "You already have a lawyer."

She pulled herself up dramatically. "I have a lawyer. Oh, yes, because my father and grandfather had a lawyer. The Pernots never change. It's absurd to think that Rowland can handle this case. He hasn't been in a courtroom for years."

The excitement was a little too rich for Paynter's thin blood: He hawked, shaking like a clothesline in a stiff wind. He wiped his eyes and said, "I'm not as spry as I was ten years ago."

Ten years, hell! Thirty maybe. He should have retired with the Cleveland administration. I sat back. I had a pretty good idea what was coming and I waited for it.

Karen Pernot looked directly at me. "I need a change of counsel in this matter, Mr. Jordan. Will you represent me?"

I cocked my head at Paynter. "That wouldn't be ethical."

"Who cares? Will you?"

I started to shake my head but she cut me short.

"Rowland will withdraw, won't you, Rowland?" She said it like an army sergeant asking a recruit to get out of bed.

"Certainly, my dear." He gave me a hopeful and somewhat pleading look. "It's quite all right, Jordan, really. Karen does need a younger man, a fighter, I should say. Truth of the matter is I'm practically retired. Haven't been active for some time, just a little estate work for old clients. I'd consider it a kindness if you'd come in—really I would."

I sat as motionless as a statue in the city square.

Karen's eyes were shaded. "There you are. Then it's all settled, isn't it, Mr. Jordan? What has to be done?"

Paynter said, "Only the formalities, my dear. I'll send Mr. Jordan the substitution papers immediately." His smile was a little taut. "Is that quite satisfactory?"

I laughed. "That was pretty well done. It seems I'm in the case whether I like it or not. There doesn't seem to be any reason why I shouldn't make a fee out of it."

She nodded vigorously. "Splendid. I'm so happy."

Paynter asked if he could be of any further service, and when she told him no he looked several years younger and trotted through the red curtains as eagerly as if he were chasing a ballet dancer.

Karen Pernot poured a drink and handed me the glass. Cassini already had one.

"Good," he said, fingering his mustache. "Now we are making progress."

I tasted my drink and looked at him over the rim of my glass.

"How stupid of me," Karen said. "You two haven't met. This is Rudolf Cassini, my vocal coach."

He clicked his heels and bent stiffly at the waist. His manners were phonier than a zircon.

"I'm to star in an operetta Rudy composed," Karen confided.

"I gathered as much," I said dryly.

"You will be sensational, *carissima*," he assured her.

I said offhandedly, "And all he needs is the money to produce it."

He put down his drink. "I beg your pardon."

I ignored him. "May I congratulate you, Miss Pernot. Handing me this case was a neatly arranged operation. I imagine you talked the whole thing over with Paynter before I got here."

She dropped her eyes. "Yes. You're very bright. Does it make any difference?"

"Some," I said. "With all the fancy high-priced legal talent around, how come you picked me?"

"*Signor!*" said Cassini, his eyes hooded. "Your remark before——"

Karen said sharply, "Rudy! Please don't disturb us."

"Don't inhibit him," I said. "What's on your mind, Cassini?"

"The tenor of your remark," he said, wearing a dark scowl and trying to look like a member of the Black Hand Society. "I did not like it."

"Tsk, tsk!" I said. "That's too bad." I turned negligently away from him and looked at the girl. "May I ask you a question?"

"Of course."

"Do you need your uncle's money to help back this operetta?"

She glanced at Cassini. "Why, yes. I was going to use some of it for that."

"And if you didn't get the money there would be no production?"

She moved her shoulders faintly.

I looked at Cassini. "That's it. That gives you a motive for killing the only witness who could hurt Karen's claim to her uncle's dough. Hiring me won't stop me from looking for the killer and if he should happen to be a close friend of my client——" I spread my fingers.

She put her head back and showed me her lovely alabaster throat and let out a peal of laughter. "Rudy!" she gasped. "You're accusing Rudy! Oh, that's very funny."

Cassini paled. "I do not see anything funny." He toyed nervously with his mustache.

"Getting back to my original question," I said. "What made you decide to retain me?"

"Must I have another reason?" she asked.

"Uh-huh. Rowland was too old. All right. But he'd be likely to suggest someone he knew better. After all, this case involves a lot of money and I'm a total stranger."

She lowered her lashes and fidgeted with the buckle of her belt. "If I had another reason, what would it be?"

"Perhaps this," I said. "The newspapers are hinting that Verna Ford may have tipped me off to something. Assuming I had such information, as an ally of yours I might or might not use it."

She glanced up. "Are you always so frank?"

"No. Sometimes I'm secretive and tricky. A lawyer is in a peculiar position. A client's problems are his problems. If you want me to help you I have to know exactly what's in your mind."

She smiled brightly. "You make me sound very complex.
I'm very simple, really. As a matter of fact, we did not go
into this blind. We made inquiries about you. I need the
money and under the circumstances you seemed the one
most likely to get it for me."

"Why?"

"Just look at it. You're a lawyer. Verna Ford went to
see you, maybe to ask your advice. Someone was afraid of
that visit and in trying to prevent it killed her. But not soon
enough. You were right. I do think she told you something.
And so if Quimby's claim was to be beaten you looked like
the man for the job."

She knew nothing about the Cambreau divorce. That much
was clear. I took another drink of the bourbon. Cassini had
seated himself at the piano stool and was staring moodily
into his glass.

Without preamble I said, "Verna Ford was here yesterday
morning."

"There," she said triumphantly. "You see. I was right.
She did speak to you. She told you about her visit."

I couldn't see where this line of reasoning would hurt so
I let her keep it.

"What brought her here?"

"My request," she admitted tranquilly. "I asked her
to come."

I said, "That's not good form—trying to make a deal
with your opponent's witness."

"Oh," she said lightly, "those things never trouble
me. Too many ethics restrict one's activities. Don't you
think so?"

"Tell me about the visit," I said.

"Rowland was floundering around, getting nowhere very
swiftly, and I felt I had to do something. Frankly, Mr.
Jordan, I was prepared to take any action that would get me
Uncle Jim's money."

"Even murder?"

"I hadn't considered that," she said.

"Or bribing witnesses?"

"If necessary. Finish your drink. I'll freshen it up for you. The wine cellar is better stocked than my bank account."

The drink slid down my throat as smoothly as a drop of oil. "As long as you're my client," I said, "you'll have to behave yourself."

She stooped to refill my glass. She looked up, her eyes bright. "An awful lot of money is involved."

"Money is nice," I said. "Handy to have. I like it as much as the next guy, but not so much I'd be willing to wink my eyes if it turned out you had anything to do with that brandy she drank."

Cassini slapped his glass down on the piano. He came to his feet, his eyes dark and angry.

"Get up!" He was breathing heavily.

I looked him over. He was wiry and compact. I took a slow drink and sighed.

"Get on your feet," he said thinly.

I said to the girl in a peevish voice, "Oh, send him away. Get him out of here before I hurt him. He makes me nervous."

Cassini made low, harsh noises deep in his throat.

Karen looked at him, her eyes curious, and she said softly but evenly, "I think you'd better go out for a walk, Rudy. This is business. It won't interest you."

I needed a lightning rod to handle the glare he gave me. But he spun on his toes and went out. I looked at the girl and smiled. We were quite alone. She glided over to an enormous velvet sofa and let herself be swallowed up by it, drawing up her trim legs and getting comfortable. Her eyes were a little dreamy.

"There," she said softly. "That's better, isn't it? Now we're quite alone. We can have a nice cozy chat. Come over and sit down beside me."

I brought my glass with me, wallowing through the rug. I sat down and touched the thick nap with my toes.

"Where is this from?" I asked.

"Persia. It's quite old."

"I could negotiate it better with a pair of snowshoes."

"Don't let the scenery fool you," she said. "This house is mortgaged to the hilt, furnishings and all."

I inhaled tentatively. Her perfume was discreet, a little elusive, and very subtle.

"Broke, eh? But you're willing to invest this money—if you get it—in Cassini's little musical."

"It isn't bad," she said quietly. "He has talent and he knows music."

"He's a mountebank. Those things he told you, he could have picked them up any afternoon in the corridor at Carnegie Hall."

She smiled. "You don't give me credit for much judgment."

"Women are gullible," I said. "Look how the Czarina was fooled by Rasputin . . . How much money did your uncle leave?"

"About half a million."

I whistled softly. The figure was quite a bit more than Floyd Dillon had admitted. She raised her glass to mine, watching me along her lashes.

"To us," she said.

"And to Uncle Jim's money. A lot of lettuce to drop into a show."

Her expression tightened. "Why not? I've always wanted a career on the stage. This is my chance. Even if it isn't a success I'll have had the experience and the publicity."

"Half a million dollars' worth?"

She seemed annoyed. "It won't take that much. And anyway, I know all the objections. If the show had any merit some reputable producer would back it with his own money. Call it vanity. I'm going into this thing with my eyes open."

"Sure," I said. "You're a big girl now. Let's get back to Verna. How did you get her to visit you here?"

She bent forward and selected a cigarette from a lacquered box. I snapped a lighter for her. She blew some smoke into my eyes and settled back, watching me.

"Must I tell you?" she asked.

"Yes."

"I went to the Magic Lamp—that's the club she dances at—and sent her a note."

"And she showed up yesterday morning?"

"Just before lunch."

"What happened?"

She plucked a shred of tobacco from her lip, inhaled deeply, then put a sip of bourbon on top of the smoke to hold it down, and spoke ingenuously, like a schoolgirl reciting a lesson. "I wanted to ask her if she was certain that Uncle Jim was dead when she reached the scene of the accident. I suspected that she'd been bribed. But I never really had a chance to question her. She spoke first, came right out with it, boldly." Karen paused and took a light nibble on her under lip.

"What did she say?" I asked.

"She said, 'Honey, I know exactly what's on your mind. You want me to change my testimony. Maybe I will and maybe I won't. That depends on you. How much is it worth?' " Karen shook her head. "I was shocked."

Yeah, I thought, about as shocked as a combat surgeon treating a hangnail. I said, "And how much did you offer her?"

Her face stiffened. She flicked some ash off the cigarette. "I wish you wouldn't be so blunt."

"So do I. But I'm too old to change now. Did you reach any agreement?"

"Not then. I only made some vague sort of promise."

"Why?"

"Because the little trollop wanted an even fifty-fifty cut, half of everything I got."

"Nothing cheap about Verna."

"No," she said bitterly. "Not where money was concerned."

"What happened then?"

"Nothing. I told her I needed time to decide. She was very cool. She laughed at me and said, 'Half or nothing, honey. You know where to reach me.' Then she went away."

I said, "And you opened the windows to clear out the smell of jasmine."

She smiled. "It was terrible. I couldn't come back into this room for hours."

"And that same evening she was dead."

"So I understand."

I leaned back and looked up at the ceiling and thought about it. She was watching me with her cameo face placid, her small mouth slightly pursed, as if she was waiting to be kissed.

I said, "You know, of course, that one of the passengers disappeared from the scene of the accident. Did Paynter make any effort to find him?"

"No. Rowland was afraid the man might corroborate Verna's testimony. He said that one adverse witness was bad enough; but two——" She gestured helplessly.

I nodded. "He had a point. Let's get back to Cassini. You discussed lending him money?"

"Many times, naturally."

"Was he here when you spoke to Verna?"

"Yes."

"When did he leave?"

She stubbed out her cigarette deliberately before she answered. "You can't be serious. Rudy hasn't the temperament for murder. He's a musician."

I said, "Given enough provocation practically anybody can commit murder. He had a dandy motive."

She puckered her forehead and gave me a long stare. "I wish you wouldn't say that. I wish you wouldn't even think it. Let's change the subject. Your face is very brown. Sun lamp?"

"Nope. I'm tanned all over."

She lowered her lashes and then lifted them slowly. She smiled. "Could you prove it?"

"Not now," I said. "This is still supposed to be a business conference."

She pouted and moved close, putting pressure against my shoulder. Her voice was low. "Aren't we finished with that?"

"Not yet. Tell me about your uncle and this girl he married."

Her eyes were smoky and she felt like playing, but she said, "Uncle Jim was all right. Not very bright, but then he didn't have to be. He inherited his money and managed to hang onto it. He was never very handsome and I suppose that made him a little shy. He never really ran around with women, and he'd been a bachelor for so many years it was a shock to learn that he was getting married."

"All this happened recently?"

"Less than a month ago. He met Ivy in Coral Gables. She was working at the hotel. Friends told me about it. Uncle Jim was taking her everywhere; Hialeah, the dog track, all the clubs and gambling casinos. It was scandalous."

"Some of them make a living at it," I explained. "Steering the boys around to various clubs for the commissions involved."

She tossed her head, frowning, and making her mouth small. "But why did he have to marry her?"

"The older they are the harder they fall. Past middle age it rocks them like an earthquake. He was afraid of losing her and so he proposed. For her it was a chance to grab at security and perhaps a bit of luxury. Or maybe she had something else in mind—a fast divorce and a big settlement. How long were they actually married?"

"Only two days."

"After being a bachelor for sixty years?"

"Yes."

"That must have been some honeymoon."

She slapped my face as gently as the flutter of a moth's wing. "You have a nasty mind. Would you like to see a snapshot of Ivy and Uncle Jim that he sent me from Florida?"

"Very much."

She rose languidly and dug an envelope out of the violet bag that was lying on the piano, brought it back, and sat down almost in my lap. She put her cheek close to mine so that we could look at it together.

It was a glossy color print, quite clear. Two people were

standing near a swimming pool, smiling carefully, the way people smile for snapshots. A slight, balding man with a receding chin and white, spindly legs had his arm around the waist of a ripely developed redhead. She was wearing a swim suit you could stuff into a thimble. It showed a lusty body designed for heavy duty. James Pernot looked justly proud.

I whistled softly. "I hardly think Uncle Jim was the man for the job. He couldn't have lasted long anyhow."

"Must you say such things?" she asked, obviously not annoyed.

I grinned at her. She gave it back to me with usurious interest. Our noses were two inches apart.

"Doesn't Ivy look like a tramp?" she asked.

I let my nod agree with her.

"I can't understand it," she breathed. "How could he have been such a fool?"

I held up the picture. "Look at him—scrawny, shy, retiring. This was sort of a dream he'd had all his life. Can't you see him, at musical comedies and burlesque shows, sitting in the front row, with his eyes glittering and working on it in his mind, wanting one of them and too damn bashful to go out and make an offer. Then he met Ivy, young and attractive and luscious and she was nice to him and that inflated his ego. He was afraid of losing her so he proposed. That's what makes old men marry young girls. Vanity, or the pride of possession. Some of them think they're getting love and some of them know they're only buying it. What they're really buying is a pile of grief. But that is the price an old fool pays for being an old fool."

She listened raptly. "You seem to know a lot about people."

"Not so much. How about Ivy's brother? Eric Quimby."

The name was a catalytic agent. The reaction was sudden and violent. A spasm of anger blazed in her eyes.

"Quimby!" She spat out the name like an arch-backed cat against a wall. She almost choked. "That miserable, unspeakable, thieving——" She snapped her mouth and I

watched the crimson stain dissolve slowly out of her cheeks
as she brought it under control.

"You don't like him, I take it."

"I despise him. And why not? The man never even met
Uncle Jim and now he wants all his money."

"I'd be sore too."

Her brow was smooth again and she gave me a sweet
smile. She could change expressions as easily as a cha-
meleon changes color.

"That's better," I said. "Now tell me about him."

"I met him for the first time at the funeral. Ivy had written
asking him to open Uncle Jim's house. I imagine she mailed
him the keys. After the funeral he moved in himself. I went
up there one day and he wouldn't let me in. He laughed at
me. He told me to go away. He said it was his property,
that he was merely anticipating the court's decision."

"You told this to Paynter?"

"Of course."

"What did he do?"

"Nothing. You saw Rowland. If he lifts a telephone he
needs a rest cure."

"We'll fix that," I said. "We'll get a court order sealing
the house and toss him out on his ear. He'll think the house
fell on him."

She laughed delightedly. "That's wonderful; I wish I
could be there."

"Maybe you can."

She looked at me, eyes sparkling. "I could kiss you."

"First let's talk about my fee."

"I—I couldn't give you much of a retainer."

"I don't want any. I'm working on a contingency. I
gamble my time and my ability for a percentage if we win.
Okay?"

"Oh, yes."

"I won't be as greedy as Verna. Right now Dillon and
Quimby have the edge. Our job is to prove that Verna was
either lying or mistaken. And it might be a good idea to

find the missing passenger. That will take a considerable amount of doing and maybe some danger.''

"Danger?" She frowned.

"I've been warned off this case already. Somebody phoned me and offered to put me on a slab next to Verna Ford if I didn't mind my own business." I smiled. "I don't scare easily."

I stood up. She came off the sofa and stood in front of me. Her eyes were sultry. Without warning she put her arms around my neck and kissed me. She only looked fragile. She had a grip like a Greek wrestler.

The drapes separated and Rudolf Cassini stepped into the room.

"*Karen!*"

You might think he had caught us in bed. She broke away without haste.

"We're sealing a bargain, Rudy."

His mouth twitched. He did not speak.

I bowed politely. "Good-by, Miss Pernot. I'll keep you advised."

I walked across the room and through the drapes with Rudolf Cassini's eyes sticking a knife into my back.

· 11 ·

I went back to my office to see if Paynter had delivered the substitution papers. I needed them before I could proceed. A narrow-shouldered, thin-faced male dressed like a sharpy at Roseland was leaning against the wall at the end of the corridor, absorbed in a newspaper.

I reached my door, turned the knob, and almost pushed my face through the frosted glass. I blinked at the door. It was locked. It had no right to be locked. Not at that hour. I frowned and let myself in with a key. Miss Cassidy was not behind her desk, nor was there a note explaining her absence—which was very queer.

I crossed over and sat behind my own desk and phoned Paynter to learn that the papers were on their way.

I settled back to wait. I had a new client. I had a chance to make a whopping fee. I had another reason to uncover Verna Ford's killer. Footsteps tapped across the outer office.

I glanced up as the door opened. The thin-faced man I'd seen lounging in the corridor hopped across the threshold, kicked the door shut, put his back against it, and showed me the sharp edge of his teeth in a tight little smile that was not even distantly related to merriment.

He owned a small, hollow-chested frame and a sallow complexion. He wore a tight, form-fitting coat and a pearl-gray snap-brim hat with light blue stitching. His lips were thin and wide. Then I saw his eyes. The irises were dark, the pupils enormously dilated. I did not have to see the punctures in his arm. He was coked to the scalp. His eyes told me that, and the way his bladelike nose kept twitching.

He took his right hand quickly out of his coat pocket and showed me the hard shine of a nickel-plated revolver. It was an ancient, dilapidated model that looked as if it would explode in his fist if he squeezed the trigger. There was something vaguely familiar about him.

He said in an odd, whirring voice, "Remember me, Jordan?"

"Not offhand," I said, blinking at him.

Moisture darkened the edges of his smile. "Sure you do. Think back, Jordan. Remember the St. Clare Hotel and a desk clerk named Dunn . . . ?"

I frowned, thinking hard. Then it came back to me. I snapped my fingers.

"Dunn!" I said. "Harry Dunn!"

"That's it. Six years. You got a good memory."

Six years. It didn't really seem that long. I remembered I had been working out of the Postal Inspector's office then, casing a third-rate hotel for some registered mail that had disappeared. I never did find the mail, but I turned up quite

another racket. Harry Dunn, the night clerk, had been rent-
ing rooms under duplicate registration cards, later destroying
them and pocketing the money. It had made the bonding
company sore. They had sent the clerk up the river.

I put my hands on the desk. I adjusted a pleasant smile
on my face. It was as artificial as a glass eye.

"When did you get out, Harry?" I asked.

"Keep away from that phone," he barked. "Tell me,
Jordan, do you remember who sent me over?"

"You sent yourself over, Harry."

He shook his head. "No. You did. Why didn't you mind
your own business? They'd never have nailed me. You sent
me up. Six years. The bastards never gave me a parole."
A cough tore at his throat and he wiped his mouth with his
sleeve. The gun never wavered.

I hung onto my smile. "It's a gamble," I said. "You
break the law and you take a chance on getting caught."

"You pushed it. I was getting away with it smooth as
silk. They'd never have wised up." A tic was jerking spas-
tically at his mouth. His eyes were abnormally bright. His
voice came out in a slow, harsh whisper. "I've been waiting
a long time for this, Jordan. A long time."

My mouth felt very dry. I wet my lips. "You can't square
matters this way, Harry. It's no good. You'll wind up in
the chair."

He sneered. "Not this time. I'm smarter than I was six
years ago. A lot smarter. Who do you think got your secretary out of the office?"

So that was it. I didn't say anything.

He gave me a dry, whirring chuckle. "I called her and
said you were stuck in Brooklyn on something important
and for her to come right out. She swallowed it like an
oyster."

He shuffled slowly forward, his eyes concentrating on
me. I sat motionless. His face glistened moistly. The nickel-
plated gun shook a little, but not enough. I felt sweat break
out on my temples.

Suddenly the phone rang.

It jangled harshly against two sets of raw nerves. His eyes jumped at it, then jumped back to me. There were deep folds in his brow. His lips had peeled against his teeth. The tic at the corner of his mouth went crazy.

"Let it ring!" he snarled.

We stared at each other like two mongrels eying a bone while the phone clanged away, sounding louder than a five-alarm fire.

Abruptly it stopped. His lungs emptied like a punctured balloon. His tongue came out and rode slowly over his lips. He was breathing very loudly through his open mouth. He took another step toward me.

"I'm gonna rub you out, Jordan, like a chalk mark. You won't even be——"

The phone cut him short. It was ringing again with a shrill insistence.

I sat up. "Listen, Dunn, this is an office. These are office hours. That phone better be answered or somebody will come along to investigate."

He stared at me dully, still breathing hard. "Okay. Get rid of him."

I lifted the handset. Dulcy's voice came along the wire, bright and vibrant.

"Hello, darling. What kind of an office is that? I've been ringing and ringing. Don't you ever answer?"

I swallowed and said harshly, "Nothing doing, Fergus. I can't see you now."

"This isn't Fergus, darling. This is Dulcy. Remember?"

"No," I barked. "Come in next week. I'm busy. I—I'm entertaining a lady."

"Scott!" gasped Dulcy, her voice shocked.

I covered the mouthpiece and looked up grimly at Dunn and said, "It's a guy down the hall. He's in a jam and he wants to see me."

Harry Dunn was bent forward, watching me with eyes that were stiffer than glass. His hand was white around the gun. He shook his head from side to side in a panicky gesture.

"No. Tell him no."

I spoke into the mouthpiece. "Listen, Fergus, I don't care how vital it is. It's out of the question. Some other time. I—hello—hello——"

I put the phone down slowly. I lifted my eyes and dropped my jaw. I licked my lips and turned up my palms. "It's no use," I said. "He's coming anyway."

Dunn's face seemed to shrink. He looked almost as if he was going to cry. "You—you're lying," he croaked.

"Okay," I said angrily. "Then go ahead and shoot."

It reached him. It plowed through the fog of his drugged brain. I might be lying, but he could not be sure. At this very instant a man might be walking down the hall on his way to join us. Dunn's eyes spurted frantically around the room.

I pointed at the pebbled-glass door behind my desk. I kept this door locked. I never used it unless I was trying to avoid someone. He whirled past the desk, clutching at the knob with one hand and trying to stuff the gun out of sight with the other. The door held. I had so much time it was pitiful. I picked the onyx pen set off the green blotter and hit him on the back of the head.

He fell like a clubbed steer.

I bent down and took away the gun. It was a .32 caliber Smith & Wesson center-fire revolver. It looked old enough to blow apart at the first shot. I sank into my chair. My heart was still pumping. My hands felt like two lumps of cold dough.

Harry Dunn rolled over and looked at me with glazed eyes. He sat up on the floor and put his face between his fingers and began to shake. I watched him for a moment, then I took the phone and rang John Nola.

When I heard his voice I said, "Listen, Nola, there's a fellow here by the name of Harry Dunn. He got out of the can a short while ago. He's still a little stir-batty and he thinks I was responsible for sending him up. He's been bothering the life out of me."

"Heeled?"

"No. No gun."

"Call the nearest precinct."

"That isn't what I want," I said. "Can you do me a favor?"

"Maybe." He sounded cautious.

"Send a man over from your department. I want this Dunn held for a couple of days until he cools off."

"You'll have to sign a complaint anyway."

"Okay," I said. "But I want one of your men. And, incidentally, I think you ought to know that I was just retained by Karen Pernot to handle her claim."

He inhaled softly. "I'll be damned!"

"Now I have an official standing in this case."

"Does Dillon know?"

"Not yet. He will inside of an hour."

"He's going to love that. All I could get out of that dame was a cold freeze. How did you do it?"

"Charm," I said smugly.

"Yeah, and finding Verna in your apartment had nothing to do with it."

He was a very shrewd guy. "It helped," I said.

He promised to send a man right over and I hung up.

Harry Dunn looked crushed. The dope was wearing thin. He was watching me out of shocked eyes in a face the color of wet cement. He had the dull, sick look of a man coming out of an anesthetic.

I said quietly, "I'm giving you a break, Harry. I'm not sure why. You're just out of clink and if I told them you came in here and shoved a growler in my face, you know what would happen. This is the last and only time. If you bother me again, if I see your face around here, I'll plant this gun on you and see that the boys really sock it to you."

He didn't say anything. I got Cassidy's typewriter and drew up an order sealing James Pernot's Riverdale house. By the time I had finished, a messenger from Paynter arrived with the substitution papers. Almost immediately Wienick arrived and took Dunn in tow. We went down to sign a complaint.

An hour later I was on my way up to Riverdale.

· 12 ·

It was a red brick house tucked into the shoulder of a hill on a nice quiet residential street, not large or gaudy, with about twelve rooms, enough for a bachelor to be comfortable in without feeling cramped, and it had an expanse of lawn in front of it, brown now but as smooth as broadloom and bounded by a box hedge that needed a haircut. Venetian blinds were drawn on all windows. I marched up a flagged walk and touched a button and inside four chimes played a hollow tune. When nobody answered I played an encore and then kept them working until I heard footsteps.

The door opened. Only enough to show me one-half of a man's face. A protuberant and baleful eye inspected me guardedly. A voice said, "Yes?"

"Mr. Eric Quimby?"

"What about it?"

I showed him an apologetic smile. "My name," I said, "is Ira Klumbach. I'm calling with reference to policy number—" I glanced at a slip of paper as if to refresh my memory—"double A-3944 which Mr. James Pernot had with my company."

The eye glistened and the voice became interested. "What kind of a policy?"

"Life insurance."

His interest mounted like a thermometer in hot water. He sounded almost cordial. "What about it?"

I gave myself a mental pat on the back. Money seemed to be the right approach with this bird. I glanced about. He took the bait and opened the door and I stepped past him and down two steps into a dropped living room. An interior decorator had done a cute job with some bleached modern furniture, a few tricky mirror effects, and a couple of Lautrec prints—mostly bedroom scenes. Mr. James Pernot had run true to form.

Against the wall I spied two packing boxes, one nailed shut, the other half filled with the family silver. Quimby wasn't wasting much time in making his assets liquid. I looked at him.

He had a long, shrewd face with two colorless, bulging eyes, somewhat furtive, and a head of tight black wire-wool hair clipped close to a high-crowned skull. It was the face of a man who has lived a long time by his wits. He was wearing plaid trousers and a blue wool sport shirt, open at the neck. Patches of wiry hair sprouted from his throat. He indicated a box chair and I sat down and gave him a meaningless smile.

He said, "About the policy?"

"Ah, yes, the policy. It's not a very large one," I said regretfully, "only ten thousand dollars but something ought to be done about it."

His nod committed him to nothing while he waited for me to continue.

I said, "I read about Mr. Pernot's accident several weeks ago, and since I sold him the policy I was wondering if I could be of any service. You know, proof of death, and the usual formalities, filling out the forms. I try to give this service to my clients. Claims really ought to be filed as soon as possible. Of course, I don't know the exact status of the matter, but I felt that you would probably know what to do."

He eyed me curiously, brows joined in a dark line over his nose. "Haven't I seen you somewhere before?"

I smiled. "That's quite possible. I send out calendars each Christmas with my picture on them. I have my own agency."

"Who was the beneficiary on this policy?"

"The estate," I said.

He measured me carefully. "Isn't that unusual—for a man to take out an insurance policy without naming a beneficiary?"

"Oh, yes. But not so much in the case of a bachelor like Mr. Pernot. He had an excellent opportunity to get this particular policy without a rigid physical examination but he had to make up his mind fast."

Quimby took a backward step, staring at me. His neck inched out of his collar. A hard light snapped into his eyes.

"You sonovabitch!" he said.

I looked blank. "I beg your pardon."

His teeth came together with a click. His mouth was nasty. "I recognize you now. There was a shot of you in the afternoon papers. You're that shyster, Jordan."

It was just as well. I was beginning to run out of talk anyway. I said, "I figured you'd spot me sooner or later. I just wanted to come in and look around and see what was going on. That silver, for example, it still belongs to the estate. If you sell it you break the law. You don't want to break the law, do you, Quimby?"

His eyes were venomous. "You dirty no good bas——"

"Easy. That won't buy you anything but a mouthful of broken crockery. I don't mind myself but my mother's very sensitive."

The muscles in his throat got swollen. "Get out of here," he choked, "before I break your back."

"Control yourself," I said pleasantly, "or you'll pop a blood vessel. Listen and brace yourself because you're not going to like this. Karen Pernot has just switched counsel and retained me as her lawyer. From now on this case is going to be handled differently and we're starting by getting you out of this house. This whole case, from Pernot's marriage to your sister, smells like an Arabian camel. It stinks. I'm going to root it up and air it out."

Flecks of red inflamed his eyes.

"Karen Pernot! She killed my witness."

"Certainly. And very cleverly too. As a matter of fact I helped her."

That stiffened him. His eyes were bulging like cherries.

"Nuts!" I said disdainfully. "Your witness was killed only after her testimony was tied up in affidavits. What happened, Quimby? Did Verna demand a bigger cut? Were you scared she'd sell out to the opposition? Did it seem like a good idea to salt her away?"

He leaped back as if he'd been stuck. "What!" he yelped. "Are you trying to say that I——" The rest of it was strangled against his larynx. His mouth curled bitterly.

I shrugged. "Why not? The newspapers are raising hell. The mayor is climbing on the commissioner's back and the commissioner is passing the buck to the boys, and there's a D.A. with ambitions, and they'd all love to ease the pressure by rigging somebody for the crime. Just to cool the heat. I tell you, Quimby, I could tailor you to meet specifications."

It was nonsense, of course, and I knew it and he knew it, but I had the distinct impression from the worried look on his face that there were some things he wouldn't want anyone to know about. His brown face cleared slowly and became crafty.

"You're full of wind. Who do you think you're kidding?"

"Not you, Quimby. Nobody could kid you. You know all the answers."

"Enough to keep you guessing, shyster."

"Don't use that word. I don't like it. Where did you get the poison you slipped into the brandy?"

He bent forward, his face sharp and mean.

"And there's another item," I said. "That diamond tiepin belonging to your brother-in-law, the one you gave Verna as a bribe."

His mouth pulled down and his tongue licked his upper lip. He was watching me tightly and narrowly.

"Verna told me a couple of things," I went on. "She had a bad feeling. She was scared. She was afraid somebody was measuring her for a box."

His mouth was a thin slash. Then he laughed harshly. "You must think I'm stupid."

"Not stupid actually," I said. "Just not very smart. Sly maybe, but not really smart. For example, you gave Verna that tiepin because you didn't have enough cash to keep her happy. And that thousand bucks you dug up for her. And that silver over there in the corner that you're crating for a fast sale. That's not smart, Quimby. It adds up to too many mistakes."

His breath quickened. "You're playing the wrong tune. Go on, beat it! Blow outa here!"

"When I leave," I said, shaking my head, "we both leave. The door gets locked behind us."

The blood charged into his face like a regiment of hussar cavalry. "My sister was married to Pernot and he left her this shack."

"Did he now? Are you sure? Only if Verna Ford was telling the truth and that's open to dispute. Suppose I turn up the missing witness and he swears that she was lying. And remember, Verna was not a doctor. She could have been mistaken. Maybe Pernot was not dead but unconscious. Oh, yes, my friend, there are many wrinkles to a case like this and I'm going to iron them out."

He breathed hoarsely, "I ought to kill you!"

Behind me a female voice said, "Go ahead, Eric, just say the word and I'll splash his brains all over the place."

She had entered without a whisper of sound. I turned and saw her standing on a small platform two steps above the floor in front of an open door leading back into the house. She pushed her arm out to its full length and at the end of the arm there was a small white fist. The fist held a short-barreled .32 Colt automatic, a blunt and businesslike Banker's Special. Her lips were drawn back over small, square teeth.

She was short, solid, and a little chunky. Her face was a bit too broad but made striking by adroitly lurid make-up. She wore her dark hair in a tight braid at the top of her head. A flowered silk wrap-around was beginning to slip open. Her tiny feet were shod in red mules trimmed with white rabbit's fur. Her eyes were hostile and sullen.

"Who's the girl?" I asked.

He said, "Put the gun away, Olga. I can handle this mug."

"Yeah," she sneered, "just like you handled that guy in Cincinnati."

"Well," I said, "I see you're all set here for a nice cozy winter."

"Keep it up," the girl said. "Just keep it up."

"Put that gun away," I told her. "It doesn't even make me nervous."

"Smart guy!" she squealed. "You think you're bulletproof?"

I sighed loudly. "Half a dozen people know I'm here. If anything happened—oh, put it away." I concentrated on Quimby. "Look, I don't want any arguments. I want you to pack up and get the hell out of here. Get your stuff together, the two of you, and beat it. Find a nice quiet hotel in town and have yourselves a party until the court decides one way or the other. In the meantime, one thing is certain, you're not going to stay here."

Olga came down the two miniature steps and slithered across the carpet as smoothly as a bobcat. She didn't stop until she was not more than two paces away and then she poured out her venom.

"I knew you were trouble the minute I saw you. You're too smart, all you damned lawyers——"

She went on like that but I wasn't listening. The judo experts have evolved several neat methods for handling a person with a gun. I didn't know any of them. But I can certainly see when the safety catch on a gun is locked. That—and her proximity—made it almost too easy.

I grabbed her hand and squeezed it so that she couldn't move her fingers. Then I gave a wrenching twist and the Banker's Special bounced on the floor. She cried out and made a claw of her left hand and raked me across the cheek. I spun her back against the sofa.

Quimby lunged in with a roundhouse swing that caught

me on the side of the head and made my ear ring like an
anvil. He was crouching low, a hard, wet gleam in his eyes.

I feinted and sank one into his stomach. It was a fine
wallop. He made a noise like the plug blown out of a com-
pressed-air cylinder. As he doubled over I lifted one to the
bony point of his chin that he must have felt all the way
down to his shoes. I felt it up to my shoulder. The small
of his back connected with a scatter rug and he skidded on
that along the waxed parquetry. He began to bleed from the
corner of his mouth. He lifted his hand and spit a tooth into
it and sat there staring at it with glassy eyes.

Olga was crawling toward the gun. I kicked it out of
reach. She put her arms around my leg and bit it. She had
a strong jaw and strong teeth. I let out a yell and tried to
kick her loose. It was no good. I had to pull her off by the
hair. The braid came loose and fell around her shoulders
like a black rope. She dug her teeth into my wrist.

Quimby floundered to his feet. I didn't think he had it in
him but by God he was on the march again. I pulled free
of the girl. He waded in, clumsy and stunned, like a wounded
rhino. "Boy!" I said. "You're a lulu!" I measured him
carefully and hit him in the throat. He sat down again. His
face was green. He was finished fighting.

I turned just in time to see the girl fling a book end. I
ducked and it struck the wall, sending a shower of loose
plaster along the molding. I coursed into her and we fell on
top of the sofa. She fought with her feet, hands, and teeth.
She kicked, writhed, and twisted. The silk wrap-around
hung in tatters. She was wearing nothing underneath. Her
thighs were white and muscular, her bosom firm, and the
skin glistened like new ivory.

"Jesus!" I breathed. "If you go on like this, you're going
to get yourself raped."

There was a brief furious spasm and then she collapsed.
She lay there, limp and panting. I climbed to my feet.

I went over and picked up the gun and broke out the
magazine and emptied the clip. I looked down into the

breech and made sure there was no shell lodged in the chamber. I already had Harry Dunn's nickel-plated revolver. I was building a collection I didn't want. I tossed this one into a corner and put the shells into my pocket.

Then I took out a paper and waved it in the air.

I said, "You're looking at a court order sealing this house until the surrogate qualifies an administrator. In thirty minutes I'm coming back here with a sheriff to execute the order. If you're not packed and out of here I'm going to prosecute you for breaking, entering, trespassing, grand larceny, assault with a deadly weapon, and everything else in the book." I jabbed a finger toward the packing boxes. "The silver stays here."

I strode out of there like a crusader. Behind me I felt two pairs of eyes burning with anger and frustration. I closed the door gently.

When I returned half an hour later, both Quimby and the girl were gone.

So was the silver.

· 13 ·

I spent the next two hours at LaGuardia Field, making inquiries. The plane which had brought the Pernots north was listed as Flight 7 and the stewardess on that trip was a girl named Janet Ross. She turned out to be a slender, self-possessed young lady. She recalled that the plane had made a forced landing in North Carolina and that most of the passengers had become jittery and insisted on completing the trip by rail. This left only about eight passengers and she was under the impression that she would recognize any of the men.

Then I went over to the Southern Airways administration office and got a list of the passengers who had left the plane in New York. I looked them over on my way back to the Drummond. I instantly eliminated two women, and also James and Ivy Pernot, which left four names. Two of these resided in Queens and probably would not have asked for transportation back to Manhattan. Either of the two remaining men, Kenneth Towner or George Gaxton, might be the missing witness.

It was already evening when I debarked from the cab. I went into the lobby and Dulcy, very lovely in a leopard jacket and no hat on her burnished hair, came forward and took my arm. Her smile brightened the gloomy room like a signal flare. We moved toward the elevators as if we had been doing the same thing for a long time.

When we emerged, she stopped me in the hall, facing me, her eyes troubled. "I was worried about you, Scott. That crazy business on the telephone—all that talk about a man named Fergus—I knew there was something wrong and——"

I put my arms around her and kissed her. She clung to me fiercely.

"Well!" she gasped. "That was nice. Did it have any special significance?"

"A reward," I said. "Your call saved my life. A guy who thought I was responsible for sending him to prison came into the office, wound up like a dollar watch, and wanted to shoot me. When you rang it helped me outfox him."

It worried her. She touched my cheek. "Those scratches, Scott. You look like you tried to seduce a reluctant alligator."

I grinned and told her about Olga.

"Well," she murmured, "come inside and let me clean it before you get rabies."

When we snapped the light on in the living room we found Bob Cambreau sprawled out on the sofa, sleeping, a bottle of Five Star Hennessy on the floor near his fingers.

Dulcy shook her head. "We'll have to wake him for dinner. He certainly can't exist solely on a liquid diet."

She followed me to the bathroom and watched, without modesty, while I stripped to the waist and whipped soap into a lather on my face.

I said, "Thanks for clearing my office of reporters this morning and letting Cassidy get some work done."

"Think nothing of it," she said airily. "You'll find me a great help in many ways. On long, wintry evenings and on rainy afternoons and when you want coffee in bed . . ."

"You make it sound very attractive," I mumbled, scraping the blade across my chin.

"And I have extraordinary powers of deduction, if you'll just confide in me." She paused. "You missed a spot. Are the police doing anything, or are you the only one working on it?"

"The police are working," I said, "a little with their brains and a little with their night sticks. But I wouldn't underestimate the forces of law and order in this town. They found Verna's boy friend in her room and arrested him. The District Attorney was thinking about an indictment, but I have an idea I changed his mind. The boy friend retained me as his lawyer."

"Is he guilty?"

"I doubt it."

"Who is?"

"An Armenian named Tikisian living at the Waldorf."

She grinned. "I'm sorry. You've only had twenty-four hours. I didn't really think you were that good."

The phone rang and she ran to get it. She was back in a moment saying that Nola was on the wire. I dried my hands and went into the living room.

"Hello, Lieutenant."

"Don't you ever hang around your office?" He sounded a bit edgy.

"On occasion. What's up?"

"You're going to love this, Jordan. That snowbird friend of yours, Harry Dunn, is out of the cooler."

I stood motionless, gripping the phone. I had wanted

Dunn in the can for a couple of days at least. "How did it happen?"

"This is a democracy," Nola said. "You can't hold a guy incommunicado here. Dunn went up for a preliminary hearing and bail was set and a guy came along and posted it."

"And who was this good Samaritan?" I asked tightly.

"A big piece of hard-boiled junk known as Janeiro—Steve Janeiro. Ever hear of him?"

"Should I have?"

"Maybe. Here's the rub. Janeiro is a lad who does odd jobs for a guy you certainly have heard about. A certain Mr. Leo Arnim."

I felt my stomach tighten like a fist. I didn't say anything.

"Yeah," said Nola tiredly, "I know what you're thinking. Leo Arnim runs the Magic Lamp and the late lamented Verna Ford worked for him. Is there a connection? Is there a tie-up? Where does Dunn fit into the picture?"

"I don't know," I said heavily. "I don't know. And I don't like it one damn bit."

"Well, I thought you ought to hear about it. So long." And he clicked off.

I dropped the phone slowly. I could feel a pulse hammering against my temple. I stood very still, tight-lipped.

Dulcy was watching me. "Would it help to talk about it?" she asked softly.

I shook my head, snapping out of it. "Baby," I said, "we're going out tonight. We're going dancing at a dive called the Magic Lamp."

She nodded, quickly aware that something was in the wind. "I'm ready," she said. "You get dressed and I'll rouse Bob."

I went into the bedroom and jumped into a fresh outfit. I wore a blue suit and a white shirt and a garnet-red tie. I felt like wearing a .45 and a small assortment of derringers.

When I came into the living room again, Dulcy was standing over Bob, looking frustrated. He was still sleeping.

"I can't wake him," she said. "It would take a five-gun salute."

I found a bottle in the liquor cabinet and brought it close to his ear and yanked the cork out with a loud pop. He sat erect with a jerk, batting his eyes.

"Double brandy, waiter," he said in a furry voice. "And make it snappy."

"Cut the comedy," I told him. "Freshen up; we're going out."

"Time to eat," Dulcy said.

He yawned widely. "Where are we going, children?"

"A hot spot called the Magic Lamp."

He pulled his brows together in an uneven line. He gave me a long, intent stare. Then he stood up and wiped his hands along his thighs. "Isn't that the *bistro* where Verna Ford used to dance?"

"The same. Know who runs it?"

He shrugged, still watching me oddly.

"A gentleman by the name of Leo Arnim," I said. "I had a chap locked up this afternoon for threatening to shoot me, and this same Arnim seems to have sprung him out of jail. I'd like to look his joint over and have a few words with him."

Bob nodded. "Okay, let's go."

We trooped to the street.

Behind the deceptive façade of a drab exterior, and down one flight, the Magic Lamp pulsed with a frenzied excitement. Its *Arabian Nights* atmosphere had all the trimmings designed to trim its patrons, from the costumed waiters wearing baggy pantaloons, red sashes, and daggers to the bronze lamps bracketed along the walls and belching puffs of gray smoke. Here it was, in a New York basement, mystery and glamor and a tinsel delusion phonier than a loan shark's smile. The dance floor was no bigger than a cigar box, and the band small and blarey. The place was packed with blank-faced girls painted like toy dolls and as bored as deaf mutes at a lecture. There were fat men who didn't have a thin chance of entertaining the girls in any other way. Wood alcohol and foul air and raucous laughter and brassy rumbas. This was Leo Arnim's club. This was where Verna Ford had nightly exhibited her talents.

A headwaiter in tails cut by an artist looked over his nose at us and shook his head. Bob stuck a bill into his willing palm and the shake miraculously became an obsequious nod. He snapped his fingers and a pair of waiters squeezed another table onto the floor.

The genie of Aladdin's lamp never performed any miracle that cold hard cash couldn't duplicate.

A swarthy, marble-eyed waiter with a pushed-in face and a malevolent twist to his mouth came over, snapped a napkin, and nodded.

I ordered bourbon for myself, Dubonnet for Dulcy, and Bob ordered a bottle of Napoleon for himself. At the next table two drunks were arguing heatedly over a girl in an indecent evening gown that exposed her back to the tail end of her spine and in front had a plunging neckline clear down to her umbilicus.

Bob's attention was riveted. He wore a drooling leer. "Look at that chassis! I think I'm falling in love."

"Stay out of it," I warned. "Those drunks are at the swinging stage."

Dulcy said, "You've been trained wrong. An early sunset is just as beautiful. You must learn to develop your aesthetic appreciation, Robert."

"Some other time," he said.

Dulcy glanced around and shuddered slightly. "This place gives me the creeps. In spite of all the revelry there's something sinister about it."

"Looks like a gold mine to me," I said.

Bob nodded. "It is. Look at the joint, packed to the rafters with people fighting to throw away their dough. There's money to be made. If you have any spare cash let me invest it for you, son. This country is due for the biggest industrial boom in its history. Just watch the market and see what happens."

"You watch it," chided Dulcy. "Scott has to keep an eye on me."

"Your heart's showing, little girl."

"That's all right," I said. "It's a wonderful heart. Shall we dance, Dulcy?"

She nodded and stood up and I ran interference for her to the floor. "We'll probably be crushed to death," I told her, "but I can't figure any other way of getting you into my arms right now."

"Dying in your arms," she murmured. "How nice!" She tucked her forehead under my chin and moved against me. "See how snug I fit?"

It was fine. We danced and I said, "Funny, but even the band sounds good, dancing with you."

"Thank you, darling. That's a real compliment."

Somebody jolted us, bringing Dulcy tight against me, and I wanted to thank him.

"Are you fond of me?" she asked suddenly.

"Very."

"Make a promise?"

"Anything."

"Be careful, Scott. I'm afraid of this place. I wouldn't want you to get hurt."

"Nothing is going to hurt me," I assured her. "I'm working on a job and if I make a lot of money I'm going to take you away to Bermuda."

"In the same stateroom?"

"Yup."

"Are you propositioning me, sir?"

"I'm offering you a job."

"Don't you want references? I worked almost four years as concubine to the Caliph of Bagdad."

"This job will last a little longer," I said. "Let's say about a lifetime."

She was silent a moment. Her eyes were misty. "Bermuda on a honeymoon. And we hardly know each other."

"I've known you all my life," I said. "I know a prize

when I see one." I swung her around and stopped dancing abruptly. I had seen something. Harry Dunn was seated at a corner of the bar with a glass in his hand and a glum look on his face. I apologized to Dulcy and brought her back to the table and then drifted over to the bar. I slid onto a stool beside Dunn and said casually, "Short stretch this time, wasn't it, Harry?"

His head jerked around. His eyes grew narrow and bitter. He said tightly, "Lemme alone, Jordan. Buzz off."

"Think back, Harry. I did you a good turn today."

"What do you want me to do—kiss you?"

"I want some information," I said.

He laughed briefly and without mirth and stared into his glass and said nothing.

"Look at it this way, Harry. I still have your gun, with your prints on it. I can change the complaint to a Sullivan Law rap. You know what that would mean."

He wet his lips, but did not look up.

I said, "You were coked up this afternoon, Harry. You didn't know what you were doing. I gave you a break. I didn't tell the law you were heeled." The barman moved in front of us and I pointed to Dunn's glass. "Two more of the same." The barman went away and did things with a shaker. I went on. "I'm going to ask you a few questions, Harry, and I want the answers."

He regarded me with wary suspicion.

"Did you know the girl who used to dance here?" I asked.

"Which one?"

"The blonde. Verna Ford."

His eyes glinted. "The squab that got whiffed off in your apartment?" He shrugged. "I saw her around. But I didn't know her well enough to pinch her thigh and get away with it."

I let that one go. "I have friends at Headquarters," I said. "They tell me that a guy named Steve Janeiro put up your bail. They said he was probably running the errand for Leo Arnim."

He put down his drink and looked up. "What about it?"

"I was wondering how well you knew Arnim. He's a little out of your class."

Dunn held up his hand and crossed two fingers. "We're pals, see, like this. We did time together. We were cellmates."

"And I guess you mentioned my name to him while you were up at Sing Sing."

"Yeah," he said thinly. "You were on my mind a lot, Jordan. I didn't have much else to think about."

"And you swore you'd get even with me when your time was up."

"I tried, didn't I?" he snarled.

The barman slid two fresh drinks across the polished mahogany. Dunn tossed his off in one gulp. I did the same. I felt like a sword-swallower. Leo Arnim must have been cutting his liquor with kerosene. I looked at Dunn. I didn't like his story. His assertion of friendship with Leo Arnim didn't ring true.

I said offhandedly, "I hear things are pretty tight in the narcotics racket. Where did you get your load yesterday?"

He froze. His jaw snapped and he gave me a swift, frightened glance. Without another word he slid off the stool and walked rapidly to a small door beside the bandstand. He opened it and disappeared.

· 14 ·

"Who was that odd-looking man?" Dulcy asked, when I joined her.

"What makes you so curious?"

"It's just that I want to know all your friends, darling."

I nodded. "And who has a better right? This fellow has a very interesting background. His name is Alonzo Viga and he used to be a Portuguese rumrunner."

A brassy fanfare choked her comment. The lights dimmed and a lemon-yellow spotlight cast an oval glare in front of the bandstand. The floor show was about to begin.

It was quite a performance and you can see its counterpart in a hundred dim cellars along the street. An anemic female in a silver wig caressed the microphone and chanted in a husky, burnt-out voice. Next, an adagio team pranced to the floor with fixed smiles pasted on their mouths, showing full sets of crockery, and knocked themselves into a state of utter exhaustion. A plump-faced baritone with effeminate hips squawled a ballad and sang an encore. For a grand finale, five maidens with faces by Max Factor, and adequately garbed for a Turkish bath, raced out, kicked their legs, wiggled their buttocks, and raced off. All this brought the house down in a thunderous ovation.

That was what Leo Arnim gave his customers and they loved it. Even Bob applauded wildly, but he couldn't have been serious.

Dulcy jumped suddenly to her feet and cried, "Look! Vivian!" She waved her hand. "Over here, Vivian."

It was indeed Vivian Cambreau. She spied Dulcy and side-stepped between tables to reach us. She greeted me, ignored Bob, and spoke to Dulcy.

"I've been looking all over for you, darling. I have a telegram forwarded from Chicago. I thought you might want it at once."

While Dulcy was tearing it open, Vivian explained, "I'm rather proud. I think I did an excellent detecting job in finding you. Dulcy's been talking about you so much, Scott, that it was easy to guess whom she was with. I phoned your apartment but you were gone. So I drove over in a cab and spoke to the doorman. He remembered when you left and he'd heard you tell the taxi driver to bring you here. Aren't I clever?"

"The original Mrs. Pinkerton," muttered Bob.

Dulcy looked up. "It's from Gil—my brother. He's flying in from the Coast and wants to spend a few days with me in Chicago." She frowned. "What shall I tell him?"

"That's simple," Vivian said. "If you want to stay with us, wire back that you're in New York and for him to come straight here."

"An excellent suggestion," I said, and was ready with a handful of silver which I dumped into Dulcy's hand. "There's a booth near the cloakroom. You can phone from there."

She stood up. "Don't go away now."

"A tank couldn't budge me," I said. She hurried away. I glanced up at Vivian. "Join us in a drink?"

"I hardly think so," she said, her manner aloof.

"Now don't go Victorian on me," I said. "You're divorcing Bob, but that doesn't mean you can't look at him. We're all grown-up and even a little civilized and if we strain ourselves maybe we can act like intelligent people."

"I just don't like the company at this table," she said.

"You weren't always so particular," put in Bob sarcastically. "Remember that hotel room in Montreal before we were married?"

Her eyes flashed. "At that time I was laboring under an odd misapprehension. I thought you were a gentleman."

"For Pete's sake!" I groaned. "Cut it out. Your marriage went on the rocks. It happens all the time. It doesn't mean you have to be at each other's throats. Stop squabbling. Sit down, Vivian."

She looked uncertain. I turned to summon a waiter for another chair but it was not necessary. The girl in the low evening gown at the next table cut loose with a piercing shriek. Her two drunk escorts went at it. One of them swung a champagne bottle, missed, struck the table with a shattering crash and a fine spray. They started to trade awkward blows.

Bob swiveled his chair and leaned forward. "A bet, Scott. Two to one on the lad with the mustache."

"Done," I said. "Twenty dollars."

Neither of us collected. A flying wedge of waiters surged in, scooped them like the cowcatcher on the *Twentieth Century Limited* and tossed them briskly into the street. It was done neatly and with dispatch and the whole thing barely consumed two minutes. That freed a chair for Vivian which I pulled around to our table.

"No more argument," I said sternly. "Sit down. I have a hunch Bob will be deserting us and I want you to stay here with Dulcy."

She sat down. Bob sighed and poured himself a long drink.

Vivian eyed me curiously. "Are you leaving?"

"For a few minutes. I have to make a social call."

Her eyes widened. "Here?"

I nodded.

"Who, Scott? Anyone I know?"

I said, "A long time ago I learned never to pique a woman's curiosity unless I meant to satisfy it. Otherwise they'll harass you to death or arrive at the most fantastic conjectures. I suppose I may as well tell you. The blonde who was supposed to act as the corespondent in your divorce used to work in this dive. I'm going to have a chat with the proprietor. He may have some information for me."

Bob finished his drink with a grunt. He looked over at us, his eyes red and his face growing flushed. He hiccupped loudly.

"That," said Vivian disgustedly, "is the sort of thing I had to endure for too many years."

"Living with you, beloved," said Bob, "would drive even Carry Nation to drink."

"That's enough!" I snapped. "What are you drinking, Vivian?"

"A Martini, very dry, please."

"No olive," remarked Bob. "Just a wee drop of strychnine."

"Ha, ha!" said Vivian. "Very funny. Who writes your material these days?"

I became aware that the swarthy waiter with the pushed-in face was at my side, standing there, watching me. For a moment it disturbed me. I gave him our orders and he took the empty glasses and lifted the brass ash tray standing in

front of me. I saw the piece of paper. It had been folded
and concealed under the tray. I covered it with my hand,
palmed it carefully and dropped it into my pocket, certain
that neither Bob nor Vivian realized anything had happened.

I glanced at the waiter. His eyes held no more expression
than two nailheads hammered into a board.

He emptied the tray, replaced it, and glided away. My
hands felt moist. I rubbed them with a napkin.

Vivian said, "Is it true, Scott, that you've been retained
by Karen Pernot?"

"Yes. Who told you?"

"Floyd. He was a bit upset."

"And where is that noted barrister this evening?"
asked Bob.

"Working," she said pointedly. "Not everyone was lucky
enough to be born with money."

"Or brains," he countered.

"At least he's occasionally sober."

"Will you stop badgering each other," I said. "I hope
a divorce puts you both in a better humor."

Bob looked at me. "How about it, Scott? While my ever
loving spouse is still here, what would you suggest?"

"Certainly not another performance like the last one," I
said. "That stuff is out, completely. Take my advice, send
Vivian to Reno, and let me contact a lawyer down there to
put in an appearance for you. Accept service of the summons
and complaint and then let the case go by default. Mental
cruelty as a cause of action will do."

"What's more," said Vivian, "it's the truth."

"Fine," Bob nodded. "This trip is on me."

"No, thanks, I'm quite capable of paying my own way."

"Yes?" He lifted his brows. "I heard from Jamison you
got into some wildcat mining stock in Canada. So if you
need any cash, my pet, I'd be——"

"No," she said coldly. "You've already been more than
generous. Floyd wouldn't hear of it."

Bob shrugged. "Okay. Get it from him—if he can chase
the moths out of his wallet."

"You're getting to be quite a wisecracker," she said scornfully.

Bob grinned and moved his chair around, switching his attention to the girl at the next table who, now that the drunks had been bounced, was without escort. He reached over and ran a finger along her bare spine. She spun around. Her eyes sparked fire.

"Hello," Bob said affably. "Lonely?"

Her eyes moved over him in a slow, speculative appraisal. She had a bold, handsome face that looked as if she'd stepped out of Elizabeth Arden's not ten minutes ago. The anger melted over it like grilled cheese. Her lips curled slowly in a broad smile that was friendly and dripping with invitation.

"I'm desolate," she said huskily.

He swung his chair to her table, taking the bottle of Napoleon with him. In no time at all their heads were close together like the heads of two conspirators in a Balkan cellar.

Vivian moved her shoulders. "That ought to keep him busy over the week end." She waved. "Here's Dulcy."

"It's all fixed," Dulcy said, smiling and sitting down. "Gil will be here in a few days." She glanced around. "Where's Bob?"

"Behind you," I said.

She looked. "The dirty libertine! To think he'd desert us for——"

"It's just as well," said Vivian. "He was getting frightfully insulting."

I stood up. "You two children stay here and don't pick up any strangers."

"Where are you going, darling?"

"On a short visit in a back room. If I'm not here by Michaelmas next surround the place with cops."

"If you're not back in fifteen minutes I'll come looking myself."

I said to Vivian, "Keep her at the table," and I turned and set a course for the bar. I stood under one of the bronze lamps that kept puffing smoke like a nervous man with a cigarette, and found the piece of paper that had been under the ash tray. I unfolded it carefully. The writing was in pencil and printed in rude capital letters.

GET OUT OF THE PERNOT CASE, JORDAN. GET OUT WHILE YOU'RE STILL ALIVE.

I pegged it away in my pocket. It was a stupid note and it was a stupid threat. I was standing there and I realized that my mouth was open. I closed it stiffly. I tried to grin but it was not successful. I took out a handkerchief and mopped the moisture off my forehead, then squared my shoulders and headed for the small door beside the bandstand.

It opened on a narrow passage with numerous doors on either side. A naked bulb glared whitely against the ceiling. One of the doors popped open and a compact little girl in a terry-cloth robe and a heavy thickness of make-up came out, hugged herself coyly, and gave me an interested look.

"Where can I find Leo Arnim?" I asked her.

A huge smile. "Won't I do, honey?"

"Not now. Meet me at Nedick's, New Year's Eve."

The smile hit the floor with a bounce. "A comedian," she said. "Last door to the left."

I was about four paces away when the last door on the left slammed open and disgorged Harry Dunn. The door closed softly on its spring. Dunn saw me and his jaw dropped and he flattened himself against the wall like a shadow. In the past thirty minutes something new had been added. A ripe, plum-colored bruise hung under his left eye and the eye itself was almost shut.

I glanced pointedly at the door behind him. "Your pal, eh, Dunn?"

He was scared. He compressed his lips. Without a word he edged past me, crablike, and then went scrambling down the corridor.

I took hold of the knob and twisted it. The door opened and I stepped quietly into Leo Arnim's office.

· 15 ·

It was a small room, nothing showy, about the same as any business office. It held a safe, a few leather chairs, a filing cabinet, and a solid oak desk. A man was sitting behind the desk, slowly rubbing the knuckles of his right hand and staring at it. I let the door close softly and put my back against it.

"Arnim?" I said.

His eyes jumped up and pinned me against the door like a butterfly. They were hard yellowish eyes above a broad nose and a thick, sensual mouth, all arranged in the usual manner on a heavy face that was bleached as white as the meat of a pompano. A face the sun didn't get much chance to shine on. A face that hated to show what its brain was thinking.

"How did you get back here?" His voice was dry and brittle and resonant.

"The usual method of locomotion," I said. "Walking."

"Take yourself out the same way."

"Later. Let's talk first, Arnim."

"Talk?" Two sharp, vertical lines dented the bridge of his nose. "Just who the hell are you?"

"The name," I said, "is Jordan."

He recognized it. His eyes grew narrow and stony and his face was bleak. He said tightly, "You're the lip involved in that Ford killing."

I nodded.

"Beat it. I don't like lawyers."

I shrugged and let it pass.

"I don't like lawyers at any time," he said tonelessly. "Especially I don't like 'em when they begin poking a nose in my business."

"I don't like tax collectors," I said, "but there isn't a hell of a lot I can do about them. It's unfortunate, but our businesses happen to make a junction at this point."

"In what way?"

"The murder of Verna Ford. I didn't ask to get involved. It was dropped in my lap. So I'm stuck with it. She used to work for you and that gives us a union of interests."

His brows folded together and he rocked back in his chair and gave me a long, wooden stare. Then he let the chair carry him forward. "Get out," he said dispassionately. "Get out while you can still move under your own steam."

I shook my head. "It's no good, Arnim. It would only make my job a little harder, that's all. I'd have to hire a private eye to do a little leg work for me and whatever had to come out would come out anyway. Why not talk to me, friendly like, and save us both time and trouble?"

He flexed his fingers and made two fists. He thought it over, clearly not liking it. His yellowish eyes measured me very carefully and he pursed his thick lips. He said suddenly, "All right. Go ahead and talk."

"Let's start with the girl."

"What about her?"

"She worked for you."

"A lot of people work for me. I run an active club here."

"True, but they don't all get killed."

A thin smile scarcely moved his lips. "Read the papers. People get killed all the time."

"True. But their employers don't shrug it off."

"So you think I'm indifferent."

"On the surface, yes."

His face hardened. "Listen, a dancer in my club goes to a guy's apartment and gets herself permanently shelved. What am I supposed to do? Fast for a week? Go to confession? Sprinkle ashes on my head? I have more than a dozen broads working for me. I don't give one whisper in hell about their morals or what they do in their spare time, including getting themselves plastered, knocked up, or murdered. It's none of my business so long as I can find replacements. I run a night club, not a dormitory. Verna Ford had been working for me only about a week. I hardly knew the dame. All right, so she's on a slab in the morgue. I don't owe her a thing and I wouldn't spend a plugged nickel to give her a fancy burial.''

It was quite a speech and I let the silence close in on top of it. After a moment I said, ''What made you give her a job in the first place? From what I know she had never entertained in public before.''

''Why not? She came here looking for work. She had enough on the ball, looks, a bit of talent, and a lot of sex. My customers like that stuff. I give it to them.''

''And you took her on?''

''Sure. I put her right on the pay roll.''

I said, ''She had a private life. What can you tell me about it?''

''Nothing. I don't get chummy with the hired help.''

''But you've seen her around the club. Was she a big drinker?''

''No more than most. They all drink these days. Too goddam much.''

''Any particular brand?''

''I wouldn't know. Ask the bartender.''

''How about men? Was she intimate with anyone in the club—waiters, musicians, entertainers?''

''I'm too busy to check that kind of stuff,'' he said contemptuously. ''Let me ask you a question, Jordan. The cops cleared you, didn't they?''

''They didn't book me for murder, if that's what you mean.''

''Then you're clear. Why don't you forget it?''

''A number of reasons. I happen to have a stake in the case.''

His eyes searched my face. ''What do you mean?''

I said, ''You read about the Pernot case?''

He nodded.

''Verna Ford was the chief witness in that business and I happen to represent one of the claimants.''

The lids shielded his eyes. ''When did this happen?''

''Today. Pernot's niece called me in.''

He drummed softly on his desk top for a moment. "You think that's wise?"

I shrugged. "She's cutting me in for a piece of the take."

He was silent for a moment. Then he said, "I guess a man has to stick to his own racket. You hinted there were other reasons."

"Yes. Two of them. And you're both of them, Arnim."

His eyes were suddenly shining and very hard. He was flexing his fingers again. "All right," he said harshly. "I'm listening."

"Let's take them one at a time," I said. "Let's talk about Harry Dunn, an ex-con and a snowbird, who came into my office this afternoon doped to his hairline and heeled with a broken-down gun and as trigger happy as a frightened soldier on night patrol. Let's open him up and see what makes him tick. I had a lucky break. I got out of that one by the width of your fingernail. I should have turned him over to the cops, gun and all, but I was too soft. I wanted to give him a chance to think it over in the cooler, and instead some hood comes along and bails him out."

Not a muscle in Leo Arnim's face moved.

"There's a curious coincidence," I said. "Or maybe it isn't a coincidence at all. The hood's name is Steve Janeiro. I hear this Steve Janeiro works for you. I already know that Verna Ford worked for you. Well, maybe Harry Dunn works for you too. Maybe he was working for you when he marched into my office and stuck a gun in my face and almost smoked me out."

Arnim's hands gripped the arms of his chair and the knuckles shone like polished ivory. He said thickly, "Dunn is a friend of mine. I heard he was in jail and I bailed him out. That's all there was. Don't read any more into it."

"A friend of yours!" I jeered. "Prison buddies! I just saw him walk out of here wearing a shiner he never got walking into a closed door. More likely a closed fist. And while we're at it, Arnim, let's iron out the whole thing. Just what is your angle? Why are you trying to scare me off this case? Did you think I'd run because one of your greasy waiters stuck a note on my table?''

He arched back. "What's that about a note?''

"Go ahead," I said disgustedly. "Act cute. Trying to scare me like I was a schoolgirl.''

He jabbed out his hand. "Let me see the note.''

"Not on your life. No, sir. Not a chance. That note goes down to Headquarters. The boys at Homicide may want to trace it in case I get into an accident that isn't an accident.''

"Let—me—see—the—note," he said harshly, spacing the words.

"Nothing doing. Call it an insurance policy. It stays with me.''

"You're sticking your neck out, Jordan.''

"Not my neck," I said and then felt the cold draft playing across it and I wheeled in time to see the door close behind a man.

"Easy," the man said, grinning broadly. "Take it easy.''

He was not carrying a gun. He didn't need a gun. He could have taken me with both hands tied behind his back. His hands swung loosely at his side, knotted up like huge mallets. He was an enormous hulk with a frame like an oil derrick and his face was vaguely reminiscent of Primo Carnera. It was a loose-featured face, thick-lipped, heavy-lidded, shovel-chinned. Everything about him was loose, his joints and the way the midnight-blue tuxedo fitted him. His small, mean eyes were canopied by beetling brows that made a furry line across the bridge of his nose. His black hair was tight and curly. Nola had called the turn. A big piece of junk. He looked like a guy who liked bullfights, especially if the bull won.

"Neat," I said. "Very neat. A button under the carpet would bring him in.''

Arnim said softly, "The note. This is the last request.''

I shook my head.

"He has a paper in his pocket, Steve. Take it away.''

Janeiro's fingers chewed into my shoulder like the jaws

of a steam shovel. My whole arm started to go numb and I shook violently loose.

"Take your paws off me," I snarled.

"The note, Jordan," said Arnim.

I looked up at Steve Janeiro. He smiled a loose, moist smile and lifted both hands and came towards me with the ponderous clumsiness of a bear on its hind legs. I sighed audibly through my nostrils.

"Aagh! Take it. Call him off. Get him away."

I pulled the note out of my pocket and threw it on the desk. Arnim unfolded it, glanced at it briefly, then dropped it into a drawer.

"I'll keep it," he said. "I don't expect you to believe this, but I didn't send that note."

I curled a lip and glared at Steve Janeiro. "So you're the nice, kind bail bondsman whose heart breaks to think that any of the boys have to spend a night in that nasty old jail."

"I sent him," said Arnim. "I told you the reason."

"As simple as that?"

"As simple as that." His eyes were veiled. "Tell me, Jordan. Have you aired your theories to the law?"

I gave him a blank look.

"Your notion," he said, "of tying everything into one neat package—Verna Ford and Harry Dunn and me."

"The cops aren't exactly imbeciles," I said. "The connection is apparent. They'll spot it sooner or later."

The big, bleached-white face sagged and looked tired. "One thing before you leave, Jordan. I don't want anything to do with the law. I can't afford it. How much will it cost to keep my name out of this mess?"

I looked at him.

"In cash, Jordan. Paid now. How much to keep me clean?"

I shook my head. "I don't know what you're trying to buy, Arnim, but whatever it is I haven't got it to sell. A girl has been murdered. The cops are working on it because that's their business. I'm working on it because I think it has a bearing on my case. There's no way of telling what's liable to come out in the wash."

I went to the door and opened it and stepped out. I walked down the narrow corridor and through the door beside the bandstand. The noise and smoke struck me with the force of a blow. I stood there, blinking at it, and thinking that none of it seemed quite real.

I joined the girls at the table.

Dulcy said, "You were gone so long I was beginning to think you'd deserted us."

"No, ma'am," I said, "not while you still have your youth and your beauty."

"Don't forget my money," she said.

"It never left my mind."

"And when I'm old and wrinkled?"

"I'll trade you in for a new model. Let's not worry about that for about forty years."

Her eyes prowled around the club. "Let's pick up a man for Vivian."

"Don't bother," said Vivian. "I'm meeting Floyd later."

"If he's working on the Pernot case," I said, "tell him he's wasting his time. He can't win."

She smiled. "He can try." She added seriously, "Scott, do you think that girl was lying about what she saw the night of the accident?"

"Verna Ford? Why not? People are apt to do a lot more than tell lies when so much money is involved."

She shook her head emphatically. "Oh, but Floyd wouldn't have anything to do with perjured testimony."

I laughed. "There's faith for you. And very touching. Listen, Dillon is a lawyer, my dear, not a saint. Almost any lawyer will flavor the facts to fit a case. Take your divorce. Suppose it had gone according to schedule. That would have been a lie, a harmless lie, but a lie just the same. Concocted, arranged, and executed all at Dillon's instigation."

Her smile was wryly one-sided. "Not quite. If Bob had been in your apartment with that girl the infidelity requirements would have been honestly met."

"You're right," I agreed. "Tell me, Vivian—Dillon is

still cagey about it—wasn't Verna Ford the girl he actually sent up to my apartment?''

"I don't know. Floyd made all the arrangements.''

I shook my head. "That was bad judgment. It was a stupid play. If anything at all went wrong her credibility for a more important case would have been impeached.''

"Perhaps,'' she said stiffly, "the divorce was most important to Floyd. Maybe she was the only girl he could find.''

Dulcy said, "Let's get out of this place. I hate it.''

I glanced around for our waiter and a thin specimen with a razor-sharp face sidled up.

"Yes, sir?''

"Where's the other one? The flat-faced buzzard with the buttonhook eyes.''

"I beg your pardon, sir.''

"The waiter who served us before.''

He shrugged faintly. "Called off the floor, I believe. May I help you, sir?''

"You're so damn polite,'' I said, "I feel like asking you to sit down with us and have a drink.''

"Thank you, sir. I'm sorry. It's against the rules.''

"Too bad,'' I said. "We're leaving anyway. Let's have a check.''

While he was bringing my change I glanced at the next table. "What's happened to Bob?'' I asked.

"The usual thing,'' said Vivian. "He's probably on his way to Atlantic City with that girl.''

I sighed heavily. "That guy is going to get belted with a Mann Act rap one of these days.''

Vivian said, "They should have gelded him when he was a boy.''

I had a comment on that, but the waiter returned, and we all rose and started to negotiate the hazardous obstacle course toward the cloakroom. The brassy music on top of the shrill voices was beginning to hurt my head; smoke fog hung over the room worse than Pittsburgh on a busy day. I was anxious to clear out before they started another floor show. That would have been the finishing touch.

I reared back like a balky horse. The back of my neck crawled. I was goggling at a sight that I didn't believe and yet it had to be true because I was seeing it with my own eyes.

Seated at a table were three people with their heads bent close together. Eric Quimby, his redoubtable girl friend, Olga, and Steve Janeiro.

I tore a path through the gauze of tobacco smoke and stood over them. "Hello, folks," I said.

Three pairs of eyes jumped up and started to hate me.

"I can't believe it," I said. "It isn't possible. If this is a coincidence then I'm the Dalai Lama of Tibet."

Olga said harshly, "Who turned over a rock and let him crawl out?"

"Well," I said, "I trust you found pleasant accommodations in town."

Quimby's jaw was thrust out and I saw the hard edges of his teeth. Janeiro lumbered to his feet and looked down at me with his dull, not too bright eyes and he said in his odd, whirring voice, "You're not wanted here, Jordan. Take a powder."

"Sure," I said. "Sure. Give my regards to Leo."

I seemed to be walking on a pair of borrowed legs that hadn't been broken in very well. I joined the girls at the cloakroom and coerced my mouth into a smile.

"Listen, Houdini," said Dulcy, "you'd better walk out ahead of me so I can keep an eye on you."

In the street, Vivian left us to keep her appointment with Floyd Dillon.

· 16 ·

We were caught in a whirlpool that night, Dulcy and I, a merry-go-round of dancing and talking and laughing and just finding each other. We went to the Carnival and then to the Stork Club to gape at the celebrities. We were very gay and maybe we were a little drunk. Every time I held her in my arms something seemed to explode in my veins. We wandered to the river and watched the glittering necklace of lights strung across the Palisades. Later we found a hansom and headed across town with the horse's hoofs rhythmically clopping against the pavement. The air was crisp and the sky an indigo blue and the night crystal-clear. We sat with a blanket over our knees and held hands.

"It's been a wonderful evening, darling."

"Come here." I kissed her.

"Umm!" She sighed contentedly. "Must I go home, darling?"

"Yes. It's getting on towards dawn."

"Can't I go home with you?"

"Careful. You tempt me."

"Why not, Scott? I'm old enough to know what I want without dissimulation. I want you, Scott, and I don't want to wait."

"Stop needling me," I said gruffly. "I'm not made of stone. You'll have me dragging you into the park."

"Would that be fun?"

I grabbed her and kissed her violently, stopping only when the carriage pulled up in front of Vivian's apartment. I took Dulcy to the door and after a lingering farewell broke reluctantly away.

The pavement was like live sponge under my feet. The sky was dark and the street lamps wore a golden shine. Life had taken on meaning and I wasn't a bit tired. I decided to walk across the park. The stars were distant and frosty.

I hurdled a wall and cut diagonally across a patch of hard turf. There hadn't been any snow for weeks and the ground was dry. I could still taste the sweetness of Dulcy's mouth. Just as I circled the bandstand on the Mall it happened without warning.

A shot fractured the stillness of the night. A bullet whined past my ear and bit viciously into the wall behind me.

I dropped like a ballast sack. It was pure reflex. The

globe of a park lamp threw a yellow blister of light at the spot on the concrete walk I had just deserted. With a kind of grim desperation I went burrowing into the shadows at the juncture of wall and earth. As I fell something hard jarred my hipbone. It was Harry Dunn's nickel-plated revolver. I hauled it out.

I lay on the cold ground, waiting, not seeing much and not breathing much either. I wormed slowly along the wall to a thicker darkness, regained my feet, and stood with my head cocked, listening. There were no sounds except the creak of a tree branch and the soft purr of a car somewhere in the park. The shadows had swallowed my assailant.

It could have been the toughest break I ever had. At that moment the car rolled around a curve in the road and piercing headlights sprayed the wall and caught me in their white glare. My shadow flung itself, immense and grotesque, against the wall.

The beam nailed me there like a spider. A perfect target. A giant bull's-eye.

Another shot exploded. I saw a spurt of flame from the muzzle spit luridly into the darkness beside a tree not fifty yards away. I arched my back, screamed like a frightened horse, threw out my arms and tumbled drunkenly to the ground. If the driver of the car heard anything, he wasn't stopping.

Somewhere a police whistle shrilled keenly. I was on my knees now, with my eyes glued hard to the tree. I saw a shadow duck out, stand uncertainly, then wheel and run. I braced the nickel-plated revolver on my left wrist and carefully squeezed the trigger.

The gun convulsed violently. The runner stiffened, staggered a few paces, then continued his rush. Darkness folded around him. I pumped out another shot just for luck. I sprang to my feet and sprinted after him. I cut across the cement walk and hurdled a bench. I cleared the bench all right but I never saw the low wire fence just beyond it. It caught the toe of my shoe and I walloped to the ground in a shattering dive.

I lay there, stunned. That cleared the gunman.

Heavy footsteps trotted up. A pocket torch blinded me in its concentric beam, glittering on the revolver in my hand.

"Drop it!" a voice jerked out. "Drop it!"

I dropped the gun. He was a big cop, much too fat for running, and his breath came hard. A police positive was ready for action in his huge palm.

"Kick it over," he ordered.

I did what he wanted.

He stooped, grunting, and picked it up. He breathed easier. Confidence rolled into him.

"He went that way," I said.

"Who?"

"The guy who ambushed me."

"Yeah," he said skeptically. "That's what they all say. You got a license for this rod?"

"No."

"Oho! That's enough right there, brother." He sniffed at the muzzle. "Who were you shooting at?"

"Pigeons," I said, still jarred and feeling lightheaded.

His chin pushed out. "What?"

"Pigeons," I said. "I was hungry."

"Wise guy, huh? What's your name?"

I exhaled heavily. "Stamboul—Felix Stamboul."

"Where you from?"

"Turkey." I got the shakes then. It was cold but my back was moist with sweat. "Listen," I growled, "there's a killer loose and he's getting away while you stand here chinning at me. Dammit! Let's do something. Let's get over to the nearest precinct house."

A short distance away there were footsteps and a voice called out, "Murphy."

"Over here."

Two men materialized out of the darkness. The big cop put his flash on them. I saw a second cop and the man he had in tow and the skin pulled tight across my chest.

"Well," I said. "Look who's here!"

He was tall and thin with a derby on his head and a trench coat flapping around his knees. Light glistened on thick-lensed glasses over a clublike nose. It was the same nose to which I had delivered a consignment of knuckles in the hallway outside my door while Verna was still lying in my living room.

The second cop said, "I heard them shots, Murph, and was high-tailing it over here when this bonzo runs smack into me. I see you got one too, huh?"

"Yeah. Your man have a gun?"

"Colt .32 in a shoulder sling. Claims to have a license. Says he's a private dick."

Murphy made a harsh sound in his throat. "One of them, eh? His gun been fired?"

"Nope. I got it right here. Full clip and no powder smell."

Murphy looked at the man with the club nose. "You runnin' away from this guy? He takin' them shots at you?"

The man shook his head.

"C'mon, let's go," Murphy said, waving his pistol to round us up.

At the precinct house, the desk sergeant, a beefy red-faced cop, glared down over his desk and made me repeat my story. He dangled the nickel-plated revolver and said, "Where'd you get this?"

"I took it away from a German admiral. Listen, call Lieutenant Nola of Homicide. He's probably home. He'll vouch for me."

"At this hour?" he snorted. "I'd be pounding a beat in Flatbush next week."

"Oh, call him. Or rout Inspector Boyce out of bed."

The sergeant eyed me dubiously. "I guess you know the mayor too."

"He's my godfather," I said.

The sergeant blinked and switched to club-nose. "Your name?"

"Emmanuel Scully."

"A private eye, eh? Let's see your papers."

Scully got out a leather folder and tossed it onto the desk. After a brief inspection the sergeant passed it back. "Working on a case?"

Scully nodded.

"What about?"

The man with the club nose squeezed out a smile. "You know better than that, sergeant. Anyway it has nothing to do with this shooting."

"So *you* say. What kind of a case?"

Scully's mouth compressed into a thin line and he shook his head.

The sergeant growled. "What were you doing in the park so late?"

"Going home."

"Aagh! Go kiss a coconut!" I snorted. "He was following me, Sarge."

"Yeah? What for?"

"Ask him."

"I'm asking you."

"Ask away. He ought to know what he was doing."

"He's a private dick. He don't have to talk."

"I'm a lawyer. Neither do I."

The sergeant's chin sank down into his collar and his face got an angry scowl on it. "I don't like lawyers any better than I like private dicks."

"That's too bad. I wonder how loud you'd yell for one if the commissioner suspended you for taking graft from all the parlor houses in this district."

I thought for a moment he was going to have apoplexy. His face got congested and he bristled like a porcupine. He sputtered incoherently for a moment, then grabbed up the phone, got Nola's number and dialed it. I heard him identify himself and then he said, "I got a lawyer here by the name of Jordan. Know him, sir?" A pause. "Yeah, he's in trouble—plenty. Carrying a weapon without a license. Firing it in Central Park . . . No, he's not drunk. He says somebody tried to pot him. I don't like the way he looks, Lieutenant, and I don't like the way he talks. He fobbed off a phony name on Patrolman Murphy. I think he knows a hell of a lot more than he's telling. He won't co-operate. We ought to toss him into the cooler."

Nola must have been talking because the sergeant kept his ear to the receiver, his eyes glaring balefully at me, and after about thirty seconds he handed me the phone without comment.

I took it and said, "Hello, Nola."

"Do I have to put a bodyguard or a governess on you?" barked Nola. "What happened?"

"Nothing much," I said. "I was walking home through the park. Somebody must have been tailing me because when I got under a light, he took a shot at me. The slug came so close I could smell it. I hit the ground and stayed there. Then, just as I got up, a pair of headlights from a passing car lit me up and *bingo*, he pumped another shot. I made believe I was hit. I yelled and fell over. That brought him out from behind the tree where he was hiding and he started running. The lighting was lousy but I squeezed a shot at him and I think I winged him because he staggered. Then he went on and I lost him when I tripped over a fence. Somebody tried to pot me and the sergeant knows it because the cops here heard four shots and only two were fired from my gun."

"Where'd you get the gun?"

"From Harry Dunn."

"You said he wasn't heeled."

"I was lying. I wanted to give him a break."

"You're a pip!" Nola growled. "You just beg for trouble. I warned you that somebody would sneak up behind you some dark night and open a leak in your back. You ought to know better than to go jaywalking around the park at three in the morning."

"What am I supposed to do?" I asked. "Buy a Sherman tank?"

"No, a coffin. Any idea who it was?"

"Sure. I have plenty of ideas but I can't boil them down. It could have been Dunn or Arnim or Janeiro or Dillon or

Quimby or any one of a dozen other citizens who don't
like me.''

He cursed without rancor, then said, ''You think you
nicked the guy?''

''I know I did.''

''Okay. We'll put Dunn on the wires and when we pick
him up we'll strip him down and search for wounds.''

''Whoever got plugged will have to be treated. Aren't
doctors supposed to report that sort of thing?''

''Sure. So what? Since when have doctors cornered the
integrity market. If I had a dime for every medico who'd
patch a guy up without making a peep to Headquarters I'd—
aagh! The hell with it! How about you? Making any progress
along your line?''

''Some. I'll tell you about it in the morning.''

''Okay. Put the sergeant on.''

I handed the phone back and after some more conversation
the sergeant disgruntledly plugged the handset into its cradle, looking as sore as a fenced-off rooster. He stared at me
hard. ''The lieutenant says to let you go.'' He jabbed a
finger at Scully. ''You—you're not clear yet. What made
you run away from the shooting?''

''Listen, Sarge,'' said Scully coolly, ''just because he
got your goat, don't bark at me.''

''Answer the question,'' the sergeant said hoarsely.

Scully shrugged faintly. ''Put yourself in my shoes. What
would you do? I'm not looking for trouble. I heard a shot
and ran away. I didn't want to get jammed up with a park
killing.''

''You were tailing this guy and you didn't see anybody else?''

''Nope.''

The sergeant swung his head violently toward the door.
''Go on, beat it, both of you! This is the lieutenant's re-
sponsibility. He'll have to answer to the inspector.''

Outside the sky was turning a dirty suède. The city had
the bleak gray look of approaching dawn. There was a sharp
bite to the air. On the sidewalk I grabbed Scully's arm and

swung him around. He didn't look real. The lumpy nose, the open mouth, the thick glasses shining like olives under the green station lights.

"That's women for you," I said. "Make a guy lose his grip. I never tumbled that you were tailing me, Scully. I don't like it. Stay away from me."

"And if I don't?"

"You'll wish you had."

"You frighten me, Jordan."

He jerked his arm loose, hawked at me, and strode off. I watched him go, his coat skirt flapping around the calves, until he turned the corner and was out of sight.

I was the only person standing on the street. A truck roared past me and backfired. Involuntarily I threw up my hands and ducked. When silence had jelled again I closed my mouth and walked three blocks. I found a cab and went home.

· 17 ·

They were getting to know me down at Headquarters and the cop on duty gave me a brief nod. Nola was behind his desk, looking tired and drawn. I was getting settled in an uncomfortable chair when the door opened and Wienick stepped in.

Nola said, "What kind of a detective are you? Sometimes I think you couldn't find a salami in a delicatessen store. I want Harry Dunn. I want him today. Understand?"

Wienick looked aggrieved. "How do we know he ain't in Mexico already?"

"Follow your nose. When a rat is scared you can smell him ten miles away. You're a cop. The city pays you a salary every week. Find Dunn."

Wienick shrugged elaborately. "Yeah, and what good does it do? We pinch him and somebody springs him. There's

too many loopholes. Bail bonds, habeas corpuses, dismiss-
als, acquittals—Jesus! I sometimes think the law was wrote
for crooks.''

"No alibis. I want Dunn." Nola's voice was cuttingly
sarcastic. "Do I have to hire the Pinkerton agency to help
the New York City Police Department? This Dunn is pretty
big, all of five-two. Think you can handle him or do you
want a couple of harness bulls along in case he gets sore?''

"Listen, Lieutenant, I can handle my weight in——"

"I know, chorus girls. Listen, Wienick, I took you off
a beat because I thought you were smart. Be smart. Bring
me Harry Dunn. A hop-head on the prowl with a hot pistol
can raise hell.''

Wienick grumbled, muttered something about a job for
the Missing Persons Bureau and departed. Nola looked at
him with a doleful smile.

"Wienick will find him. He's a good man. Now and then
he needs a little prodding.''

I said, "You really think Dunn took those shots at me in
the park?''

"How do I know? Sometimes I feel like taking a shot at
you myself.'' He shifted his weight and half closed his eyes.
"You were right about last night. You did wing the guy.
We found bloodstains on the walk where he crossed over.''
His lips grew small. "I'd sure like to see if Dunn is creased.''

"Well," I said smugly. "Deadeye Jordan. With a good
north light and any weapon no older than the Civil War I
could have laid one right through his belly button.''

"Yeah. That's all we need." He leaned back and stroked
his chin. "Where were you last night?''

"At the Magic Lamp. I had a talk with Leo Arnim.''

He lifted his brows. "So-o. About what?''

"About a note one of his waiters stuck under an ash tray
on my table, warning me to clear out of the Pernot case if
I wanted to stay alive.''

John Nola's eyes jumped open and became alert. "The
hell you say! Let's see it.''

I shook my head. "I can't.''

"Why not?" He was frowning.

"Because Steve Janeiro took it away from me." I let some air out through my nostrils. "Yeah, with his bare hands."

Nola's eyes held as much expression as two beer caps. "You sure one of his waiters planted the note?"

"I'm not even sure of my own name any more," I said. "The instant I pegged that waiter I didn't like him. Then, after it was over, the waiter was gone; he'd been taken off the floor." I spread my hands. "Cambreau was at the table, but I can't figure him for a motive. His wife had just joined us and barely seated herself when I found the note. And anyway if you can tie her into the Pernot case you're a better man than I am."

"Her boy friend is one of the lawyers."

"Sure. I thought about that. But it's too obvious and too farfetched."

Nola sat back again and pursed his lips thoughtfully. "This Arnim angle puzzles me. Frankly, I can't see him looking for trouble at this stage of the game. Remember, he's still on parole."

"How about his private life?"

"Nothing there," said Nola slowly, "at least not on the surface. He was married once, but his wife went west while he was up in Sing Sing. Last I heard she got a divorce. Since then he seems to be cold on women—won't even look at one."

I said, "Just why does he need a gorilla like Steve Janeiro?"

Nola shrugged. "A guy gets used to a bodyguard when he's in the rackets. This Janeiro is no daisy. He's done plenty of time himself and he certainly can't afford a jam, but at least he's not on parole."

I sprang the rest of my news. "Here's something else. As I was leaving the Magic Lamp I saw Eric Quimby, his girl friend, and Steve Janeiro in a huddle at the same table."

Nola brought his face up and stared at me hard. "I don't get it."

"Neither do I."

He said ruminatively, "Consider this, perhaps Quimby went to the Magic Lamp to ask questions about Verna and got to know Janeiro that way."

"It's possible," I agreed, "but they seemed like mighty close friends."

Nola stood up and paced around his small office, his brow wrinkled, pulling at the lobe of his left ear. Finally he turned. "I still like Dunn for that shooting spot. A guy like him, an ex-con, a bindle-stiff, can carry an obsession around with him for years." His eyes got grim. "If I could only get him downstairs he'd talk. He'd spill like a sprinkling can."

I looked at him with surprise. "Strong-arm stuff," I said thinly.

He detected my tone at once. His face turned wooden. "You're odd, Jordan. I don't understand you. A guy tries to pump you full of lead and you sit here looking pious and enlightened. Sure, that's very admirable. Treat them gently, you say. No third degree. Well, I used to have ideas about police brutality myself, and I still do. But you deal with criminals over a period of time and you're apt to shed some of your illusions. You can't argue or reason with hoodlums or racketeers or paid killers. The only argument they understand is a lead pipe across the chops. Maybe these men are mentally sick; I wouldn't know. Tell me, how would you handle a vicious bastard who'd sap an old man for a handful of silver? With fancy psychological double talk and a rubber hammer against his kneecap?"

I was silent. It was the longest speech I'd ever heard him make and a not ineloquent one. I felt there was something in what he said.

"Maybe you're right."

"I know I'm right," he said, subdued. "I want you to understand my position, Jordan. Too many things are happening in this case. I have a feeling there's going to be more killings and I'm damned if I know how to stop them." He chewed on his lip, then added, "You know that Southern Airways stewardess who flew the plane with James and Ivy Pernot?"

"Janet Ross?"

"Yeah. Well, she's missing. Packed up, walked out on her job, disappeared."

I didn't like that. I said, "Things are beginning to boil. Somebody's getting worried."

"You're the one I'm worried about, Jordan. The finger is on you. Somebody wants you shelved and buried deep. What are you going to do about it?"

I said quietly, "There's one thing I can do. I can drop this case and get married and sail for Bermuda tomorrow. Which I sure as hell am not going to do. You think I ought to carry a gun?"

"No," he said glumly. "I don't think anyone ought to carry a gun. I don't think they should ever have been invented." He gave me a sour smile. "I'll get you an application and we'll fill it out and run it right through. Have you got one?"

"War trophies. A Japanese Nambu and a fairly good Luger."

"Shells?"

"None."

"There's a shop across the street," he said.

And so twenty minutes later everything was arranged and I was in the supply store across the street from Headquarters, making a purchase. When I took out my wallet I found a piece of paper bearing two names: Kenneth Towner and George Gaxton. These were the two men my Southern Airways list had boiled down to, either of whom might be the missing witness.

The first one, Towner, lived uptown and I spent about an hour on a fruitless errand since he turned out to be a boy of eleven who'd been visiting his grandparents in Miami, convalescing from a siege of pneumonia. He'd arrived on Flight 7 all right, but his father had called for him at the airport.

That left only George Gaxton.

A search of the phone directory told me that he was a diamond importer with an address on Park Lane. I went

down there directly. Park Lane, a narrow thoroughfare, runs
the city of Amsterdam a close race as a diamond center. In
a narrow building on the third floor, a simple legend on a
frosted-glass door said:

GEORGE GAXTON

GEMS

I opened the door and stepped inside. The outer office
was presided over by a dark beauty in a black satin dress,
fully packed. Lacquered hair, ivory skin, and a mouth that
was a bright splash of crimson. Her smile was full of per-
sonality.

"May I help you?"

"Yes," I said, "but not here." Annoyance rather than
demureness developed a pinkish tint in her face. "I'd like
to see Mr. Gaxton."

"Have you an appointment?"

"No."

"What is the nature of your business?"

"I'm from the Customs Office."

That got a reaction. She sat up stiffly and peered at me,
small worry lines puckering her brow. I extracted a card
and placed it on her desk. She picked it up and examined
it and tapped it delicately against her fingernails.

"Is this a legal matter, may I ask?"

"You may," I said. "It's a matter that's liable to develop
into almost anything."

She moistened her lips. "Has Mrs. Gaxton——" she
said, then caught herself and gnawed on her under lip. "Mr.
Gaxton is a very busy man."

"Naturally," I said. "It takes a bit of time to appraise
those stones that were smuggled past the Customs last week."

Her face grew blank. Her mouth twitched uncertainly.
She flicked the card against her teeth. Her brain was working
on both cylinders. She brought her eyes up level with mine.
They didn't seem very happy.

I leaned forward with a confidential air and said in a stage
whisper, "Listen, this is urgent. A friend of mine just got
in from Constantinople with some rubies from the late Czar's

collection. Also some emeralds and sapphires swiped from the Romanov crown.''

She pushed back against her chair. Her eyes were dark and her bosom swelled magnificently with anger. She snatched at the phone and touched a button. She said, ''There's a man here to see you. He's a lawyer and he says it's urgent . . . Yes, I'll send him right in.'' She hung up and pointed to a door behind her desk marked: PRIVATE.

I walked over and opened the door and walked in on a moonfaced man in his late forties with two chins, sociable eyes, a hearty manner, and a wheezing voice.

''A lawyer,'' he said amiably. ''Well, I hope I'm not being sued.'' He indicated a red leather chair. ''Sit down, sir.''

I got deposited and crossed my knees and said without preamble, ''How did you enjoy Florida, Mr. Gaxton?''

''Florida?'' He looked puzzled. ''That's an odd question. Don't mind telling you though. Last time I was there, back in '26, they had a hurricane. Hell of a blow. Wind took a ship right out of Biscayne Bay and hung a Ford on some telephone wires. Hell of a thing! By George, it scared the peruke off Malvina—that's my wife. She looked like the dickens!'' His stomach rocked with laughter. ''She looks like the dickens anyway.''

I waited till he had his breath. Then I looked at him and said, ''How about that trip you made three weeks ago?''

He sat erect and blinked vapidly. ''Who me? Three weeks ago? Florida?''

I nodded.

He shook his head with emphasis. ''You're mistaken, sir.''

''I hardly think so,'' I said. ''Let me refresh your memory. A little over two weeks ago you returned from Miami aboard a Southern Airways plane on Flight 7, landed at LaGuardia Field and headed toward Manhattan in a Cadillac that crashed, killing three people, and leaving you the sole survivor. For some reason you left the scene of the accident. I'd like to know why.''

He was watching me, transfixed. Then his lips puffed out with alarm. "You're crazy."

"I will be soon," I said. "Look, Gaxton, to save time I'll lay my cards on the table. You've been reading about the Pernot case in the papers?"

His chin bobbed up and down and he looked ill.

"Then you know that one of the occupants of that car disappeared. I traced the names of the passengers, narrowed them down, and finally wound up with yours. Running away from the accident was no crime and probably you had your reasons. Play ball with me and I'll respect those reasons."

His tongue seemed frozen to the roof of his mouth. He put his face between his hands and rocked himself back and forth. "Crazy!" he finally croaked. "You're crazy! I never got on any plane. I never flew in my life. I never was in any accident. I haven't been to Florida for twenty years."

I gritted my teeth. "Your name and address were on the passenger list. If you were not in Florida two weeks ago, where were you?"

He looked panic-stricken. It was as if someone had pulled out the stopper and let the color drain out of his face.

"It—it's blackmail!" he piped. "What do you want?"

"The truth. Where were you?"

He slumped down, exhausted. "I—I can't tell you."

I shrugged. "Then tell the police."

"*No!*" he cried. He closed his eyes and slowly opened them. He clasped his fingers in a gesture of supplication. His face was steaming. "Please, can you keep a secret?"

"If it needs keeping."

He swallowed painfully. "I was in Atlantic City. I told Malvina I was going away on a business trip. I registered in a hotel under the name of Sidney Johnson. You could check the signature. I couldn't have been in two places at the same time."

I said softly, "Don't you mean Mr. and *Mrs*. Sidney Johnson?"

A salmon-pink hue invaded his face. He nodded.

"And the girl?" I asked.

"Please . . ." He made a small pleading gesture.

"Sorry. I have to be sure. The girl outside?"

He looked like he was going to cry. That Malvina certainly had him bulldozed.

"Congratulations," I said. "She's an appetizing morsel. And don't worry about Malvina; she's probably stepping out herself." I handed him a piece of paper. "Just write 'Sidney Johnson' on this. There, that's fine." I stood up. "Somebody else may have the same name as yourself and not be listed in the directory. Or he may come from out of town. Good day, sir."

I went into the outer office. There was no smile, business or otherwise, on the brunette's face. Her stare was as frigid as the North Pole. I pointed to a silver-fox jacket hanging on the rack. She never bought that on a secretary's salary.

"Handy thing to have in Atlantic City this time of the year, isn't it?"

George Gaxton's amorous escapade was instantly confirmed by the riot of expressions that crossed her face. I smiled at her and went out of the office.

I went into Maiden Lane and started to light a cigarette, but lost my taste for it and threw it away.

· 18 ·

At six o'clock I picked Dulcy up and drove her over to the airport to meet her brother who was flying east for a brief visit. Gil Vincent turned out to be a tall, amiable guy working on an engineering project in Southern California. We hit it off immediately after the usual frantic amenities. With her arm locked in his, Dulcy said, "You'd better get to know him, Gil. He's going to be your brother-in-law."

Gil Vincent looked at us in surprise. "When did all this happen?"

"A long, long time ago," she said, "but you wouldn't understand."

He pumped my hand. "I warn you, Scott, she was always a problem child."

We kidded around for a couple of minutes, then I excused myself to make some inquiries at the Southern Airways office, but learned no more than Nola had already told me. Janet Ross had quit without explanation and dropped out of sight.

After supper I thought Dulcy and Gil would want a chance to talk alone, so I left them. It was almost eight o'clock and with nothing scheduled I decided to go down to the office and catch up on some paper work.

In lower Manhattan the streets were dark and deserted and a stiff wind whipped down between the building canyons. I went into the lobby. Two cops detached themselves from a wall and moved in on me.

They were sizable specimens with a tough, no-nonsense look about them. One of them had small, mean eyes and a florid, high-blood-pressure complexion.

"Where you goin', Mac?" he asked in a voice that had never got friendly with its owner.

"My office," I said.

"What's your name?"

"Jordan."

The two cops exchanged sharp glances.

"Give him a personal escort," the mean-eyed cop told the other.

We went into the elevator. The night operator gave me a nervous, stunned look and let his Adam's apple make two swift round trips, then he avoided my eyes. I didn't need a blueprint. Something was wrong and I felt it in the sour sensation that was gripping the pit of my stomach. In the upper hallway there was more law than you'll ever find in one place except the Policeman's Ball.

The lights were lit in my office. Most of the activity was centered about there. The cop nodded and I walked in. John Nola was standing in front of Cassidy's desk. His face was drawn and his mouth was grimly taut. His dark, grave eyes looked at me with a fixed intensity of expression.

I went close to him and let my eyes ask the question.

"It's happened," he said in a strained voice. "I warned you. There's been another killing."

I knew then what it must feel like to be trapped in a falling elevator. My insides knotted like a clenched fist.

"God! Not Cassidy, Nola?"

He didn't answer. He turned and walked briskly into my office, and I followed him.

Lying on the floor behind my desk with his lips peeled back in the rigor of death, his glassy and sightless eyes still open, was the body of Bob Cambreau. His face was vacant, the color of freshly laid cement. The front of his white shirt, chest-high, held a dark brown smear. A man was kneeling beside him.

I stood there and looked down at him. My mouth was open and I felt empty. There was a dull, throbbing ache in my head, as if a steel band was slowly compressing my brain, trying to squeeze the consciousness out of it.

Nola's hand put pressure on my arm. It seemed to help.

He said, "When the report first came in I thought it was you."

The man at Bob Cambreau's side grunted and rose off his haunches and turned pouched, restless eyes on the lieutenant.

"Well, Doc?"

"Two shots," the man said crisply. "Both bullets pierced the heart it seems. He was dead before he dropped. From the looks of the wound they were fired at close range. No powder marks however. The shells undoubtedly went through the glass door first."

"What caliber, Doc? So we'll know now what to look for."

"Hard to say offhand. I can tell you definitely when we dig out the slugs. Probably .32's of fairly high velocity." He retrieved a black bag, nodded shortly, and hurried away.

I looked over at the pebbled-glass door behind my desk.

I saw two neat holes, frosted white around the rim and radiating cracks. Nola took my arm again and piloted me to the outer office. My knee joints felt loose.

Nola hung a hip on the desk again and said, "The cleaning woman found him about seven. She went in and almost tripped over him and started yelling blue murder. Near as I can reconstruct it, this seems to be what happened: Cambreau was here in your office—you can tell me why later—and the killer came along the hall and tapped on the glass door. Cambreau heard it and went over to open the door. His prints are on the inside knob. With the light behind him, his shadow was a clear outline from the other side. The killer was standing there with a gun ready and gave it to him. The building had been pretty well cleared by that time and nobody seems to have heard the shots."

I didn't say anything.

Nola's glance was pointed. "You know, of course, who they were after."

I nodded, still dazed and wordless.

Nola said in a brittle tone, "When the killer saw that shadow against the glass he thought it was you."

I ran my tongue along parched and flaked lips.

He moved his hand in an angry gesture through his hair. "Did you have an appointment with Cambreau this evening?"

"No," I said in an apathetic voice.

"Are you sure?"

"Positive."

"What brought you down here at this hour?"

I told him about the neglected paper work.

"What brought Cambreau here?"

"I don't know," I said dully.

Nola's jaw muscles bunched. "I do," he said shortly. "He got here before your secretary closed up and told her that you wanted him to wait for you."

I couldn't understand it. It didn't make sense.

Nola went on tightly, "Something like this was bound to happen, especially after that shot at you in the park. These

guys mean business.'' He snorted bitterly. "And you didn't
want us to know that Harry Dunn had a gun. But he's not
the only one. Leo Arnim warned you off the Pernot matter.
Eric Quimby hates your guts because you threw him out of
that house. Maybe Frank Walther who was released this
morning still thinks you poisoned his girl. And we mustn't
forget Floyd Dillon whose case you're turning inside out."
He lifted his shoulders. "There's only a few with motive.
Maybe there's another assortment of citizens who want you
dead. Maybe——''

The door snapped open and Philip Lohman strode in. The
D.A. eyed me coldly, followed the direction of Nola's nod
into my office. He reappeared after a moment, directed some
questions at the lieutenant, and listened grimly to what I
had already heard. Then he stared at me through slitted
eyes.

"So it's catching up with you, eh, Jordan?"

I made no comment.

"Where were you between six and seven?"

"Having dinner with some friends," I said dully.

His lips twitched and he looked at Nola. "Who was on
duty at the elevator. Night man?"

"Not till seven. That wouldn't mean anything anyway.
There are stairs coming up that lead into a delivery area.
The killer didn't have to be seen."

"Ballistics have anything to work on?"

Nola shook his head. "Not yet. He was probably killed
with a revolver."

Lohman's brows contracted in a frown. "What do you
mean?"

"Shells are ejected only by automatics. We didn't find
any in the hall."

He nodded as if it was old stuff to him. "Naturally. Have
you searched the building?"

"We're still working on it; halls, lavatories, refuse cans,
air shafts, incinerator . . ."

"Good. Any fingerprints on the outside knob?"

"Only Jordan's. They might have been there for days."

Lohman's face sharpened and he swung on me, his eyes stone-hard and his voice level. "I'm moving in, Jordan, personally. There will be no more bungling or interference from you, understand? From now on we're going to get action. You've been throwing yourself around in a reckless and highly irresponsible manner. I haven't liked your attitude from the start. That's over and done with. You're going to talk and you're going to talk now and you're going to talk straight."

Suddenly I was hot with anger. Anger flared up inside me. My eyes were burning.

"That's too goddam bad," I said savagely. "Who the hell do you think you're threatening—some ten-cent panhandler out of the morning line-up? A friend of mine has just been murdered in cold blood and nothing you can say will bluff me out of doing what I think is right. Neither you nor your gang of political panderers can stop me. Shove that up your chimney."

His face turned pale. He said in a choking voice, "You can't defy the authority of my office and get away with it. I'll——"

"You'll what?" I growled. "Go ahead and tell me."

"I'll put you behind bars as a material witness."

"Bull! I don't know anything about this and you have no way of proving that I do." I paced around the room. Suddenly I punched viciously at the filing cabinet, wanting to feel the ache in my fist. Then I turned and looked at him. "We're doing this all wrong, Lohman. Hell, I don't want to fight you. I want to help you catch the killer and fry him. If you have any questions, go ahead and ask them."

He reeled back. He was surprised and only partly mollified. A shrewd look glinted in his gray eyes.

"I think you'll find it pays to string along with me, Jordan. I can light a fire under you on a lot of things. The police blotter on that Central Park shooting says you were carrying a gun without a license. Co-operate and we'll let it go. There must be a tie-up between that shooting and this murder. You wounded the man in the park. Who was he?"

"I don't know," I said.

"You saw him well enough to hit him."

"It was a lucky shot. I was firing at a shadow."

He fingered the pince-nez off his nose and his eyes grew thin. "You're trying to shield somebody."

I opened my mouth and then closed it slowly. I said quietly, "You're kidding, aren't you, Lohman? You're not really serious. Why would I try to shield anyone?"

"Because identification at this time might jeopardize your chances of winning the Pernot case."

I spread my legs and stared at him and gave a short, harsh laugh. "You can't believe that, not actually, Lohman, because if you do you're an even bigger fool than I thought."

His jaw set with a hard click. He thrust his face close to mine and grated in a voice taut as a mandolin string, "You're skating on thin ice, Jordan. There are a lot of things you're going to account for. Verna Ford went to your apartment with something on her mind and somebody tried to prevent her from talking to you. I want to know what it was. And I want to know why you were so anxious to get her boy friend released from custody. And just how did you talk Karen Pernot into substituting you as her attorney. You've been guilty of a breach of professional ethics, concealing vital evidence, interfering in a murder investigation, violating the Sullivan Act and engaging in a gun fight. Now you're going to do exactly as you're told or you're going to find yourself in a cell."

He stopped, his nostrils flaring widely with labored breathing.

"Are you finished?" I said nastily. "Then listen to me, Lohman. You're a pompous, brainless bag of hot air. Your thick-skulled ideas are the conclusions of an asinine and muddle-headed mind. It proves how sloppy the public is about electing public officials. I'm leaving here now. If you think you can stop me and make it stick, go ahead." I glanced at Nola. "So long, Lieutenant. I'll talk this over some other time."

I opened the door and went out into the hall. Lohman did

not call out. The cop there made no move to stop me. I took the elevator to the street and started walking. I was shaken and angry and a little scared. I have no recollection where I went or how far I walked, but when I looked at my strap watch finally, almost two hours had passed.

At ten o'clock I was standing at the door of Vivian Cambreau's apartment with my finger on the bell. Dulcy opened the door. Her face was pained and wan and her eyes red from weeping. She nodded wordlessly and squeezed my hand and led me into the living room. Gil stood grimly with his back against a drawn shade. Floyd Dillon sat on the couch with an arm around Vivian's shoulder.

Vivian's face looked stunned and haggard. She saw me and a tear trickled down her cheek. She was shredding a handkerchief between tense fingers. The flesh under her eyes was dark.

"Oh, Scott . . ." she whispered brokenly.

What can you say? Are there words to assuage the pain of death? They had been separated, of course, and it was not as if a man she deeply loved had been killed. But they had been married and they had lived together and those years must have meant something. And to have him go out as he did was a tearing shock. I had never supposed Vivian completely insensitive. She put her hand up and began very quietly to sob.

"Now, Vivian," Dillon said firmly. "You've got to get hold of yourself."

After a moment she looked up at me out of a streaked face. "The police say it was a mistake."

"It seems that way," I said soberly.

Dulcy came over quickly and took my hand, clasping it with a kind of fierce intensity. "Oh, Scott, they were after you."

I did not say anything.

Gil's fists were knotted at his sides, pressed tightly against his thighs. "But who? Why?"

"I can't answer the first question," I said. "The second

seems obvious. Someone is under the impression that I know something I am not supposed to know.''

Dulcy said, "We're going away, darling. We'll leave until this thing cools off."

Gil said, "You're going away all right. You're coming back to California with me."

She shook her head. "No, Gil, I'm sorry, but I'm staying with Scott. Please don't insist."

Gil compressed his lips but did not press the subject.

Dillon smiled faintly. "Well," he said, "at any rate this settles the divorce problem."

Dulcy stiffened and her eyes snapped. "What a heartless thing to say!"

He shrugged. "I'm simply being frank. Cambreau is dead and it's all very tragic, but Vivian no longer loved him and I'd be a hypocrite to act grief-stricken."

Dulcy was watching him with incredulous eyes. "But he had so much to live for."

"If you mean money, yes," Dillon murmured. "I rather imagine he'd have drunk himself to death in another year. The fact remains that I didn't like Cambreau alive and I see no reason to like him any better now that he is dead. I am frank enough to say so rather than sit here and look pious."

"Please—Floyd——" Vivian pleaded.

I was burning. But I kept a tight rein on myself because this was neither the time nor the place to handle Dillon the way I would have liked. I spoke in a restrained voice to Vivian.

"As soon as the medical examiner's office releases the body I'll have Bob moved to a chapel."

She thanked me with her eyes. Then they grew cloudy and perturbed. "Scott," she said hesitantly, "this thing that happened tonight—did it have anything to do with the Pernot case?"

I shrugged. "Probably. We're working on that assumption."

She seemed to shrivel back on the couch. "You men!" she cried bitterly. "Can't you settle that horrible mess and put an end to all this violence? I can't have any peace. Something may happen to you or to Floyd at any moment. You won't be safe anywhere.''

Dulcy was a prompt ally. "She's right, Scott. Settle the case and let's go away.''

Dillon looked indifferent. His face exhibited as much expression as the City Hall cornerstone. So far as he knew I had uncovered nothing to change the complexion of the case and he still had it sewed up.

"Well, Dillon," I asked him quietly, "how about it?''

He gave me a distant freeze.

"Withdraw Quimby's claim," I said, "and I'll advise my client to give you fifty bucks each.''

He heaved up off the couch. Bright patches flamed in his cheeks. He said with controlled fury, "I've had just about enough of your clowning, Jordan. And that business of kicking Quimby out of his house——''

"*His* house!'' I cut in. "If Rowland Paynter hadn't been a senile old idiot he'd have kicked Quimby out the day he moved in.''

"Scott,'' Dulcy cried in a shocked tone.

I looked at her and shook my head. Bob was dead and the girls were wounded and here I was arguing with Dillon. I felt like a heel.

"I'm sorry,'' I said. "If I can be of any help, Vivian, just call on me. See you tomorrow, Dulcy.'' I nodded at Gil and went out.

· 19 ·

We buried Bob in his family plot at Woodlawn. I remember it was a bitter cold Saturday morning. There was a heavy gray overcast in the leaden sky. The earth was hard and unyielding. Dulcy stood at my side, trembling. Behind a black veil Vivian's face was invisible, but her shoulders were bowed and shaking. I remember thinking what a horrible ordeal civilized people thrust upon themselves with funerals. It seems a pointless thing to parade one's grief before an audience and there must be a better way of saying this last farewell. A grave is so grimly final. It was depressing and I was glad when it was over.

Afterwards Dulcy and I drove Gil back to the airport. He had delayed his trip until after the funeral and he was flying back west immediately. A huge four-engined plane wheeled and banked against the sky. He looked at Dulcy and asked again if she wouldn't go away with him, at least until the situation here had cleared.

She shook her head. "I'm staying with Scott."

Gil gave us a wry smile. "I know better than to argue with a woman. Take care of her, Scott."

His plane was on the runway now and we waved him aboard and then he was gone. We watched the ship until it was pin-pointed against the horizon and then we went back to the car and drove home.

We found John Nola in my apartment, sitting in a chair, waiting, his eyes half closed and a half-burned cigarette limp in his mouth. He was still wearing a dark tailored coat and a maroon muffler. He stood up when he saw Dulcy— they'd already met—and explained that the porter had let him in.

I watched him obliquely. "Just a social visit, John, or is something up?"

"Felt like talking," he said.

"Fine. Fix us a couple of drinks, Dulcy. You know where to find the stuff." I sank into a chair and stretched out. "Thought you might show up at the funeral."

He shook his head. "I don't like cemeteries. The only time they'll get me there is when they plant me." He looked away and examined a spot on the wall. "I've been thinking of putting a man on your tail, Jordan, as a precaution."

I was having none of that and I told him so.

He said, "Well, it's your life. I'm doing what I can. I have two men watching Harry Dunn's rooming house. He hasn't showed up since Cambreau was killed."

"The way you're trying to rig Dunn for this crime wave, it looks like you've placed him near my office at the time of the shooting."

Nola shook his head slowly. "No. But we know Walther was there a little after six."

I sat erect and looked at him hard. "What does Walther say about it?"

"Nothing. But only because we haven't quizzed him. We haven't quizzed him because we can't find him either. He hasn't been back to his ship in three days."

Dulcy came back with the bourbon. Nola took one, wondering aloud if it wouldn't be wise to have the contents chemically analyzed before he tasted it. He took a boy-sized sip and put the glass down. Dulcy pulled the hassock beside my chair and sat on it. Nola tucked a fresh cigarette between his lips and lit it from the old one. I settled back comfortably and fingered gently the fine down on the back of Dulcy's neck.

I said, "You're concentrating on Harry Dunn and Walther while it seems to me that Quimby is just as likely a prospect. He has no idea why Verna came to see me. He probably believes that she told me something inimical to his interests. I gave him plenty of reason to hate me. Besides tossing him out of Pernot's house he thinks I'm up to some legal skulduggery that may gyp him out of close to half a million dollars."

Nola kept his gaze level. "How about Floyd Dillon?"

"Ditto. He knows what Verna was doing in my apartment but he doesn't know what else I may have found out. He knows I'm working on the case. He may even think I've located the missing witness. He wants to win this case because he's going to marry Vivian Cambreau and she's an expensive addition to his overhead. Winning the Pernot case will net him as heavy a fee as a lawyer can expect to make.

And money still stands in my book as a paramount motive for murder.''

He blew a smoke ring and watched it flatten against the ceiling and drift away. He smiled faintly. "You're doing fine. How about Leo Arnim?"

"Arnim is linked to Verna Ford who worked for him. He's also tied in some way to Harry Dunn. And he's gone to considerable trouble trying to frighten me out of the case.''

"Steve Janeiro?" he asked quietly.

"Why not?" I said. "By profession Janeiro is a torpedo. He certainly isn't too squeamish to use a gun if the price is right. We know that he works for Arnim and he seems on extremely friendly terms with Eric Quimby.''

Nola leaned over and detachedly flicked some ash into a tray. He looked up at me. "There's your own client.''

"Karen Pernot? By all means, let us include her. Why not? This is murder and we ought to put everybody under the glass. Well, what about her? Here is an angle that's thinner than cellophane and twice as transparent but let's have a look at it anyway. She has a boy friend named Rudolf Cassini, supposedly a voice teacher and a composer, more probably a gigolo and a charlatan. He has written what purports to be a musical play and he has promised her the leading role—if she backs it. She's hot about the idea— getting on the stage is almost an obsession with her—only she hasn't the money. But she is willing to use her uncle's inheritance when and if she gets it. By smoking me they might throw suspicion on Quimby or Dillon and bring the whole brew to a boil that may force a settlement. There's enough money in the estate for all concerned. Sure, it sounds like a harebrained theory but what is more stupid than murder in the first place.''

Nola gave me a slow nod. "All right. That includes everyone except yourself and Mrs. Cambreau.''

"Right," I said, "I could have killed Bob and a damn clever job too, making it appear that the bullet had my name on it. And I certainly had plenty of opportunity to knock off Verna Ford. Only you'll have to figure out a motive for yourself. As a motive for Vivian Cambreau, try this one on for size. She's slated to marry Floyd Dillon. By airing the divorce fiasco I might get him suspended and injure his status as a breadwinner. It doesn't fit? Okay, figure out a better one.''

Nola's smile was devoid of amusement. He ground out his cigarette and began torturing the lobe of his ear. He looked up and said, ''How about that shamus who was in the park the night you almost got nicked?''

''Emmanuel Scully?'' I nodded shortly. We had almost forgotten the man with the lumpy nose. ''There is a guy who might bear some investigation. My guess is that he was working for Dillon. And if he was it is barely possible that he stumbled onto something hot. The idea may have occurred to him that with the proper handling he could make himself some money.''

Dulcy sat up, her face eager. She looked at me and then at Nola. ''Look,'' she said excitedly, ''if this Scully is a blackmailer and Scott was on the verge of destroying his business, mightn't he sneak into the building and put a bullet through the office door? After all, he was in the park that night too.''

I smiled over her head at Nola. ''But his gun wasn't fired that night, baby.''

''Naturally,'' she breathed. ''That would be too obvious. He could have had two guns and quickly buried one.''

Nola frowned at her. He took another boy-sized sip of his bourbon and stood up. ''I think I'll pay Mr. Scully a visit. Want to come along?''

I was about to refuse when Dulcy said, ''Go ahead, Scott. We'll stay home tonight. I'll prepare dinner. You'll find it ready when you get back.''

I looked at her dubiously. ''It isn't possible. Can you cook too?''

Her smile was dazzling. ''Like a French cook, darling.

Duck, grouse, soufflé, anything your heart likes, and if we have company I can roast a whole pig on a spit.''

"Not in my living room, baby." I kissed her on top of the head. "This will be a preview. Go ahead, and expect me back in about an hour."

She was rattling dishes around in the pantry even before we had the door closed.

We found Scully in a small apartment that held some lumpy mohair furniture and smelled like a Bowery saloon. When he saw me at the door his body arched back like a frightened kangaroo. He tried to pull the "privileged communications'' act, but Nola gave him short shrift on that. Murder had been done twice and was coming up a third time and if Scully liked the detecting business he'd come clean or by God he'd wish he had.

So Scully talked. Dillon had hired him originally to catch Bob Cambreau and Verna Ford in my apartment. After Verna died and I went on the prowl, Dillon was scared lest I turn up the missing witness and spring it on him in court. Scully was ordered to tail me. He stuck close to Dulcy and me that night and followed me into Central Park, but he was dead tired and figured that I was going home and that he could pick me up in the morning. He was heading for one of the exits when he heard the shot and started running. That was why he had not spotted my attacker.

He didn't know much about Verna. She had worked in Irene's Dance Studio and used to room with another girl from there named Muriel Evans. The two girls lived in the same building.

We left him and went out into the street and pulled oxygen into our lungs. Nola regarded me stolidly, but he wasn't really seeing me because his eyes were remote and fixed on some thoughts that seemed to be getting born somewhere in his brain. His lips were puckered and he shook his head, then he sighed and said softly, "A girl was killed on purpose and a man was killed by mistake, and while you're trotting blithely around somebody is plotting how to cash in your chips, Jordan. Watch yourself.''

My laugh sounded phony even to me. Nothing further was said till we reached his car. "How about coming back to my place for potluck?" I asked.

"You don't mean it," he said, smiling quietly. "You don't really want me around. She's quite a girl."

He climbed into the car, waved casually and drove away. The sky had darkened ominously and muted thunder rumbled hoarsely in the distance. I lifted my coat collar and headed back.

I found that Dulcy had made no idle promise. It was miraculous. A bridge table set with a folded white sheet, candles in saucers for atmosphere, a string quartet on the radio. Then the big surprise. Lean, tender pot roast, broccoli, crisp shoestring potatoes, topped off with biscuit tortoni and strawberries. We opened a bottle of sauterne and had a party.

"Come here," I said when we were finished, and pulled her over to the sofa and down on my lap. "You're incredible. How did you do it?"

Her eyes reflected the smile on her mouth. "I can't fib to you, darling. It was quite simple. You can really thank Mr. Birds Eye."

"What!"

"Uh-huh. Frozen foods. All packed like a block of wood and ready to heat."

"What next?" I said. "We're making strides. Pretty soon you'll be able to buy babies in Gimbel's basement."

"What a horrid thought!" She shook her head emphatically. "We wouldn't like that, would we, darling?"

"Nope. The conventional method was good enough for my grandfather and it's good enough for me."

Lightning streaked across the sky outside and a few tentative raindrops slapped against the window. Dulcy stirred softly in my lap, then turned her head so that she could look at me.

"Preparing dinner kept me busy, Scott. I guess it's fear but I feel empty when you're gone."

"Don't worry," I told her reassuringly. "The killer will be laying low until the heat cools."

She shook her head and her brow puckered. "I'm not sure. He's frightened now and he's worried that you'll see it—who he is—and he may decide to strike again fast. He could catch you off balance."

"You worry too much, baby. I bear a charmed life."

"Why don't the police do something?"

"They're working on it. But it's too complicated. They're boring all along the case, looking for an opening."

"Bob never had a chance, did he?"

"Not even a prayer. That's the way killers work, suddenly and without warning."

Her eyes looked squarely into mine. "I know it's hopeless asking you to quit, darling, and so I'm not going to do it. I know how easy it would be just to step out of this case, but I know, too, that there are some things a man has to do. Maybe you could have been persuaded before Bob was murdered, but I guess it's too late now. He was your friend. You can't just forget that. And besides, it's a bad thing to let an evil idea have a clear road because of fear, because people are afraid to fight back. It's just that it's too hard for me to know you're in danger."

I looked at her without speaking. We didn't have to speak. Then I pulled her close and kissed her. Her shoulder was smooth and firm under my fingers.

After a while she said in a small, shaky voice, "You can propose again if you like, darling. This happens to be my mating season and I'm especially receptive."

"It's the rain," I said. "Rain always affects me like this. Stimulates my libido. Maybe we'd better forget Bermuda and spend our honeymoon in India during the monsoons."

"Gee, Mr. Jordan," she laughed. "I'm nuts about you."

We sat there in the dimness, listening to the drumming of the rain. Lightning flickered fitfully against the walls. I lifted her up and got to my feet.

"It's getting late, baby," I said. "I think I'd better be taking you back to Vivian's."

She sighed, but got her coat. We went to the door and stopped there. We were facing each other. Her eyes were shining. I heard her breathing. We moved together hard until she was flat against me. I had her in my arms and I was kissing her with a kind of hungry ferocity.

She whimpered softly. Her mouth opened. I felt the blood coursing in my veins.

"Scott——"

"Yes."

"I don't want to go home in the rain."

I picked her up. My heart was pounding. I carried her across the room. Her fingers dug into my shoulders.

· 20 ·

She was sleeping when I awoke the next morning. She was smiling. Her coppery hair was splayed out on the pillow, glinting in the sunlight. I shaved and showered and came out smelling coffee. I went to the door and got the morning paper and the phone rang.

It was Vivian, sounding agitated. "Scott, where's Dulcy? She hasn't been home all night."

"She's here with me," I said.

A shocked gasp. Then silence.

"Don't worry about her," I said. "She's all right."

She remained speechless for another moment. Then she said, "I'd like to talk to you, Scott. When can I see you?"

"This morning, in my office."

"I'll be there." She hung up.

I went into the pantry and watched Dulcy from the doorway. She turned and gave me a radiant smile. There was no false modesty, no shyness, no regret.

"I guess I'll have to make an honest woman of you, baby. Better start buying a trousseau."

"Shall I buy some Hindu saris, darling?"

I let her see that I was puzzled.

"If we're going to India on our honeymoon, I mean."

I grinned. "Let's stick to Bermuda."

"How do you like your eggs, Scott?"

"In pairs," I said. "Each fried on the same side."

She had set the bridge table and I sat down and looked over the paper. The Pernot case was relegated to the fourth page with no new developments. Dulcy came over with a platter.

"How does it look, darling?"

"Very gloomy," I said. "According to a Harvard scientist the world is doomed. The next atom bomb may set off a chain reaction that will blow the earth apart."

"I mean the eggs, silly."

"Oh! Beautiful. Don't fret though. Here's an item by a Yale scientist who says the Harvard scientist is off his trolley and no such thing can possibly happen."

"That's comforting. Eat your eggs, darling."

After breakfast I kissed her soundly, and walked out of there feeling comfortably domestic. When I entered the office Cassidy glanced up with simulated astonishment.

"Don't tell me you're actually going to do some work here today."

I leaned down and put an arm around her.

"None of that," she said primly. "I ought to quit you cold and get a job with the Marx Brothers. I might find some peace and quiet. Here's your mail."

I took four letters into my office. The first three were routine. The fourth was not. It was an illustrated advertisement torn from a newspaper. It showed a black coffin hinged open at one end. The text read:

Exceptionally strong casket. Lined with satin and matching pillow. Silver extension handles. Engraved name plate. Entire service including embalming, dressing, limousine, and one dozen folding chairs—only $225.

I stared at it and breathed out softly and closed my mouth.
I didn't think it was a joke. A murderer was warning me
that he meant business. I pulled out my copy of Shakespeare,
the one with the hollow interior that held the fifth of bourbon
and was pouring a drink when Cassidy called on the inter-
com to say that Vivian Cambreau was waiting. I had her
come in.

The black dress was stunning. Even in mourning she
managed to look fashionably groomed. She saw the bottle
and arched her brows. "Drinking, Scott? At this hour?"

I nodded. "It's a habit I'm liable to develop until more
normal times. I certainly need one. How about you, Vivian?"

She shook her head, smiling faintly. "Thank you, no."

I took a long pull. The alcohol sneaked into my blood
and I felt less shaky. I gave the bourbon back to the Bard
and put the book away. Then I settled against my chair and
waited for her to speak. She sat on the edge of the seat,
clasping and unclasping her purse, her teeth fumbling uncertainly with her lip.

Finally she looked up. "I don't think Floyd is going to
like this," she said, "but you were Bob's lawyer, Scott,
and you knew all about his affairs and have most of his
papers, and I wish you'd handle things for me."

I nodded, not particularly surprised; the request was not
unusual. Besides she didn't want Dillon to have too intimate
a knowledge of her finances. "Be glad to, Vivian. Have
you discussed this with Dillon?"

"Not yet. I shan't mention it unless he does. I suppose
the taxes will be very high."

"Naturally." I explained about the taxes and the probable
size of the estate. I said, "While you're here you can sign
some papers and we'll get right to work."

She took out a small gold pen and was busily figuring
on the back of an envelope when I went to the outer office
and found some testamentary forms for Cassidy to fill. Vivian was still hard at it when I rejoined her.

She smiled ruefully. "It seems I'm in partnership with

Uncle Sam." Then her eyes got troubled. "Scott, about Dulcy——"

"Don't worry," I said.

"But she can't stay at your place like——"

"Forget it," I said. "This is different."

She shrugged. "All right, you don't want to talk about it." She put her hands together. "Are the police making any progress, Scott?"

"A little. They're looking for a couple of suspects."

The inner ends of her brows lifted unevenly. She looked down at her hands. Her voice was low, almost a whisper. "I was awake all night with the most dreadful thoughts. About Bob and Floyd. They hated each other and . . . Oh, I don't know . . . I guess I'm unstrung. I shan't ever sleep again until this thing is solved."

"We'll all sleep better when it's over," I said.

A shudder rippled over her body. "Lord, I hope——"

The buzzer sounded. I picked up the handset.

"A visitor," said Cassidy.

"Man or woman?"

"Man. A Mr. Leo Arnim."

"So . . . How about the Cambreau papers."

"Almost ready."

I had her bring them in. We spread them out for Vivian's signature. I stood up and promised to call Vivian as soon as anything turned up. Then I let her out through the pebbled-glass door behind my desk.

"All right, Cassidy. Send Arnim in."

Leo Arnim eased himself into the chair just vacated by Vivian. His square bleached-white face was composed. He crossed his knees and folded thick hands over them. I glanced pointedly over his shoulder.

"Alone? No muscle man in case our interview is not satisfactory."

He shook his head. "Don't bear down on your humor too hard."

"What do you want, Arnim?"

His gaze was steady. "To make you an offer."

I answered him with a pair of doubtfully suspicious eyes.
He said, "I need a lawyer. I want you to represent me."
"To do what?"
"To keep me out of trouble."
I elevated a brow. "What kind of trouble?"
"None yet. Maybe there won't be any." He pulled a
large wallet from his inside breast pocket and extracted a
thin packet of bills. He laid them out carefully and delib-
erately, one at a time, along the edge of my desk. There
were five. One thousand dollars apiece. He sat back and
brought his eyes up to mine. "They're yours, Jordan. You
may have to earn them and then again you may not."
"Are you anticipating trouble?"
He shrugged. "That depends largely on you."
I looked at the bills. They were lovely. They were tempt-
ing. Five thousand dollars is a lot of money. Business was
picking up. Everybody seemed to be wanting my services.
I didn't think I was that good. I leaned forward and said,
"I don't think five thousand dollars will cover it."
There was no movement in his face, not even a flicker
of the eyes. "I'm prepared to meet any reasonable demand.
How much?"
"That's hard to say, Arnim. I could give you exact figures
for slugging a union organizer or framing a political rival,
but this is a little harder. If you're offering me this money
in case it turns out that you poisoned Verna Ford or shot
Bob Cambreau and you want me to keep it covered or to
defend you, then there isn't any amount you can add to it.
There isn't even enough in the Federal Reserve Bank."
I picked up a pencil and put the eraser against the bills
and flipped them one by one off the edge of the desk. They
fluttered to the floor and arranged themselves around his
feet. Leo Arnim did not look down. He kept his eyes on
mine. They were cold and bleak. A muscle throbbed in his
thick throat. He let out a harsh breath.
"Pick them up, Jordan."
"Pick them up yourself. They're yours, not mine."
We stared at each other. His face was stiff and maybe a

little whiter, if it could possibly get any whiter, but with no particular expression beyond that. No emotion, no anger. A man who can control himself like that is a dangerous antagonist.

He bent down to gather the bills. As he did so his sleeve hiked up and I saw something. I saw the white edge of a gauze bandage above his right wrist.

I should have kept silent. I should have let him go and then called Nola. That would have been the smart thing to do. So of course I lunged across the desk and grabbed at his sleeve and yanked it up.

There it was all right. A bandage, neatly and carefully wound halfway up his forearm.

He twisted away with a strangled sound. He crouched back. There was plenty of emotion in his face now. Raw anger and hatred. His eyes were mean and dangerous.

I backed away. My head was buzzing. I said in a low, even voice, "I shot a guy in Central Park, Arnim. I could have shot him in the arm. Is that what the bandage is for? Is it there to cover a bullet wound?"

He let out a harsh, ragged breath. His eyes were ringed and red. Then the anger faded and his face got set in its usual impassive mold.

"All right," he said. "You think you picked up something. Try and use it."

He stuffed the bills carelessly into his pocket, turned, and strode from the room.

I sat down again and waited until my breathing was normal. Then I picked up the phone and rang Nola. I told him the story. "You may need a court order," I said, "but we won't have to look much farther if there's a bullet hole in his arm."

Nola said swiftly, "I'll work on it at once. Sit tight until you hear from me."

I hung up slowly. I sat there, wondering if the break was at hand. I felt jumpier than an absconding bank clerk. Time was important now and it might be some hours before Nola could locate Arnim, longer if Arnim elected to hide out. I

sat back, thinking about it. There still remained a lot of
angles. I remembered what Emmanuel Scully had told us
about Verna's former roommate, Muriel Evans. I put on
my coat and hat and told Cassidy I was going out.

Irene, of Irene's Dance Studio, was a meaty woman in
a sequin-spangled gown. She had a waxy complexion, a
politician's voice, and the musty aroma usually found in
old basements. I told her I'd been recommended for samba
lessons and expressly instructed to ask for Muriel Evans. I
finally pried it out of her that Muriel Evans had taken the
day off.

I caught a subway to Queens. A kid came through with
the early afternoon papers and I bought one and read a piece
about Bob Cambreau. It had a pretty good picture of him.

It was a four-story walk-up recently dressed with a coat
of stucco and red paint on the fire escapes. The mailboxes
told me Verna Ford lived on the top floor and Muriel Evans
directly below her. I hiked up and stopped on the last landing
to catch my breath. I knew that Verna's apartment had not
yet been released by the police. I was thinking they might
have overlooked something.

The door was a cinch. It had an old, common lock that
snapped back after a bit of manipulating. A patent lock
would have given me some trouble.

The room held an assortment of furniture, a divan with
too many pillows, a gate-legged table, two plush chairs,
and plenty of evidence that the police had been there and
not been very neat about it. I went over that room like a
miser fondling a piece of gold. I felt the pillows, tested the
divan, lifted the carpet, examined the underside of chairs,
neglecting nothing and finding nothing.

I drifted into the bedroom. It held a bed, a dresser, a
closet and a bureau. I went over to the bureau, yanked out
the drawers and dumped the contents onto the bed. I sifted
through the usual junk a woman collects. Nothing to get
excited about. I got down on my hands and knees in front

of the bureau and wedged my head between slats and lighted a match. Something caught my eye. It was a piece of paper stuck under a strip of inner molding.

I slipped it free and straightened my back. It was a pawn ticket. The date said it was only a week old. I folded it and tucked it away in my wallet. I tossed everything back into the drawers, replaced them, then looked around and went over to the closet. I turned the knob and pulled the door open and froze to my toenails.

A gun came out of the closet. It looked like a Walther double-action automatic pocket model. It pointed at a spot six inches above my navel. The gun was almost lost in Steve Janeiro's enormous palm. He ducked his head forward and stepped out of the closet. I backed away from him.

"Well," I gulped in a voice shakier than the Bank of China. "Fancy meeting you here."

A slow grin stretched moistly at his loose mouth. His teeth were almost as big as those of a horse. He himself looked bigger to me at that moment than a horse. His eyes were dull and flat.

"You're a nervy guy, Jordan," he said. "Who sent you here?"

"The Homicide boys," I said. "They gave me a key to the joint."

"You alone?"

I shook my head. "There's a cop waiting downstairs in a squad car."

He lumbered backward to the window and shot a fast look. It was a back view. He snorted disgustedly. His eyes sharpened. "The cop comin' up?"

I shrugged indifferently. "That depends on how long I take."

He tucked the gun away in an underarm holster. He didn't really need it anyway. His brows were folded in concentration. It wasn't easy work for him.

I said, "Looks like we both had the same idea. What were you looking for, Steve?"

He wiped his hands along his thighs and scowled and

said nothing. I lit a cigarette to show him how casually I was taking it. I looked at him.

"I thought Leo Arnim wasn't interested in Verna."

Steve Janeiro bobbed his head. "Leo isn't."

I gave him a polite sneer. "Don't peddle that to me," I said. "Leo sent you here, didn't he?"

His eyes got sullen. "No. I came here on my own."

"It might be a good idea to tell me about it, Steve."

He stared down at his shoes. They looked like Indian war canoes. He brought his eyes up and a crafty glint had crawled into their flat opacity.

"This ain't any of your business, Jordan. But just so you don't make any wrong cracks to the law, I'll tell you." He lifted two picklelike fingers and pressed them tight. "Verna and me were like this, see? I gave her some junk and I wanted it back. I came here looking for it."

"What kind of junk?"

"A couple of trinkets I wouldn't want the cops to trace." His jaw set and he leaned at me to give me a narrow-eyed glare. "I got them trinkets in a jewelry store one night after closing hours. I can't have the cops pinning no more raps on me. My record won't take it." He breathed out with a rasp. "You tell anybody about finding me here, Jordan, and I'll break you in half like a matchstick, understand?"

"What made you hide in the closet, Steve?"

"Your key in the lock. What the hell, I got no business here. The cops would love to catch me stepping over the line." He tugged at the brim of his wide pork-pie hat. He looked at me hard. "I'm gettin' outa here. Remember, you didn't see me. I don't want no law climbing my back. Leo neither. Especially Leo, get it?"

He lumbered past me and opened the door and stepped out. I was alone with a pumping heart and cold, wet sweat along the entire length of my spine. Janeiro's cruel, insensitive eyes said that he would kill a man as casually as I would crush a spider.

I found nothing of further interest in Verna's bedroom. I left the place, closed the door softly, and descended one

flight. I stood on the landing, with my head on one side,
listening. Beyond Muriel Evans's door I heard the strains
of a piano. What floored me was the melody. I had heard
this music a few days ago. I had heard it in Karen Pernot's
living room.

I touched my finger to the buzzer.

The door opened and a platinum blonde with a small nose
and a rather large mouth frowned a question at me from
very wise and very old aquamarine eyes. The music had
stopped.

I gave her my best smile. "Irene sent me."

It was not a bright start. We both knew it was a lie. Her
eyes and her mouth got small. "Irene never sends anybody
here," she said in a sharp, shrill voice. "What do you
want?"

"A little information, Muriel."

Her face was watchful and suspicious. "About what?"

"About Verna Ford."

She jerked her head back and slammed the door in my face.
Almost but not quite. I had a foot wedged against the jamb.
I leaned my weight against the door and she fell back with
a startled gasp. She bit on a knuckle, holding her shoulders
high, staring at me with a frightened fixity of expression.

I stepped across the threshold. The room was almost an
exact duplicate of the one above, except for an old upright
piano against the wall.

A man sat on the piano stool with his back to the instrument.
It was Rudolf Cassini.

· 21 ·

He was as surprised to see me as I was to see him. But he
seemed to like the idea a lot less.

"Well!" I breathed. "The maestro himself."

Cassini didn't budge. He sat on the stool, transfixed, watching me frozenly. His eyes began to look unhappy.

"This is a nice snug hide-out, Rudy." I leered at him. "Are you giving a singing lesson?"

His lips twitched and he put his hands on his knees and squeezed them. Muriel Evans shifted a pair of worrying eyes from me to Cassini and back again, blinking rapidly.

"You know this guy, Rudy?" she asked.

He nodded, but did not speak.

I said, "Or are you looking for another investor for your show, Rudy?"

He got to his feet and reached for a midnight-blue Homburg on top of the piano.

"Don't leave on my account," I said.

Muriel chipped at the air with her hand. "What is this? What's going on?"

Cassini looked at her with a face that was wishing it was somewhere else.

"Who is he?" she demanded.

Cassini's long, thin fingers fluttered expressively. He managed finally to say, "He—he's a lawyer. His name is Jordan—Scott Jordan."

It was like having a pitched ball go through your fingers and belt you in the face. She reeled back. Her face went gray and angular. You might think I'd been introduced as Count Dracula. She looked at me in a hypnotized way and whispered, "Jordan!" and closed her eyes as if she was going to faint.

"Listen, Muriel," I said quickly and earnestly, "you were Verna's friend and she was killed in my apartment and I know how you must feel. You've been hearing a lot of nonsense. I had nothing to do with her death. Clear that out of your mind. It's not true. I don't know who killed her, but I want to find the man who did. I think you can help me."

Her eyes opened slowly. Her voice was barely audible. "What do you want?"

"Information, Muriel. You were the only friend she had.

Girls confide in each other. We're up against a blank wall because we know so little about Verna. Anything, any little shred of information may turn the page for us. I need your help.''

She trembled. Verna's death had scared her. She didn't know what to do. Her eyes turned to Cassini for advice. He ducked his head at her with a jerky motion.

"It's all right, Muriel. You can talk to Jordan." He had been edging toward the door and now his hand was on the knob.

"When will I see you?" she asked plaintively.

"Soon," he said hurriedly. "I will call."

The door opened and closed and he was gone. I gave Muriel a calm and reassuring smile and shook out a couple of cigarettes and gave her one. I held a match for her. She filled her lungs with smoke and let it leak out in twin streams from her nostrils. She sat down. Some of the color seeped back into her face.

I decided not to question her about Cassini. But their presence together was a new and confusing wrinkle. Steve Janeiro and Verna Ford. Cassini and Muriel Evans. The frayed strands of a lot of lives were being spun together.

I said, "You were pretty close to Verna, weren't you?"

She nodded. "Yes. I was her best friend, at least until two weeks ago when she seemed to change."

"Change? In what way?"

Her mouth pulled down. "It's hard to explain. Verna seemed to draw inside herself, like she had a secret and wanted to be alone with it. Then there was the money. I don't know where she got it, but there seemed to be quite a lot. She went on buying sprees and bought all new clothes."

"Where did this money come from?"

"I wish I knew." Muriel gave me a smile that was mostly on one side of her face. "Money was an obsession with Verna, almost a madness. She never had much as a kid. She came from a very poor family that lived in Hell's Kitchen and she used to talk about money a lot. She was always saying that someday she'd have more than she could spend."

The tip of her cigarette glowed red as she inhaled. "I guess there was nothing Verna wouldn't have done for money—nothing."

I tapped some ash into a tray. "Was Verna a good dancer?"

"Oh, yes. Really good. That job at the Magic Lamp was the first real break she ever got. She used to haunt the night clubs in her spare time, trying to show them what she could do." Her lips curved. "Verna figured a night club was the best place to hook a guy with big dough. Irene was plenty sore when she quit. She used to bring a lot of business to the studio."

I nodded. Somebody was cooking corned beef and cabbage and the smell sifted heavily through the building. "How about her boy friends?"

She shrugged. "They came and went. Men always chased after Verna. But she could handle them." A small frown wrinkled her forehead. She said thoughtfully, "There was one guy towards the end that she seemed to like more than the others."

I sat up. "Can you describe him?"

She screwed up her eyes, trying to remember. "He was big, sort of athletic-looking. He always came and took her away in a taxi. I met them once on the stairs, but Verna didn't introduce us." She gave me the one-sided smile again. "That's how I know she liked him."

The description didn't mean anything. There are a lot of big athletic-looking guys around the city.

"How about Frank Walther?"

"Walther!" she snorted. "Verna was just playing him for a sucker. He always had a lot of cash when his ship docked, back pay, but Verna managed to run through it fast enough. He'd buy her anything she wanted. He was nuts about her."

"Just the playmate for a lonely sailor," I said. "Tell me, whose car was she driving the night that Cadillac cracked up?"

"Ours. We bought it together, secondhand, and took turns using it."

"Did she ever talk about the Pernot case?"

Muriel shook her head. "Verna was very cagey about that. When I'd ask her about it all I'd get would be a kind of funny smile. She hinted once that it was the big break she was waiting for."

"How about Steve Janeiro?"

"Who?"

"Janeiro. A big, ugly brute who worked for her boss at the Magic Lamp. He says they used to be sweeties."

"Never heard of him," she said firmly.

I stood up and turned towards the window. "But it could happen without your knowing about it."

"Yes, I guess so, only——" Her voice chopped off. She gasped sharply and came to her feet. I stared at her. Her slim body was rigid as a golf stick. She stood there, jabbing a finger at me, as motionless as a bird transfixed in midflight. Her mouth began to form soundless words.

I goggled at her. "What is it?" I asked sharply.

Her face was as brittle as glass. I saw the dark roots at the base of her platinum hair and I saw the muscles twitching in her throat. She was on the verge of tossing a wingding. I opened my hand and walloped her across the face.

It left a red welt that slowly faded. Her eyes blinked and she made a sobbing noise. But the tension had snapped. I took hold of her shoulders.

"What is it, Muriel? What's wrong?"

"That's him!" she said in a strained whisper. "That's the man!" She was pointing at the folded newspaper in my pocket.

I picked it out. "What man?"

"The picture," she breathed. "He's the man I saw with Verna."

I looked at it. Under the caption MURDERED BROKER was Bob Cambreau's face.

I got an idea then what it must feel like to fall through a hole in the ice. "Are you sure?" I asked harshly.

"Yes. That's him all right." Her eyes met mine, white ringed. "And now he's been killed too."

It didn't make sense. Bob Cambreau and Verna Ford. Or did it? He'd been seeing her. Going out together. Had come here to her apartment. And all the time he'd never breathed a word about it—not a whisper.

I looked at her hard. "You mean to say you never recognized his picture before?"

She shook her head. "I never look at the papers. They make me nervous since Verna went over the edge."

"Don't the girls at the studio ever talk about it?"

"No. Irene doesn't like us to mention the case."

I stood there, trying to whip some order into the chaos. It was no use. It needed a quiet simmering. Right now my brain was turning over like a revved-up engine. I ground out my cigarette and let Muriel get composed again. I asked some more questions but she was dry. I thanked her and went down to the street.

It was colder in Queens. The streets were noisy. A gang of kids were playing stick ball and insulting each other. I got out my wallet and looked at the pawn ticket I had taken from Verna's bureau. A cab rolled along and I waved him down.

Three golden balls glittered in the afternoon sun. The pawnshop's windows were cluttered with everything from a pearl-handled lorgnette to a pair of brass knuckles. I went inside. Opening the door had touched off a bell and a man emerged from the shadows in the rear and pulled a light cord. A butter-colored, twenty-watt lamp glowed overhead. He sidled behind the cashier's cage, peering out through the grille at me from shrewd, calculating eyes. He was a leathery little item with a slipping dental plate that he kept clicking back into place with his tongue.

"Good day, sir," he said.

"Is it?" I asked. "How can you tell from here?"

He chuckled. He didn't think it was funny, but he chuckled anyway. "What can I do for you, sir?"

I placed the pawn ticket on the ledge in front of him. He clipped a pair of glasses to his nose, smiling, and examined the ticket. The smile ran away like a mouse through a hole.

His mouth pulled down at the corners. He looked up flatly. "You are not the lady who pledged this item."

"Obviously. However, I am the man who is going to redeem it."

"Why doesn't the lady come herself?"

"Because she sent me."

He put the tips of his fingers together and studied me with infinite care. "You know what this item is?"

"The skeleton of Alexander the Great," I said impatiently. "Come now, haul it out."

His face fell. "You have the money?" He seemed a little bitter.

"Right here." I tapped my breast pocket.

"Cash?"

"Cash, traveler's checks and banker's notes. I like to go well-heeled." His caginess was beginning to pique my curiosity.

"Two hundred dollars?"

"Easy," I assured him. "Don't worry. Let's get on with our business."

He shrugged, turned, and kneeled down at a squat, black safe, twisted the dial, swung open a heavy door, rummaged inside, and came up with a yellow envelope. He slit it open and reached in and with great reverence picked out a diamond clasp. The light in the store was dim, but the clasp glittered brilliantly. The pawnbroker shook his head and gave me a slow, sad smile.

"Ach! Such a lovely piece!" He sighed from his stomach. "Small but neat—fifteen baguette diamonds, set in platinum and silver, with rubies and emeralds, only chips maybe, but such workmanship. In a store like Lantier's you would pay ten thousand if you would pay a nickel for such a bauble."

He fingered it caressingly. "It made me feel like Morgan just to have it in the store."

I took a blank check out of my wallet and unscrewed a fountain pen.

His hand jumped out at me. "No," he squeaked. "Nothing doing. No checks."

I looked at him. "What's wrong? Do I look like a crook?"

He shrugged enormously. "Who can tell crooks from honest men these days? Only last week a fine-looking gent, a man who looked like a Supreme Court judge, gave me a check which it bounced so hard it cracked the showcase. Please, my friend, you said cash—make it cash."

I filled in the check and waved it. "You haven't any choice," I said. "Take it or leave it. The check or the cops."

He argued vehemently, but he knew he was waging a losing battle. The deal was finally consummated when I identified myself. But he lingered reluctantly.

"How do I know you have a right to the clasp?" He looked at me with his eyes hooded. "You see, I know what happened to the girl. I read it in the papers and remembered her name."

I said, "She did not come by the pin honestly. I represent the true owners. I'm willing to redeem it just to save time. If you prefer you can turn it over to the police. But you'll lose two hundred dollars."

"Two hundred dollars I don't want to lose," he said with conviction.

The check and the clasp changed hands.

"Why did the girl take such a small sum?" I asked.

He lifted his palms. "All she wanted I think was to keep the pin in my safe."

It sounded plausible. I left him with his sorrow and repaired immediately to Lantier's on Fifth Avenue, a very grave establishment with the somber atmosphere of a funeral chapel. The manager recognized the pin at once.

"Why, yes," he said promptly. "We designed that pin for Miss Karen Pernot. It was a gift from her uncle. He was one of our most esteemed customers."

"How long ago?"

"About a year, I'd judge. I can look it up in the records, if you'd care to wait."

"That's all right. Thank you very much."

The street was brisk and clear. The same certainly did not apply to my skull.

· 22 ·

I wandered up Fifth Avenue, hardly noticing the sleek tide of women that drifted past me with their acquisitive eyes devouring the opulent window displays. Atlas, with the weight of the world on his shoulders, had nothing on me. On Seventy-fifth Street I cut east, crossed the street, and climbed the stairs.

The same mule-faced maid in the same black alpaca dress admitted me and led me into the same semicircular room and put me into the big box-shaped sofa. Miss Pernot, she said, would join me in a moment. Before the ponderous red drapes had a chance to settle behind her, they broke open again and Rudolf Cassini stepped into the room.

His dark face still looked unhappy. He covered half the distance towards me, blinked uncertainly, licked his lips, and said, "I—I'd like a word with you, Jordan."

"Fire away," I said.

"Would you do me a favor?"

I shrugged. "Perhaps."

"It—it's about Muriel Evans," he said earnestly. "I wouldn't want Karen to know that you saw me . . ." He made a vague, helpless gesture. "Karen is a very jealous girl."

"Is she?"

He sent a quick, nervous glance over his shoulder. "Yes. Would you promise not to mention anything about——"

I said, "Listen, Cassini, I'll promise this much: if it doesn't interfere with anything I'm trying to do, you have nothing to worry about."

His eyes brightened.

"On one condition," I added.

"Anything," he said promptly.

"I want to know what you were doing in Muriel Evans's apartment, and how you got to know her."

He lowered his eyes a bit sheepishly, or as sheepishly as a guy like Cassini can look. He said, "After Karen's uncle

died and Verna Ford came forward with her story, I tried
to do a little investigating of my own. I went to the dance
studio where she used to work and there I met Muriel. We
got—" he shrugged expressively—"well, we got friendly."

"That sounds logical," I said.

He was still in the process of thanking me when Karen
Pernot floated in. Her compact body wore a royal-blue host-
ess gown and her cameo face wore a cordial smile. "What
a pleasant surprise," she said. Her eyes found Cassini.
"Rudy, darling, we have some business to discuss. Come
back this evening. And please tell Clara to bring us some
bourbon."

When all that had been attended to, she joined me on the
sofa. She sat so close you couldn't have squeezed the queen
of spades between us. Her mouth was serious and her dark
eyes concerned.

"I was horrified when I read about that dreadful shooting
in your office. I tried to reach you, but you're never in."
Her fingers curled around my arm. "You're pretty valuable
to me, Scott—I may call you Scott, mayn't I?"

"You may."

"Promise me you'll be careful."

"I'll be careful."

"Good." She smiled as if the world had suddenly become
a much finer place to live in. "How are things coming?"

"Fair. We're making a little progress, nothing sensational, but I'm hoping something big will crack at any moment."

"Perhaps we ought to celebrate," she said. "Tomorrow
is my birthday."

"Quite a coincidence," I said. "I have a present for
you."

She pressed my arm lightly. "You're psychic. I love
presents. Let's have a drink on it."

She poured some bourbon into a pair of thin jiggers and
we touched glasses. It was fine bourbon. The distiller hadn't
become impatient. It was smooth as a hummingbird's wing.
She turned to me with a shine in her eyes.

"I'm terribly excited. What is it?"

I took out my handkerchief and unfolded it in her lap. The diamond clasp glittered under the chandelier, sparking fire from a thousand different facets. She caught her breath. Her eyes were riveted tightly to it. They were dark and blank and a little frightened. Then she lifted her chin and laughed a high, tinkling laugh that seemed a full octave too high for her larynx.

"How wonderful!" she whispered. "Where did you get it?"

"From a pawnbroker."

She blinked at me, the smile hanging on.

I said, "This pawnbroker got it from Verna Ford. The sixty-four dollar question is, where did Verna Ford get it?"

She had another drink, looking at me over the rim of the glass. She turned the clasp over in her fingers, then said brightly, "I'll bet she got it from Eric Quimby."

"Why do you say that?"

The words tumbled out. "It's simple. You see, several months ago I broke the catch and Uncle Jim said he would have it fixed. He took it but he never returned it. Quimby must have found it in the house and given it to Verna."

"Why would he do that?"

"As a bribe—to pay for her testimony."

"Where would Uncle Jim be apt to take the clasp for repairs?"

"Lantier's, I suppose. Does it make any difference?"

"Some," I said. "I was there today and they never mentioned it. The catch seems to be all right now."

Her cheeks flushed slowly. I looked at her sideways, as you'd look at a child suspected of fibbing.

"You think I'm lying," she said. "Don't you?"

"Uh-huh."

She bit her lip. "Then why don't you say so?"

"All right. You're lying."

She stood up quickly. Her eyes were dark. Exasperation was in her voice. "You're the most distrustful man I ever met."

"Why not?" I said grimly. "In the past few days every-thing has happened to me that can happen to a guy. I've been warned and threatened by notes, letters, and pictures of coffins. A strange girl was poisoned in my apartment. Cops have pulled me out of bed in the middle of the night. An assortment of guns have been pointed at me and a few of them fired. I've been dreaming about my own obituaries. Scott Jordan, died suddenly of lead poisoning. Omit flow-ers. I've been lied to and misled from hell to breakfast by everybody in the case. You're my client. I'm trying to help you. How can I help you if you lie to me too? You're the one person I want the truth from—now and always."

She worked her fingers together, her lower lip drooping sulkily. After a moment her eyes grew solemn and she said, "You won't be angry?"

"I won't be angry."

She sat down again and relaxed and said frankly, "I did lie to you. I gave Verna the clasp. I was wearing it that afternoon she came here and she saw it and wanted it. She said she'd change her testimony. I gave her the clasp as a token of good faith."

"What else did you promise her?"

"Twenty per cent of all the money I got from Uncle Jim's estate."

"But she died too soon," I said.

She dipped her head. "Much too soon."

"And why didn't you tell me all this before?"

Her mouth pouted. "You promised not to scold. I didn't think it was important once Verna was dead."

"Of course it was important. Just look at it. Suppose she had taken your offer to Quimby and asked him to better it. What would his reaction be? He'd want to kill her."

"Exactly," she said intently. "And that's just what hap-pened. He killed her."

I looked at the ceiling and murmured, "Give me strength."

"You can prove it," she said stubbornly. "You can pin it on him. Oh, I'd like to be there when he got what was coming to him. I'd laugh myself sick."

I shook my head. "We're a long way from that. In the meantime you owe me two hundred dollars. That's what it cost to redeem the clasp."

"So little?" She looked outraged.

"Verna wasn't selling it. Just depositing it for safekeeping." That seemed to make her feel better. I added, "Suppose Verna had double-crossed you."

She shook her head ingenuously. "Oh, she wouldn't have done that."

"Not much," I said dryly. "You didn't know Verna."

She was silent for a moment. Then she said, "Shall I give you a check now?"

"It can wait."

More silence. She put her head down and looked up at me as if we were playing a game. "You're still angry. You think I have some more secrets."

"Have you?"

"No," she said seriously. "Honest. I want you to believe me. From now on I'm going to tell you the truth."

"That will be dandy."

She brought her face slowly around in front of mine. The dark eyes were now limpid. "Because I trust you," she said gently. "And I like you. And I want you to like me."

"I do like you," I said. She gave me a smile I felt in my ankles. I changed the subject. "Here's something that ought to please you. Eric Quimby no longer lives in Uncle Jim's house."

She sat up eagerly. "What happened?"

"I threw him out."

Her face glowed. "How wonderful!" she breathed.

"On his ear," I added. "Bag and baggage. Him and Olga."

"Olga?" She looked puzzled.

"The girl he had living there with him."

"In Uncle Jim's house?" she queried in a horrified tone.

"It's a house," I said, "not a monastery."

"But living there with a woman——"

"Don't look so shocked," I said. "You can't stop that

sort of thing. The church, the army, and the Napoleonic Code have all been trying to for years."

Her face changed. She laughed. She switched expressions and moods like other women change hats. She said, "I guess you think I'm a prude. I'm not really." She lifted her chin and slowly dropped her lashes. "Please kiss me, Scott." Her lips glistened.

I picked up my jigger and tossed off what was left of the bourbon. I didn't do anything else. After a moment her eyes fluttered open. I said, "You're forgetting Rudy."

"Rudy!" she said. "He's good at some things. This isn't one of them. So you're a man with scruples."

"No serious ones," I said. "It's just that I was engaged last night. I don't think I ought to start philandering until next week."

"Engaged?" Her eyes were speculative under half-lowered lids. "Is she pretty?"

"Passable. Somebody has to like the plain ones."

Her teeth glistened as she smiled at me. "Of course you're joking. She's probably very beautiful. Well, be careful, my friend. I usually get what I want."

"You're spoiled."

"Perhaps." She shrugged faintly. "I hate being thwarted. I learned how to get what I wanted when I was a child. With a slight change in technique it still works."

"A woman ought not to expose herself so clinically," I said.

"You'd see through me anyway." Her smile was affable. "And this way you may think I'm engagingly frank. Can I go up to Uncle Jim's tomorrow?"

"Nope. It's been locked and sealed by court order. It stays that way until the surrogate appoints an administrator."

She looked disappointed. "When will the case be reached?"

"In a couple of weeks. It's on the calendar. Tell me, do you know anything about a diamond tiepin your uncle used to wear?"

"Why, yes," she said slowly. "Why do you ask?"

"Lieutenant Nola found it among Verna's possessions."

"There you are," she stated flatly. "Quimby gave it to her."

"Maybe she took it off your uncle after the accident."

"Oh, no." She shook her head emphatically. "I saw it in his house after he left for Florida."

I shook my head in admiration. "I don't know whether you're lying or telling the truth and this time I'm not sure I want to know."

She leaned at me with an intense expression. "It *is* true. We must win this case. I've got to have that money."

"To back Cassini's show?"

"For myself, not for him. Can't you understand? I have always wanted to sing. And I have always wanted fame. I want to see my name in lights. I want to hear my voice in a theater filled with people. I want to hear the roar of applause. Is that so strange? And nothing is going to destroy that dream, nothing." She stood up. "Don't you think I'd be a success. Listen . . ."

She sat down at the piano and began to play one of Cassini's melodies. She sang. Her voice had a clear, low quality and in the bottom register some genuine beauty. She was not one of those microphone whisperers. She could fill a room. When she finished she looked at me fixedly.

"Well . . . ?"

"I liked it," I said. "You're all right."

She came forward quickly, a sudden glow in her eyes. "Listen, Scott, I have an idea. Why don't you help back Rudy's show?"

"Me?" I shook my head. "Not a chance. I'm a lawyer, not an angel. If I make any money in my racket I don't want to lose it in another man's. Not long ago I filed a petition in bankruptcy for a producer who had been in the business all his life. His judgment was supposed to have been infallible. Yet in his last show he laid an egg that would have made a turkey scream with agony. No, thanks. I'd as soon put my money on a crooked jockey."

She sighed resignedly. "It was just an idea."

I started to reach for the bourbon, decided that I had filled my quota, and instead got to my feet.

Her eyes widened. "You're leaving?"

I nodded.

"Will I hear from you soon?"

"The moment something breaks."

"Sooner," she said, "if you decide to break your engagement."

Her smile was warmer than the sun on Waikiki in mid-August.

· 23 ·

I had that tired, grated feeling that comes from too much thinking and too much emotion. I walked along the street and wondered how Nola had made out with Leo Arnim—what the bandage on Arnim's wrist had shown. Nola must have nabbed him. I recalled that Arnim could not stake out because his parole prohibited him from leaving the state and he had to report regularly.

I found a phone booth in a drugstore and rang Headquarters. Nola was not there and they didn't seem to know when he'd be back. I sat there in the booth and held up my ideas and reappraised them in the light of new developments.

It was plausible to assume that Verna had made demands on Quimby. She was a girl who would recognize an opportunity when she saw one. It wouldn't have to jump up and hit her in the face. If I could show that her depositions were perjurious and inspired by bribery, Dillon's case would crack like imitation leather. I decided to have a look at his possessions.

I dialed Floyd Dillon's office. He was out and that was my first break. I spoke to his secretary in a hard, authoritative, official tone: "Police Headquarters. Where can we find Eric Quimby?"

She began to stutter doubtfully.

"Can it, sister. This is official business. We got no time to play. Dillon has the address. Look it up in the files and hop on it."

"Just a moment, sir," she replied meekly. The phone crackled for a moment then she was back. "Mr. Quimby has a room at the Marvin."

I thanked her and hung up and went out and jumped on a bus. Fifteen minutes later I was drifting through the lobby of a third-rate hotel on East Twenty-ninth that smelled a thousand years old, was bare of furniture, but held some potted palms that nobody had bothered to water in a decade or so. A bored desk clerk with patent leather hair and no chin did not look up at me. I picked up the house phone and asked the operator for Mr. Eric Quimby.

The earpiece made buzzing noises but there was no response and that was my second break. "Mr. Quimby does not answer."

"We had an appointment," I said irritably to the operator. "Are you certain you're ringing the right room?"

"Yes, sir—Mr. Quimby, 405—there's no answer."

"Okay." I made a clucking noise and hung up.

The desk clerk was still buried in his own thoughts. I ambled casually over to the naked-ribbed elevator and let its creaking cables hike me up to the fourth floor. I was hoping that Quimby's door would not be too much of a problem.

A tiny woman with kinky gray hair was running a sweeper along the threadbare carpet. She looked up at me with a toothless smile. I gave it right back to her. I stopped in front of 405 and began a search through my pockets. I let a frown darken my face. She had stopped working to watch me. I picked a half dollar out of my pocket and wandered toward her, spinning it in the air.

"Must have left my key in the box," I said. "Could you——"

She speared the coin like a Dodger shortstop. The grin was very wide now and showed a tooth here and there. She

detached a huge key ring from a safety pin and turned a
passkey in the lock. "There you are, sir," she said.

I smiled and thanked her and closed the door behind me
until the spring lock snapped firmly. I was alone.

Quimby and Olga were not living as luxuriously as they
had up in Riverdale. The room contained a lumpy double
bed, a chenille spread that looked as if it had served time
as a towel in a public washroom, chairs, a rickety desk, and
a door that led into a bathroom. The bureau top held enough
feminine toilet articles for an amateur theatrical society.

I opened the closet door. Quimby's clothes divided the
space with Olga's. His pockets failed to turn up anything
more significant than a couple of toothpicks and two Indian-
head nickels. I turned and pulled out the bureau drawers,
sifting through their contents, trying to leave everything
exactly as I found it. Here was an assortment of shirts and
feminine underthings. I learned only that Olga's tastes leaned
to peach-colored slips with lace borders.

On the rack at the foot of the bed there was a heavy
canvas-covered piece of luggage. I stooped and saw that it
was locked. I was fumbling around with it when the noise
of a key being fitted into the door froze me solid. Voices
spoke in the hall and a woman laughed.

Quimby and Olga had returned. My heart lurched violently. Being caught here was one jam Nola would not be
able to gloss over. That made it perfect.

Breaking and entering. Attempted larceny. And beyond
that there was still the little matter of my professional reputation. A lawyer does not sneak into his adversary's room
to search for evidence. Dillon would not like that. The Bar
Association would not like it. And probably the judges at
Special Sessions would not like it. To say nothing about
Eric Quimby's legal right to put a bullet through an intruder
with absolute impunity. I was trapped in a spot tighter than
a fat woman's shoe.

I sprang at the closet and literally caught myself in mid-
air. I stopped so short it almost stood me on my ear. They
would head for the closet first—to hang up their hats and

coats. The spring lock on the door clicked back. My eyes spurted frantically around the room. The door began to move inward.

"What a day!" Quimby's voice complained. "First thing I'm gonna take a shower."

"I just want to lie down and get some rest," said Olga.

A whippet never moved any faster. I dove headlong to the floor and whirled under the bed. Just in time.

They came into the room and took off their hats and coats and hung them in the closet.

"When'll we eat?" Quimby asked.

"Later, honey. I'm too tired now."

Quimby laughed softly. "What you need is a shower, kid. Pep you up. Come on, take one with me."

"You're crazy," she said. "That's all you ever think about."

"What's wrong with it?" He came over to the bed and sat down heavily. The springs rested on my spine. I pushed my face into the carpet, tasting lint.

Olga said acidly, "God, how I hate this rathole! If it wasn't for that bastard, Jordan, we'd still be living in style."

"Don't worry about Jordan," Quimby said grimly. "A guy like that ain't long for this earth."

"Yeah? I can't wait. I wish he'd got it that night instead of Cambreau."

One of Quimby's shoes hit the floor. A stockinged foot hung twelve inches from my face. He said, "I got a feeling that Jordan is next on the undertaker's list."

She moved over and sat down beside him on the bed and the wooden slats quivered against my back and sprayed a cloud of dust motes around my nose.

Quimby laughed lightly. "Every time you come near me, baby, I get ideas. Come here."

"Stop, Eric . . ."

There was a muffled sound and a brief struggle. Olga started to giggle but it ended abruptly with a sharp exclamation. "Ouch! What's that sticking me?"

"Nothing," Quimby breathed.

"It's the gun!" Her voice was thin and strained. "You're wearing that gun again. I thought you got rid of it. You promised me you would."

"Forget it," he said harshly.

"No. Listen, Eric—please listen—we got a chance to make some real money for the first time in our lives. Don't go spoiling it by getting crazy. You know how you are when you get a temper. We'll wind up without any money and in trouble. Better get rid of that gun."

"Goddamned if you don't think it was me that fogged Cambreau. Jesus, it's right there in your face! You think I went after Jordan and got the wrong guy. Use your head, baby. Would I make a dumb play like that? Hell, if I was after Jordan I'd stick the barrel of the gun right down his throat before I started pumping."

"Oh, Eric . . ." she wailed.

"What the hell's eating you anyway?" he asked gruffly. "You getting soft, kid?"

"I'm not soft. I'm scared. How do we know the cops won't walk in on us any minute and begin asking questions? If they catch you with a gun they're liable to start digging up stuff we don't want them to know anything about."

Quimby was silent for a moment, then he said thoughtfully, "I got to be ready for anything that comes along. Somebody's playing this game pretty rough. Just remember this, baby, if the cops get nosy, we were together the night Cambreau got shot. Right here in this room, understand?"

"Yes," she said in a small, slow voice. "Right here in this room."

"That's the idea. Stick to it, baby." He got up off the bed. "I hope that damned maid left some towels."

The girl stood up too and moved in front of him. "Unzip me, honey, before you go."

He laughed softly and I heard the scratch of a zipper and the rustle of cloth. There was another tussle. That Quimby was a beaut!

Olga squealed. "Your hands are so cold."

"Jesus, baby, your skin is like milk. Stop wriggling."

"Don't, Eric—you crazy fool—not now——"

"Turn around," he breathed thickly.

"Eric . . ."

They scuffled and floundered over onto the bed. Dust showered down. I felt a sneeze gathering intensity high against my sinus. I squashed my nose against the floor and prayed silently. Above me Olga made little catlike noises. My face was burning. I was drenched.

A sharp knock sounded against the door.

Silence hung over the room.

"Who is it?" whispered Olga in a scared voice.

The doorknob rattled violently. A voice called out, "Open the door."

Quimby got up and went over to the door and opened it a crack. He sucked in a sharp breath. "*Leo!*" he said, sounding stunned.

The door opened wide and Quimby backed into the room. A pair of shoes advanced and kicked the door shut.

Leo Arnim's voice spoke quietly. "Who's the dame?"

"She's all right, Leo."

"Get rid of her."

"Listen you——" Olga bleated.

"Get her out of here."

"Yeah, sure, Leo. Beat it, Olga. We got some business to talk over. Come back later."

She did not argue. She stood up and got her coat and went out, closing the door softly behind her. The two men stood facing each other. Then Quimby laughed breathlessly, a laugh that had nothing at all to do with being amused.

"I was glad to hear about your parole, Leo."

Arnim snorted. "You didn't give one whistle in hell about it."

More silence.

"I hear you were in my club a couple of nights ago."

"Yeah, Leo."

Arnim's voice was mildly purring. "Why didn't you come back and talk to me? After all, you're Ivy's brother. You know how I used to feel about her."

"I figured you were busy, Leo. I didn't want to bother you."

"Very considerate. You're changing, Eric. What brought you there?"

"Just wanted to look around, Leo."

"See anything?"

"Yeah, Leo, it's a nice layout."

"It wouldn't be that you came there because of the Ford dame, would it?" Arnim asked.

"The Ford dame? Who's she?"

"Don't peddle that drool on me." Arnim's voice had turned to acid. "I know what happened to Ivy. I can read the papers. So your little sister hooked a millionaire in Florida, eh? And now she's dead and you're trying to muscle in on the estate."

Quimby did not speak. Silence seemed to fold over the room like a thick fog. I held my breath. So Leo Arnim knew Ivy Pernot. And he knew Eric Quimby. It didn't have to mean anything.

Arnim was talking again, in a low, careful voice. "Quite a coincidence, wasn't it, Eric, that your star witness happened to work for me. She must have had you dancing at the end of a string, if I knew Verna. So you came to the club trying to get a line on her."

Quimby exhaled sharply. His voice had become heavy and tired. "Okay, Leo," he said. "I guess there isn't anything I can do if you want to put the squeeze on us. We'll have to cut you in. There's plenty of dough to go around. You——"

"Shut up!" Arnim said icily. "I don't want a nickel of the Pernot money. Not a goddamned cent, understand? I want no part of the case. I don't want to be tied up with the Ford girl any more than I have to. I can't have the cops on my back. I wouldn't even want them to wise up that I ever knew you—or Ivy."

"Sure, Leo. Anything you say."

Arnim grunted and walked over to the door and then turned and said in a voice that was harsh and strangled with leashed fury, "Stay away from the club. And stay away from me, understand? We don't know each other. If you ever come near me or near the club again, I'll kill you. Is that clear?"

"You can trust me, Leo."

"Yeah, like I can trust a starving rat. Who's this chippy with you?"

"Just a girl, Leo."

"She know anything about me?"

"Not a thing. She's dumb, Leo."

"Keep her that way." He opened the door and added woodenly, "Remember, stay away from me." The door closed behind him.

Quimby stood motionless, dragging air into his lungs with a rasping sound. His feet were flat on the floor. His voice was low and raw with obscenity. Suddenly he stopped cursing and gave a grinding laugh. He grew silent and then went into the bathroom. I heard him draw the shower curtain and after that there was the swift rush of pressured water.

I rolled out from under the bed. I wasted no time. I got out of there like a stallion breaking from the barrier at Hialeah.

• 24 •

I kept moving until I found a phone booth several blocks away. I rang Headquarters again and learned that Nola had returned but could not at the moment be reached. I couldn't wait. I had to see him and talk to him. I went out and jumped into a cab.

When I walked into Nola's office, he was there, sitting behind his battered desk, moody-eyed and glum-faced. Smoke drifted upward from a forgotten cigarette. He looked up and gave me a slow, dour smile.

"Did you see Arnim?" I asked.

He nodded.

"How did it go?"

He shrugged. "No soap. Not even a lather."

"But his arm was bandaged. I saw it. Certainly something must have happened."

He discarded the cigarette. "It did. Arnim had an accident about two weeks ago. He was driving his Chrysler up on the Bronx River Parkway and had a blowout and lost control of the wheel. His car jumped the road and whaled into a tree."

"Who says so?" I asked, disappointed.

"Arnim does—and two state troopers who witnessed the whole thing. They were right behind him when it happened. He seemed shaken up and they drove him to a doctor in Mount Vernon. Bone in his forearm was chipped."

"You checked all this?"

"In person. A record of the accident is on the police blotter and I spoke to the troopers myself. Spoke to the doctor too." Nola grimaced. "That's the hell of being a cop. You turn over a rock and you never know what you're going to find—a water bug or a snake."

I nodded. "I've been working myself. I have a few items of interest, but don't ask me how I got them because if I told you, you'd have to book me on half a dozen charges. First, I got it from Janeiro's own mouth that he was more than just a casual acquaintance of Verna Ford. I learned, too, that Leo Arnim has known Quimby for some time. That he's afraid of being seen with him or having the police find out about it. He also knew Quimby's sister, Mrs. Ivy Pernot. And if that doesn't add enough to the confusion I learned that Bob Cambreau had been squiring Verna Ford about town."

Nola was scowling. "What do you make of it?"

"I don't know. It seems to tie everybody into a wet knot that I'd like to see you unravel."

He shook his head and gave me an empty-eyed look.

I said, "Any trace of Harry Dunn?"

"Not yet."

"Frank Walther?"

"Not a sign. His ship sails tomorrow and he'll have to turn up or be stranded."

"Maybe he can't show up."

Nola centered a searching glance on my face.

I said, "You placed Walther at my office building about the time Cambreau was shot. Suppose he recognized the killer and spoke up and had to be immediately liquidated."

Nola chewed on his lips. "Another homicide and this whole department is slated for a shake-up. I wish——"

He stopped to answer the phone. He listened briefly, then covered the mouthpiece and looked up. His eyes glinted. "It's Wienick. He just spotted Harry Dunn sneaking back into his rooming house."

I got excited. "Listen, Nola, hold everything. Let me go over there and talk to Dunn. I think I can handle him."

He was staring at me, his jaw hard.

I said swiftly, "Keep Wienick on tap. If it's no good you can always grab Dunn and use your own methods. But first let me have a crack at him."

Nola ruminated, his brows bent together, then he nodded and rumbled instructions to Wienick. He hung up and said to me, "I ought to be back in uniform. I'm letting you do this on a hunch. I can't see how you can foul things up any more than they are. Go ahead." He gave me an address and added, "Top floor rear."

Shadows were lengthening over the city when I reached Harry Dunn's rooming house fifteen minutes later. At this time of the year it gets dark early. I saw Wienick lounging inconspicuously in a doorway across the street. The hall door stood open. I went in and climbed four flights of worn, grooved stairs, past peeling wallpaper. The place was heavy with the sour smell of forgotten meals.

On the top floor I put an ear against Dunn's door and listened to the meaningless sounds of a man moving around. I knocked softly and the sounds within stopped. I knocked again. After a moment he asked in a cautious voice who it was.

"Jordan," I said. "Open up, Dunn."

A key turned and the door opened. Dunn's face was oyster white and fear peered out of his bloodshot eyes. He was taut, haggard, edgy. He was scared. I have seen healthier-looking corpses.

I went in and closed the door. It was a small depressing room. Overhead a grimy, rectangular skylight grudgingly admitted what was left of a fast dying sun. A door, slightly ajar, showed a bathroom about the size of a closet.

Dunn backed up and perched on the edge of the bed and licked his lips and looked at me guardedly.

"Where have you been, Harry?" I asked him.

"Around."

I shook my head. "You'll have to do better than that. A lot better. There's a lot of things that need explaining. Two people have been murdered. The Homicide Bureau is in a stew. The newspapers and the commissioner and the outraged public are all climbing on their backs. They need a fall guy. With your record and your connection with the case you're a cinch to be tailored for the rap."

His lips twitched nervously. "They can't pin anything on me."

"Maybe. I wouldn't be too sure. It's been done before. I'll make a deal with you, Harry. You have some information. I want it. Play ball with me and I'll go to bat for you. I'm in solid down at Headquarters and you know that's no idle chatter. At this very moment there's an urgent pickup order out on you. If the cops nab you, and they will, they have a few tricks that will make you sing louder than a Wagnerian soprano. Use your head, Dunn. I can save you a lot of grief, a lot of punishment."

His lips jerked and he squirmed back. He seemed to be cracking like Mussolini's legions. "What—what do you want?" His voice was a barely audible whisper.

"That first time you came to my office," I said, "where did you get the drugs and the gun?"

His jaw went slack and he shivered. He was scared again. He made his mouth tight.

"Don't be a fool," I grated. "I know where you got the stuff. I can almost guess what happened. Arnim was afraid of me. He was afraid that I knew something he didn't want known. There's only one way you can really silence a guy. He wanted me chilled off and he picked you for the job. You came along and fell into his lap. He knew about the hate that's been rankling your guts. So he put the needles in you. He got you hopped up and sent you out with a gun. You were supposed to put me on ice. But when that little scheme backfired, and you wound up in the clink, he was afraid the snow in you would melt and you'd chirp a story to the cops, so he sent Steve Janeiro down to bail you out. And all the time you thought he was your pal. Some pal! That's worth a laugh, isn't it, Harry?"

I paused to let him digest it. It didn't sit very well.

I said, "Arnim gave you that gun, didn't he Harry?"

"Yes," he whispered.

"And that night when I met you coming out of his office with a shiner—he had just slugged you. Why?"

Dunn spread his fingers in a puzzled gesture. "I can't figure it, Jordan. All I told him was that I was outside talking to you. He went wild. He hit me and swore if I ever opened my yap again he'd close it for good."

"What's Arnim scared of, Harry?"

"I don't know."

"He's trying to hide something. What is it?"

"I don't know."

"You're lying," I said.

Dunn's teeth snapped and his fingers plucked nervously at the bedcovers.

I put my face close to his. "You'd better talk, Dunn. I'm through with reasoning."

His tongue coiled out over his lips. "Listen, I swear——"

"Goddammit! A friend of mine has been murdered. It could have been me. Talk up."

He seemed to wilt, but he kept shaking his head.

I grabbed him by the throat, anger flaring hotly. I shook him like a pair of dice. His teeth were rattling.

"Talk, damn you, talk———"

His face darkened and his eyes rolled. His lips turned
blue and he made choking noises. He started to sag under
my clenched hand. I let him go and stepped back. He was
tugging frantically at his collar, gasping for air. Incoherent
mumbling came from his swollen lips. I heard him say,
"Water."

I turned and went into the undersized bathroom. There
didn't seem to be any light in there. I groped for the faucet
and ran a thin trickle of water. I held a glass and waited for
it to fill.

Behind me there was the sudden crash of breaking glass.

I whirled to see Harry Dunn sitting up stiffly on the bed.
His thin face was turned upward, popeyed with terror, staring at a jagged hole in the skylight.

On the roof, looking down at him with fixed eyes, kneeled
Steve Janeiro. The big man had broken the skylight with
the muzzle of his gun. He was crouched low, deliberately
aiming through the shattered pane. He had arrived at a
moment when I was out of sight. And so intent was he on
his target that he failed to spot me standing there in the
murky doorway.

Harry Dunn, his face ashen under the stunned blankness
of his eyes, kept his face turned upward. It was frozen,
except for the movement of his lips. He kept moving them
very slowly, like a goldfish in a bowl, but no sounds came
out. Steve Janeiro shot him three times.

The impact knocked Harry Dunn back across the bed so
that his head thumped against the wall. The wall kept him
propped up. A crimson smear blossomed on his shirt. His
tongue lolled out thickly and his fingers twitched spasmod-
ically.

I managed to get off one shot through the skylight, but
it was too late. Steve Janeiro had already faded against the
darkening sky, and all I did was knock some more glass on
the bed. I stood there, impaled, staring stupidly at the tendril
of smoke that curled lazily from the muzzle of my gun.

Dunn's mouth made a bubbling noise. I looked at him.

His eyes were still open but now the lids were folding slowly over them. I saw a feeble pulse fluttering in his throat. The man should have been dead but he was alive and it was incredible.

Footsteps pounded up the stairs and Wienick burst into the room.

He saw Dunn, and he saw the gun in my fist, and his eyes widened with stark incredulity. He whispered in a hoarse voice, "Sweet Jesus! Now you've done it."

"Don't be an ass!" I breathed hoarsely, pointing to the shattered skylight. "It was Steve Janeiro, He came across the roof from another building."

Wienick whirled back out of the door, hauling his gun from its holster, and slamming down the stairs three at a time. But I knew that he was too late. By now Steve Janeiro was in the street and gone.

I looked at Dunn. His face was still and as white as paper, but his fingers were moving.

I went quickly downstairs, past gaping, frightened faces, to call an ambulance.

· 25 ·

We sat, John Nola and I, in the hospital waiting room, looking at each other like two politicians hearing bad election results. At best, Harry Dunn had only the slimmest kind of a chance. By some miracle all three bullets had missed his heart, but shock and the loss of blood were very great. His life hung by a spider's thread and now they were giving him his third transfusion.

Nola said heavily, "Boiled down, it looks like this: Leo Arnim sent Dunn over to your office to kill you. We do not know his motive, but presumably it had something to do

with Verna Ford's visit to your apartment. When Dunn
fizzled the job, he was maneuvered out of jail and then,
because Arnim couldn't trust him to keep his mouth shut,
he ordered Janeiro to erase him. Unfortunately, you were
there at the time and saw the whole thing.''

I frowned at him. "Why do you say 'unfortunately'?"

"Why not? It's unfortunate for Janeiro, unfortunate for
Arnim, and unfortunate for you. If Dunn dies your testimony
will send Janeiro to the chair. He can't let that ride. He or
Arnim or some outside talent will be called in to rub you
out of the picture.''

I felt chilled. "Then do something. Janeiro is in hiding,
but you can pick up Arnim and sock him away.''

"On what charge? Remember, we're still speculating.''

The door opened and the doctor looked in. ''You can see
Dunn now.''

"How is he, Doc?" I asked.

"Fading fast, but he's conscious now and I can't say how
long it will last.''

We followed him down a silent white corridor with its
pungent antiseptic odor and into a small white room.

Harry Dunn's face wore the pinched and sunken look of
approaching death. His eyes were hollow and burning. I
went over and put my lips close to his ear. In a low, delib-
erate voice I said, "Can you hear me, Dunn? This is Jordan.''

His eyelids flickered. That was the only sign of recog-
nition.

"We both know who fogged you, Dunn," I said. "But
only you know why.''

His lips moved soundlessly.

"Did Arnim send Steve Janeiro after you?"

His voice was a whisper from a bottomless well. "No . . .
they had a fight . . . Arnim threw Janeiro out of the club . . .''

I felt weak. This was just fine. It threw our nice clean
theories overboard.

"Then Janeiro was acting on his own. Why did he shoot
you?"

Dunn closed his eyes. His face was wet clay. He said in a raggedly torn whisper, "Because I saw him . . . fixing a bullet wound . . . on his side . . ." Dunn's breath came out in a harsh whistle and his bloodless lips hung slack.

The doctor closed in determinedly. "I'm sorry, but you'll have to leave now."

"One more question," I pleaded urgently. I bent down again. "Dunn, can you hear me? The bullet wound—did Janeiro get it when I shot him in the park?"

His chin moved faintly and then his face relaxed and went flaccid. Almost instantaneously it grew rigid. Swiftly the doctor applied his stethoscope and listened. He looked up and shrugged and pulled the sheet over Dunn's face and said matter-of-factly, "That's all, gentlemen, he's gone."

I followed Nola into the corridor. Our eyes met. "Just like that," he said tonelessly.

"In a split second," I said. "The transition from life to death is swift."

He nodded. "At least we learned that it was Janeiro who shot at you in the park. He could have done that under orders from Arnim."

I shook my head thoughtfully. "I hardly think so. We were wrong. Dunn told us that Arnim had tied a can to Janeiro. If Arnim had any killing to do he'd do it himself. Janeiro was probably good for a little muscle work, but Arnim wouldn't send him out on a kill and then fire him and raise bad blood. The point is, why would he kill me at all?"

"Because you know something."

I shook my head. "Maybe it's buried somewheres, but I can't dig it out."

"Think, boy, think hard."

I pressed my temples. "It's no use. My head is blown up like a pumpkin."

The doctor came out of the room and Nola beckoned him over. "Doctor," he said, "I want you to do me a favor. I want to keep Dunn's death under wraps for a time. Can you keep it a secret?"

The doctor nodded, frowning. "Perhaps. I don't understand."

"It's a hunch," Nola said. "If we keep the killer over a barrel, something may pop."

"I'll do my best. I'll pass the word along."

"Fine, especially the switchboard. If anyone calls, his condition is about the same, he may even pull through."

The doctor hurried away to attend to it. Nola offered to drive me home. We went out and got into the car. An idea had been chasing around in my head and I said, "Let's try this on for size: Walther was seen around my office when Cambreau was killed. We know that Cambreau had been running around with Verna. Maybe he found that out and followed him there and put a slug into him."

Nola lifted his shoulders. "I don't like it. Men stick pretty close to type. Walther is not the kind who'd shoot a guy through a closed door. It wouldn't give him any pleasure, not if his motive was jealousy or revenge. What's more I think Cambreau's death was a mistake. The killer was after you. We must remember that both killings, Verna's and Cambreau's, were part of the same pattern. Will you say that Walther also killed Verna? If that is so, and I doubt it, then it disregards Arnim's patent interest in the case and this latest caper of Janeiro. It also disregards Dillon and Quimby and the whole Pernot business."

He was right, of course. "I didn't think much of the idea myself," I admitted. "I guess I'm too close to this thing to see it in the right perspective."

Nola tooled the car deftly through a traffic jam and was silent.

I said, "Since your mind is clicking so efficiently, maybe you can explain Cambreau's friendship with Verna."

"That's not hard. I've been thinking about it. Cambreau had been up to Floyd Dillon's office to discuss his divorce and he may have seen her there. He was a chaser. A blonde like Verna would attract him. He followed her out of the office and picked her up. She would easily size him up as a good touch."

That sounded logical. I asked, "What about Arnim now?"

"We'll put a tail on him, give him some rope. But I don't think he'll make a move." He paused. "As for you, my friend, I give you absolutely gratis at the city's expense a couple of men to dog your heels. If we can't stop anybody from putting a bullet into your back, we can sure as hell grab him for it."

"No fuss," I said mildly. "The idea rather appeals to me. My luck can't hold out forever."

Nola pulled up before the Drummond. I got out and waved to him and then went into the lobby and upstairs. I opened the door and Dulcy came at me with a rush. She looked up at me, her face serious.

"Listen, darling, do you want me to retire to a convent?"

"Heaven forbid!"

"I will," she said, "if anything happens to you. I've been listening to the radio reports about this new shooting."

"There's nothing to worry about," I said. "Nola is planting Headquarters men all around me. I'm safer than a baby in a crib." I sniffed at the air like a terrier. "What smells so fine?"

"Supper," she said. "We're staying home tonight where I can keep an eye on you."

"You're going to make some man a fine, dutiful wife. Where do I file an application?"

"It's already filed and under consideration. Go wash your hands. Supper will be ready in a moment."

I performed the necessary ablutions and when I came out the bridge table was set with a steaming lamb stew. I looked at Dulcy from the corner of my eyes. "Mr. Birds Eye again?"

"Uh-huh."

"Maybe I'd better marry him."

She made a face and ordered me to work. When I finally sat back with a groan, she smiled at me and sighed. "I wish you could stay here for a week."

"That's a splendid idea," I said, "but I have to make a living."

Her chin was firm. "When this case is over, you're going to have a new kind of practice. I'll bring you the clients."

"You? How?"

"There are ways," she said airily. "I can stick petticoats in escalators and loosen wheels on Fifth Avenue busses. All you need is a little ingenuity."

"Sure," I said, "and we'll be spending our honeymoon in jail."

"Then we'll bribe the turnkey to give us the same cell." The phone rang. "Don't answer it," she said. It kept ringing. I went over and picked it up.

"Hello."

"Jordan?" The voice sounded familiar. It was strained and hoarse.

"Speaking," I said.

"Steve Janeiro. Don't try to trace this call. I'm in a booth and I'll be outa here in a minute. I gotta talk to you, Jordan."

I laughed thinly. "Your brains are loose. What do you take me for?"

"Listen," he said urgently, "I gotta see you. I want to make a deal."

"Make it with the cops."

"No cops." His voice was feverish. "Only you. I trust you, Jordan."

"But I don't trust you."

"I tell you I know something that will blow the Pernot case wide open and make you a sack of dough. I'll sell it to you."

"For what?"

"To keep your flap buttoned about what you saw in Dunn's room."

"Impossible," I said. "The cops know I was there."

"Tell 'em you were mistaken. It was too dark to recognize me. You can change your mind."

"You're whistling up the wrong tree, Janeiro. I can't perjure myself for a potential killer."

His teeth snapped audibly. "Listen," he said, his voice taut with desperation, "Dunn ain't dead yet. Until he drops off they can't pin a murder rap on me. But I'm in a hole, see? I'm a three-time loser and even if they convict me for assault with a gun it would send me over for life. I'll risk that, but I don't want to burn.''

"Nothing doing," I said flatly.

"Wait. If Dunn dies the whole deal is off. You can talk your piece and I'll hit out for Mexico. That'll clear your conscience. But if he lives, you didn't recognize me.''

I almost laughed. Nola's hunch had been right. Janeiro did not know Harry Dunn was already dead. And so I made a promise that was no promise at all and I did it without a scruple.

"Okay, Janeiro," I said. "If Dunn lives the guy I saw at the skylight had a red mustache and gold teeth. If he dies, it was you. Spill your story.''

He sucked in a harsh breath. "I'm tearing a hole in my pocket. This could have made me plenty. Well, here goes. It's about Quimby's sister.''

"Ivy Pernot? What about her?''

"She was never married to James Pernot.''

"You're cracked. I saw the marriage license myself.''

"They were married all right." He laughed thinly. "Yeah, but it never took. She already had a husband.''

I was tight with expectancy. "Who?''

"This will kill you. She was married to Leo Arnim.''

I stood there, my jaw hanging, stunned. Then I said slowly, "Are you sure?''

"Positive. I got a couple of snapshots showing Leo and Ivy together, one in her wedding dress. I'll send them to you. They won't do me any good. So long, Jordan.''

"One moment," I almost yelled. "How did you learn all this?''

He was under pressure now, worried, talking fast. "I heard the Ford squab putting the bite on Leo for a thousand bucks. He didn't know I was in his apartment. I guessed it had something to do with the Pernot case and I cased his joint one night while he was in the club and dug it up.''

"What were you doing in Verna's room when I caught you in the closet?''

"Looking for more evidence. I gotta go now, Jordan. I've been in here too long.''

I was beginning to see some light. Another link dropped into place. I said, "So you went to Quimby and braced him for a cut of the Pernot money to keep your mouth shut."

"You're bright, Jordan. That's it."

I plowed on. "Last question. Is that why you went after me in the park, because you were afraid I'd wreck Quimby's chance to collect?"

"Yeah. He didn't have the guts for a job like that. He's yellower than a piece of crayon. But it's all water under the bridge now. Remember your promise. So long, Counselor."

He hung up. Dulcy was watching me with shadowed eyes. I stood there and let the thoughts go tumbling around in my brain looking for likely roosting places. They juggled around and arranged themselves in a pattern that began to make a little sense. I knew, too, why Janeiro had attacked Harry Dunn. As a three-time loser, a conviction for assault with a deadly weapon would mean a life sentence. He would never be able to trust Dunn.

I called Nola. It was getting to be a habit. After listening to the story he told me to get down to Centre Street at once.

Dulcy looked disappointed. "You're going away again."

"Just for a little while, baby. You stay here and keep the door locked. Don't open it for anyone."

"I went shopping today for our trip to Bermuda," she said. "I bought a wonderful new bathing suit that hasn't any straps and practically no back and very little front. If you stay home I'll let you see how I look in it."

"You tempt a man beyond human resistance," I told her. "It'll have to keep for a while."

She saw me to the door and out.

• 26 •

The inspector's office was warm and thick with smoke and charged with the tension of the three men listening to me.

Boyce, Lohman, and Nola were ranged around the room.
Boyce was impassive; Nola was brooding; and Philip Lohman sat hinged forward, his jaw tight and his eyes hostile.

I said, "It was like betting on a horse race with a guy
who doesn't know the race is over. Harry Dunn had something on Janeiro. He spied Janeiro changing a bandage on
his hip and realized immediately what had happened, that
Janeiro had probably been wounded by my random shot in
the park. After Cambreau's death, the heat was turned on
Dunn. Janeiro was afraid that Dunn would try to take the
heat off himself by switching it to the big boy. As a three-
time loser he couldn't afford to be picked up on any charge.
He had to reduce this risk by eliminating Dunn. Naturally
he didn't anticipate my witnessing the whole thing. It was
a tough break. He was boxed in. He doesn't want to burn.
Like all killers he's a miserable coward at heart. Even a life
sentence looked better than the electric chair and he was
willing to bargain for any concession he could get. He was
trying to beat the life rap by selling me this information."

Lohman rubbed his hands. "We'll have a Grand Jury
indictment first thing in the morning." He looked at Boyce.
"When will he be brought in?"

Boyce shrugged. "The dragnet is out." A frown pulled
his brows together. "I still don't know who killed Verna
Ford."

Lohman favored him with a pitying look. "It's clear to
me. Arnim killed her."

"I'm not so sure," murmured Nola.

"Well, I am." Lohman looked smug. "I have some
evidence of which you gentlemen are not aware. One of my
investigators found the Ross girl."

I sat up. "The Southern Airways stewardess? Found her
where?"

"In New Jersey, visiting some relatives. She was paid
twenty-five hundred dollars to leave the state and get out
of sight."

"By whom?" I asked sharply.

"She can't say. The deal was made by phone and the

money sent by mail. A man phoned her and asked if she'd take that sum to disappear. Twenty-five hundred dollars is a lot of money to a working girl. She agreed and received the money the following day.''

"What made her talk up at this point?"

Lohman smiled thinly. "Fear," he said. "The desire for self-preservation. The fact that several people had been killed and that she might be next on the list. We made out a rather strong case."

The door opened and Dillon appeared. His eyes moved around the room and centered on the District Attorney.

"You sent for me?" His face exhibited worry.

Lohman inclined his head. "Yes. In connection with the Pernot case. Have a seat. We're going to thrash this thing out if it takes all night. Since you're Quimby's lawyer I think you ought to be in on it. Besides, there are some questions we want answered."

Dillon got deposited in the chair indicated and lifted his Roman nose in an attitude of frankness. "I'm quite ready to co-operate."

"Fine," Lohman said sardonically. "Three people had to get killed before we could all gather in a nice spirit of collaboration. Did you know that the marriage of James and Ivy Pernot was bigamous?"

Dillon's mouth flapped open and he half rose out of the chair. His eyes widened with shock. "What!"

"Precisely. Ivy had a husband when she married James Pernot in Florida."

"Who?" Dillon whispered.

"She was married to Leo Arnim."

Dillon looked jarred to the heels. He slumped back, speechless.

"Because," continued Lohman with relish, "if you were aware of that fact and continued to prosecute Quimby's claim, you were guilty of a serious breach of professional ethics, to say nothing about suborning perjury. And far worse, keeping silent in the face of all this violence and murder makes you criminally responsible."

Dillon paled. His mouth was working. "Naturally," he said, "had I known the facts I would never have touched the case."

"Naturally. A possible fee in five or six figures would not affect your principles. We lawyers are beyond reproach, aren't we? Well, we shall see."

Dillon's hands were clenched over his knees. The door opened and Wienick looked in. "Arnim is here now."

Boyce said, "Send him in."

Leo Arnim came into the room. His heavy, white face surveyed us bleakly and impassively. He kept his hands in the pockets of his coat, the thumbs hanging out.

Lohman waved at a chair. "Have a seat, Arnim."

"Sorry," Arnim told him shortly. "I can't stay long."

"No?" Lohman's smile was fleeting. "Well, we shall see. Perhaps you won't mind answering a few questions." He was very polite and polished and slick, and enjoying himself hugely. He was an actor performing for the rest of us, showing how clever he was. "I suppose you've heard about Steve Janeiro and Harry Dunn."

Arnim nodded stonily.

"Did you know that Dunn was dead?"

No change of expression moved any feature in Arnim's face. He said coldly, "I'm not interested."

Lohman lifted his brows in a high arch. "Ah, but Janeiro was employed by you."

"Not to kill Dunn. We broke connections yesterday. I fired him."

"Why, may I ask?"

"We had a difference of opinion."

"About what?"

"About who killed Trotsky."

A slow flush darkened Lohman's face. He drew himself up. "Watch your tongue, Arnim. You're in no position to act flip. As a matter of fact, you're in serious trouble. Several murders have been committed and we can definitely link you with at least one of them."

Arnim stared at him inscrutably. "I haven't heard you say anything yet."

Lohman thrust out his jaw. "Then listen to this: the first victim, Verna Ford, was a witness in a case concerning the survival of a woman called Ivy Pernot. This woman was your wife." He paused to watch Arnim's reaction. Leo Arnim stiffened like a board and his eyes became as thin as the edge of a worn dime. Lohman nodded with satisfaction. "Ah, I see this hits you. If the fact that she was your wife became known the survival case would collapse. It had to be kept a secret so Eric Quimby could inherit Pernot's estate through his sister, Ivy. I say that you were in on this scheme. I say further that the relationship was discovered by Verna Ford. According to Janeiro, the girl was blackmailing you. I say that you killed her to ensure silence. You gave her a bottle of brandy that had been poisoned and she took it to Jordan's apartment and drank it there and died. Will you deny it?"

Arnim took a long breath and let it out slowly. His face was grim. He stood there, flexing his fingers, staring at Lohman, and he said in a toneless voice, "I will deny it. Ivy was not my wife. She divorced me in Las Vegas while I was serving a term in prison. The final papers were mailed to me there."

It staggered Lohman. It dropped the bottom clean out of his hypothesis and moved Dillon's case right back into the running. It jolted all of us. I sat very still in my seat, thinking hard. Divorced or not, the fact still remained that Verna had been blackmailing Arnim. Why? The question prodded at me.

And then, without any warning whatever, the cold, hard light of logical deduction flashed on me. My brain must have been working subconsciously on it for a long time.

I stood up and moistened my lips. I said quietly, "Tell me, Arnim, would an inspection of your bank account show a recent withdrawal of twenty-five hundred dollars?"

His eyes were blank. "What are you getting at?"

"The money you paid Janet Ross to leave the state."

Nola's chin jerked up. "Arnim?" he asked querulously.

"You people are dull," I said. "He had to get rid of her

because she might recognize him as a passenger on the Southern Airways plane, Flight 7, from Miami—*the missing witness.*''

Arnim's eyes held a brittle shine between narrowed lids. He hulked forward, staring at me.

In a way I felt sorry for him. I said softly, "Yes, Ivy had bought herself a divorce but to you it was only a piece of paper. It made no difference because you still loved her. You loved her enough to risk your freedom and your future. And so when the vine brought news that she was in Florida, you flew down to see her. Perhaps you thought you could talk her into coming back to you. You flew down, secretly of course, because being on parole you could not leave the state and had no legitimate reason for doing so. You made a reservation under a name picked at random from the city directory. But when you got there, it was too late. Ivy had just married James Pernot and was on the point of flying back to New York. So you came along on the same plane. Maybe you arranged with her to take Pernot to the cleaners. It doesn't matter. At any rate you were in that limousine crack-up on the highway back to Manhattan in which they were both killed.''

Leo Arnim was breathing heavily out of a lopsided mouth. Lohman and Boyce were watching us with a fixed intensity.

Nola said, frowning, "You mean he came out of that accident without a scratch?''

"Not at all. He fractured his wrist. Compared with the others it was a slight injury. Freak accidents like that happen all the time. Last year a plane crashed and everyone was killed but a small child. Arnim was probably knocked unconscious. When he came around he knew that he had to get away before anyone saw him, else he might be sent back to prison to finish his term for breaking parole by leaving the state. That was a very real danger. So he crawled away and somehow got back to the city. He did not at that time know that Verna had already seen him and gone for help. The next day he got out his car and drove along the Bronx River Parkway and faked an accident. He waited until he spotted a couple of troopers and then deliberately drove into a tree. Those cops were his alibi. To explain the injury sustained in the earlier accident. As it turned out, he actually needed that alibi because you questioned him.''

Arnim's face was knotted like a fist. Beads of sweat stood out on it as if he had just come in out of a lashing rain. His eyes burned at me with a deadly hatred.

I went on carefully. ''And then one day Verna Ford walked into his club and recognized him. That was in the cards. She had been making the rounds, looking for work, and it was only a matter of time before she hit the Magic Lamp. And immediately she knew she had something. She sized up the situation at once and put the squeeze on him. She wanted a job as a featured dancer and he gave it to her. He couldn't help himself. It must have been like trying to fill a jug with no bottom. Verna would milk it dry. She was that kind of a girl.''

Lohman planted himself squarely before Arnim and said in a clear voice, ''Arnim, I'm charging you with the murder of Verna Ford.''

Leo Arnim swallowed hard.

''You killed her to eliminate threats of exposure about your flight south. You tried to kill Jordan too, because you were afraid he knew or might learn the truth, but you got Cambreau by mistake.''

Arnim took a backward step, his upper lip curled in. His eyes were bitter. ''That's a lie! I did not kill the Ford girl and I never saw Cambreau in my life.''

''We know that,'' put in Boyce. ''You shot him through a door.''

''How about that threatening note your waiter shoved under Jordan's plate.'' It was Nola now, ganging up on him.

Arnim shook his head stiffly. His eyes were flat. ''I want my lawyer.''

That was all he would say. They couldn't shake another word out of him. Boyce had him taken away. Lohman went out to talk to the reporters. I glanced at Nola, but his eyes were staring at some distant horizon, brooding, lost in thought. I seemed to have been forgotten.

I went out and down to the street and began walking. My head felt heavy and my muscles were intolerably weary. I had covered only two blocks when a man fell into step beside me and touched my arm. It was Floyd Dillon.

"I'd like a word with you, Jordan." He sounded worried.

"I'm listening," I said.

"About the Pernot case—I think we ought to come to some sort of an agreement——"

"Sure," I said. "You want to settle. I don't blame you. That Las Vegas decree isn't worth the paper it's written on. Ivy was never a bona fide resident of Nevada. Arnim was never personally served, nor did he ever submit to the jurisdiction of the court. I can have the whole thing set aside. Ivy's marriage to James Pernot is invalid and Quimby's claim to the estate isn't worth a sneeze in hell."

He coughed uncertainly. "Well, now, I'm not so sure——"

"Listen,". I said promptly, "I'm anxious to get out of town. I'm tired and sick to death of this whole thing. I want to get far away from it. Let's go over to my office and call our respective clients. I can't promise anything because Karen Pernot hates Quimby. On the other hand, setting aside the divorce and invalidating Pernot's marriage would take a lot of time and money. If you can get Quimby to settle for ten per cent, I'll try to convince my client to accept the offer."

He didn't like it. He'd been seeing a swollen fee. He took a long time, thinking. Then discretion advised him to make the best of a bad deal.

I said, "As a matter of fact, even ten per cent will amount to a fairly large figure."

"You don't leave me much choice," he said glumly. "All right, I agree."

We went directly to my office and got settled. I rang Karen Pernot and told her the story and after batting it around for a while she gave me the green light. The long delay if she failed to negotiate was what finally persuaded her. I handed the phone to Dillon and he dialed the Marvin and spoke to Olga. Quimby, she said, had gone down for a moment but would call us back and he gave her the number.

"This calls for a drink," I said sociably, sitting back and reaching out my copy of Shakespeare and extracting the bourbon from its hollow interior. I got two glasses and poured and proffered one to Dillon, smiling affably. "No need for bad blood," I said. "With me married to Dulcy and you to Vivian, I suppose we'll be some sort of in-laws."

As we lifted our glasses the phone rang. I lowered my glass and replaced it with the mouthpiece of the instrument. "Hello," I said.

"Mr. Dillon?" It was Eric Quimby's voice.

I held out the handset and he took it with his free hand. "Hello, Quimby," he said soberly. "I called to explain about some new developments. I am not going to upbraid you for concealing certain——" He stopped short and looked up and the phone fell out of his hand, clattering to the floor.

There was a frightened look in Floyd Dillon's eyes. He was still holding the empty glass, clenching it. There was a crunching sound and the glass shattered like powder, and his fingers began to bleed. His face turned blue and a violent spasm shook his body. His eyes were bulging horribly and his tongue stuck out, swollen and discolored.

"Dillon!" I cried hoarsely. "For God's sake, what is it?"

He didn't answer. His neck went rigid and he grabbed it with both hands, lifting himself half out of the chair. Then he uttered a gurgling sound and pitched forward, sprawling onto the floor.

I was on my feet. I looked down at my glass and jerked my hand away. I stooped over Dillon with my palm against his chest. The beat was there, but seemed to be ebbing fast. His features remained distorted, but the convulsions had stopped and he was an inert mass.

I hefted him over my shoulder and staggered into the hall, jabbing at the elevator button until the car arrived. In no time at all I was in the street and dumping him into a taxi. "Hospital," I yelled at the driver.

He was a good man. He tore a hole through traffic with one hand on the horn and never took it off until we were at the emergency entrance.

"Poison," I snapped at the intern. "About fifteen minutes ago."

He didn't even feel for a pulse. Those lads learn to work fast. "Stomach pump," he said crisply to a nurse. "Emergency. Let's go." They wheeled Dillon away.

I was alone then, with all the strength out of me, drained. I walked on caving knees to the lobby and called Nola and then went back to the waiting room.

Presently the intern appeared. He was back too soon, it seemed, and I was afraid. I looked up at him. "Gone?"

"Nope." The intern was very young. He smiled. "Dr. Preisic is handling it. We've got him cleaned out and I think he'll make it."

"What was it?"

"Cyanide. I'll need some information for the law."

"It's already done," I said. "They're on their way now."

He nodded and settled for a few routine answers.

"Anything I can do?" I asked.

He shook his head. "We're giving him stimulants and oxygen now. It's touch and go but I think he'll lick it." He went away confidently.

After a while Nola found me and pulled up a chair. Strain had cut white lines around his mouth and his jaw was set. I told him the whole story.

He sucked in his lips. "Any ideas?"

"Who knows? Anybody could have got into my office. Clients, the cleaning woman, the building super, my own secretary." I shivered. "I had a drink of that stuff to my mouth when the phone rang. That's the second time I was saved, literally, by the bell."

He nodded. "You look like hell. Let yourself go, shake a little. What are they doing with Dillon?"

"The usual, stomach pump, stimulants——"

"Any chance?"

"They think so, but cyanide is deadly stuff and anything may happen."

"Cyanide, eh?" A questioning frown dented his brow. "Where's the bottle?"

"My office. On the desk."

He regarded me queerly. "The cleaning woman been there yet?"

"I don't think so," I said, missing the point. "Why?"

His eyes hardened. "She's liable to walk in there and spot that bottle and take a pull at it herself. Where's a phone? The hell with it! I'll go over there myself." He clamped his hat over his head and ducked out swiftly.

I sat there for a long time, waiting for news and thinking. Footsteps whispered past in the corridor. Somewhere a woman groaned. A nurse came in and looked at me. But I sat there, and a pressure began to build up inside me, like steam in a boiler, until there was an actual ache in my chest. I got up, stiff-legged, and went down to the street.

· 27 ·

Vivian came to the door in an evening dress of spun silver, her hair brushed loose over her shoulders, black and lustrous, her figure striking and strong. Surprise flitted across her eyes.

"Why, Scott!" she exclaimed. "I was expecting Floyd. Come on in."

A chrome cocktail shaker, a bowl of cracked ice, bottles, and two long, gleaming glasses were ready. She put me in a chair and tipped her head appraisingly.

"You're glum tonight, Scott. What's wrong? Have a scrap with Dulcy?"

I shook my head and looked down at my hands. "Get a grip on yourself, Vivian. I have some unpleasant news."

The smile died and her eyes widened. "Has . . . what is it?"

"Dillon," I said quietly. "He's in the hospital."

Her mouth quivered and she looked down at me, stricken. "An accident!" It was almost a moan. "Oh, God, is he— is he——"

"No," I said. "Take it soft, Vivian, it could be worse. He's not dead—he's sick, very sick, but he's in good hands and coming along."

She sank into a chair and steadied a trembling lip with her teeth. After a moment, she said, "I'm all right now. How bad is he? What happened?"

"Poison," I said simply. "Cyanide."

Her eyes jumped open.

"He was with me when he drank it. He was almost gone in the twinkling of an eye, but I managed to get him to a hospital and they pumped him clean and he has better than a fifty-fifty chance."

"Poison!" she whispered. "But why, Scott, why? Where did he get it?"

"From my office bottle. I gave it to him."

She swallowed hard, leaning forward.

I said, "We were about to settle the Pernot case and I gave him a drink to celebrate. I missed a dose myself by the grace of God and a streak of luck. Otherwise, we might be lying up there in my office now, dead, the both of us."

She came fluidly to her feet. "What hospital? I'm going to him."

"No. Not now, Vivian. Later perhaps. There's nothing you can do and they wouldn't let you see him anyway; he's still unconscious. Sit down. You're white as chalk, Vivian. Better have a drink. I don't want you passing out on me."

She went over to the servette and poured herself a long drink. She stood there, her back to me, while a quiver seemed to shake her body. Then she turned and smiled wanly and put the drink down her throat. She came back and stood near me.

"You look pretty bad yourself, Scott. It must have been

a dreadful ordeal. There's some bourbon on the table. Help yourself."

I did need a drink. I needed one badly. It wouldn't help much, but I went over and poured one and brought it back to the chair and sat down, holding it in my hand.

She moistened her lips. "How did Floyd happen to be in your office at this hour?"

"We met at Headquarters. Things boiled over tonight. The D.A. just arrested Leo Arnim and charged him with the murder of Verna Ford."

She gaped at me. "Leo Arnim?"

I nodded. "It seems she recognized him as the missing witness. He'd been a passenger on that plane from Miami. Arnim is an ex-convict and he'd broken parole to fly south. That meant he could be sent back to prison and Verna was putting the bite on him. They say he killed her because he was afraid she'd talk."

"Then he . . . he killed Bob too."

I shrugged. "So the D.A. claims. I doubt it."

Her thin eyebrows made a wavering line. She was watching me, her eyes restless.

I said, "I've thought it all out, Vivian, and I believe I know the truth. I'll tell you." I inhaled and lifted the glass and took a mouthful of bourbon and tossed my head back. I looked at her and let my lips pull into a stiff grin. She put her fingers to her throat and beads of moisture condensed on her forehead and I saw her upper lip twitch a little.

Suddenly I held up the glass and gave it a petrified stare. I lurched to my feet and the glass bounced on the floor and rolled away. I held my breath. I held it until my lungs ached. I kept on holding it and I felt the blood pounding into my face. I could see my face in the mantel mirror across the room. I saw it grow dark and blue and distorted. My knees wavered and I began to sway.

Vivian stood tautly, her knuckles pushed into her mouth, between her teeth. There was a deep rumbling in my head and my ears roared. I staggered toward her and she shrank back with a frightened gasp. A hoarse animal noise got strangled in my throat and I reeled drunkenly. I crashed against a chair. Then I floundered against the window, clutching at the drapes, and they came down in a rending tear as I tumbled to the floor, writhing under them. Then I lay limp and quiet.

Silence. The minutes dragged on leaden feet. No sound at all except her raggedly harsh breathing. Time was suspended.

Then I heard her heels click across the floor, heard her pick up the phone. She said in a cool, normal voice, "Hello . . . Superintendent, please . . . Mr. Crowley? How are you? This is Mrs. Cambreau in 604 . . . Will you do me a favor, please? I'm on my way to the country tomorrow, first thing in the morning, and I want to pack. Would you get my trunk from the storage room? The large one, please, and thank you so much."

I lay very quiet, hardly breathing. She moved about quietly. A glass tinkled. Presently the bell rang and she went out of the room to answer the door.

"You're very sweet, Mr. Crowley." The words drifted in to me. "Just leave it right here in the foyer. That's all right. I can manage. And thank you again." The door closed. The latch clicked. The chain guard slid into its notch.

There was a scraping noise. She was dragging the trunk into the living room. And then she was standing over me and the window drape wandered off my face as she tugged it loose. The tip of her shoe tested my ribs. She laughed briefly, a short, unpleasant laugh.

"Your streak of luck ran out, my friend," she said nastily. "Oh, you had it coming all right. You had it coming for a long time. I was afraid of you from the first moment. The police were dull, but you, my friend, you were the real danger. Now you can rot in hell where you belong."

Her fingers were icy against my neck as they curled around my coat collar and she began to drag me along the floor. She was incredibly strong.

The phone shrilled. She tensed and stood listening to it. She went away and I heard her talking. "Yes, this is Mrs.

Cambreau . . . I understand, Nurse . . . You say he's conscious and that he asked you to call me and say he's all
right. Thank you. You're very kind.''

She came back into the room and walked around to the
trunk and stopped dead. Her face went a blotchy, smeared
white. A scream froze solid in her hung jaw. Her eyes raced
frantically around the room and then she saw me.

I was sitting comfortably on the couch, knees crossed,
smoking a cigarette. I blew a gray plume into the air.

She shrank back, gave a whimper, and began to shake.

"On the contrary, Vivian," I said. "My luck hasn't run
out at all.''

"The liquor," she croaked.

"In the drape, where I spit it out. You're losing your
touch, baby. That was a clumsy gesture you made with the
bourbon. You were in too much of a hurry—too desperate.
That's not good. The delicate art of murder calls for a fine
touch and careful planning. I rather hurried you, didn't I?''

Her mouth drooled open and the juncture of her jaw began
to twitch crazily.

"I feel proud," I said. "That was a pretty good imitation
of a man being poisoned. But then why not? I just saw Floyd
Dillon go through the same thing. Only he wasn't acting.''

Her eyes were bleak.

I said stonily, "Tonight while I was in the hospital, I
thought of something Nola once said: that a girl had been
deliberately poisoned and a man killed by mistake. He was
talking about Verna and Bob. And the thought struck me
that maybe he was wrong, maybe it was the other way
around. Maybe a girl was killed by mistake and a man
deliberately murdered. And the more I thought about it, the
more the idea appealed to me.

"Everything fitted so neatly. All the little inexplicable
pieces suddenly popped into place. Verna never brought
that brandy with her. You brought it to my apartment because you knew it was Bob's favorite drink, and you knew
he'd go for it the instant he saw it. You knew too—from
what Dillon told you about the divorce raid—that my door

would be open. The fact that Bob might have a drinking party with Verna never fazed you in the slightest. Two people would die. So what? There's lots of people in the world. But you didn't figure on Bob. He went and got drunk somewhere else and never showed up and your whole scheme collapsed.''

Her mouth stretched down and she took a trembling breath. "No, Scott, that's not true. You don't know what you're saying. I had no reason to kill Bob. He was giving me a divorce and he'd made a generous settlement——''

"Which you promptly lost on the stock market. You didn't want Bob, but you didn't want a divorce either. What you wanted was his money. And the best way to get it was to kill him while he was your husband.''

"Scott—listen——''

"No," I said harshly. "You listen. What can you say after trying to kill me right here in this room? What were you going to do with the trunk, darling? Drop it in a mountain lake? Bury it in the country? Not a bad idea, but not original. Not as clever as shooting Bob through a closed door so it would look like he'd been killed by mistake. That showed real virtuosity. Yes, in some ways you were pretty good. How did you get him into my office? It doesn't matter, really. You got him there and it was ingenious and you had the lot of us fooled. You simply walked into the building, climbed the stairs, tapped on the door, and when Bob sauntered over you gave it to him, right through the glass. Where is the gun, Vivian? Did you get rid of it yet?''

Her eyes burned feverishly. She did not speak.

"That was taking advantage of the trouble raised by the Pernot case. Chalk one up for you, baby. And that note, threatening me if I didn't drop the case. A fine red herring. You had it ready in your purse all the time, intending to drop it into my pocket. But then those drunks at the Magic Lamp had a fight and drew everybody's attention and you grabbed the opportunity to slip it under my tray. Poor Leo! He thought somebody was trying to cross him. He played right into your hands by taking it away from me." I shook

my head contemptuously. "But that other business—the
picture of the coffin—that was corny, darling. You must
have really been worried. It didn't fit in at all and you should
have known it wouldn't scare me worth a damn."

She was crouching against the trunk, haggard and a thousand years old and not beautiful any more at all. Her lips
were curled in, leaving her teeth naked and white. It gave
her a predatory look. She found her voice.

"You poor stupid fool!" she said quickly. "You're only
guessing. You could never prove it."

"You think not, baby? Wait till you hear what a good
prosecutor can do with it. There are other things too. That
day you came to my office and asked me to handle Bob's
estate, you saw where I kept my liquor and you had plenty
of time to fix me a cyanide highball. I was getting too close,
wasn't I, and you were beginning to be afraid of me. Were
you wearing gloves that day? Probably not. I don't remember. The police are checking the bottle now for prints. And
wait till my secretary tells the story to a jury . . . the motive—the opportunity——"

Her hands flew up to her throat. "I didn't. I didn't. You're
lying——"

"Am I? And speaking of gloves, where is the mate to
that lilac glove you dropped in my apartment the afternoon
you went there to plant the brandy. Until now I thought it
belonged to Verna, because I never suspected another woman
of having been there. But she was wearing a green outfit
that day and not even Verna's taste was bad enough for a
combination like that. But you, my dear, you were wearing
orchid when I saw you in Dillon's apartment that first night.
Those colors match fine. Orchid and lilac. Is the glove still
here? Will the police find it when they arrive in a few
minutes?"

"The police!" she whispered.

"Sure. What did you expect? They're on their way up
now."

She drew herself up straight, her eyes abnormally bright,
and shining like a cat's eyes, and she steadied herself against

the trunk. She couldn't hold it. Suddenly her face broke and she put out her hands tragically. Her voice trailing the end of a long breath was thin and urgent.

"Don't do this to me, Scott. You can fix it. It isn't too late. Save me. I'll give you anything you want. Bob left more money than we could ever spend. You can have most of it. Only save me——"

"Nothing doing," I said roughly. "I have to live with myself. Besides I couldn't trust you."

"You can, Scott, you can——"

I shook my head. "No. You've killed and you'll kill again. You have the taste of blood. It would never do to have anyone know your secret and stay alive. I want to be able to sleep."

Her face was upraised, streaked. "I'll go away, Scott. I'll leave the country. I'll do anything you say. Have pity——"

"By God," I laughed harshly. "That's rich. You killed my friend and you just tried to kill me and now you have the gall to stand there and ask me for pity. Nothing doing, my friend, not a chance. You're going to stand trial and you're going to the chair. They don't like to execute women in this state but they've done it. Stand still, Vivian. Don't move. I don't want you destroying that bottle of bourbon. That's going to be the clincher. Wait till the prosecutor holds it up to the jury and shows how you tried to poison me. Your third victim. And how you got the super to bring up a trunk to get rid of the body. You'll look damn funny with that rich black hair of yours shaved to the skull and the electrodes against your bare scalp. It's not a bad way to die, Vivian, no worse than poison or bullets. The worst part is knowing that it's coming and waiting for it. Verna and Bob never knew. They were lucky. And it doesn't take long. Two thousand volts that knock you against the straps and turn you black——"

"Stop it!" she screamed, her lips twisted.

"You killed Bob, didn't you?" I said relentlessly.

"Yes, yes, I killed him. I hated him. I always hated him.

All I ever wanted was his money. But the price of living with him was too high. You can't imagine what it was like." She moved toward me, wringing her hands. "Give me a chance, Scott, please. You can swing it."

"What happened to your nerve, Vivian?" I demanded remorselessly. "You've already killed two people."

She was very close to me now. "He drove me. He was getting impatient, pressing me to go to Reno. I had to do something. I'd lost all my money. I was confused. I didn't know what I was doing."

"How did you get him into my office?"

She was like a person drowning. "I rang his club and left a message for him to wait there."

"But you were confused," I echoed sarcastically. "You didn't know what you were doing. How do you think that explanation will sound to a jury?"

Her fingers plucked frenziedly at my sleeve. "I won't let them take me. Help me, Scott——"

I tore my arm free. "Like hell! What shall I say to the cops?"

"There's Leo Arnim," she said in a desperate gush of words. "The police think he did it. He's only a gangster. Nobody will miss him."

"No. Arnim doesn't deserve my sympathy but I'm certainly not going to stand by and see him burn for a murder you committed. I have my conscience, such as it is."

She clutched at my hands, her breathing shredded and torn. "We were always friends, Scott. How can you be so ruthless?"

"Ruthless?" I sneered. "That's a laugh. That's just like a killer—giving no quarter and then begging for pity and mercy and compassion. Ruthless? What were you thinking when you fixed my drink a little while ago? Was it tenderness, an abiding love, a desire to shield me from this evil world? And you talk about being ruthless."

She backed away, her face working, the muscles jerking the features awkwardly out of shape. "You must believe me, Scott. I saw the moment you walked in that you knew what happened and I was frightened. I got panicky.''

"Were you panicky when you poisoned my office bottle? What do you take me for, an imbecile?"

She pried her teeth away from her bottom lip, leaving it flecked red and the only color in her face. She said with desperation, "There's the money, Scott—so much money——"

And then I stuck it to her. The *coup de grâce*. The finishing touch. I laughed. A short, derisive laugh.

"The money," I said, leering. "Yes, there's the money. Of course. But I'm going to get it anyway. For you see, my pet, Bob's money will go to Dulcy. She's his cousin. And I'm going to marry Dulcy."

Her pupils darkened and dilated. Her nostrils flared. I have never seen so much terror and hatred in a look. Then she whirled and raced through the bedroom. I did not move. I did not try to stop her. I heard the bathroom door bang shut and the latch click. There was a finality to it, like turning the last page of a book.

I stood motionless. My face felt brittle, as if it would crack like old parchment if I even moved my mouth. I did not smile. There was no smile in me. I stood with my head cocked in a listening attitude.

And then I heard it. A soft thump. The noise a body would make in falling.

I do not know how long I stood there after that, but presently I became aware that the bell was ringing. I went to the door and opened it and stared out at Nola. His eyes moved past my shoulder into the apartment, then jumped back to mine. They were cold and searching and as hard as stone.

"How did you know?" I asked as he came in.

"I got to thinking about it," he said, "and every time I asked myself a question I came up with the same answer." He nodded at the trunk. "Looks like she was getting ready to pull out."

"She's pulled out already," I said quietly.

His eyes grew icy. "You let her go?"

"Only as far as the bathroom. She's in there now."

He pivoted sharply and strode through the bedroom and twisted the knob. He struck the panels with his knuckles. But of course there was no answer. His head came slowly around and his face was tired. "All right," he said tonelessly. "I'm listening."

"Probably cyanide," I said. "The same stuff Dillon got. She didn't seem to have much trouble getting that sort of thing. I don't know what she tried to give me, but——"

"You?"

"Yeah. Just before you got here. The moment she saw my face she knew the jig was up and she spiked a drink and gave it to me. I strung along and made believe I'd swallowed it. I went through the whole act, convulsions, blue face, everything, then I toppled and she thought I was dead. That's what the trunk's for; she had it brought up so that she could dump me into it. But I stood up and scared her witless."

His mouth drooped. "Why the elaborate act?"

"Because all I had, actually, was only a theory. Sure, you could have built it up and put a foundation under it and tied the pieces together and made a case out of it, but by then she'd have pulled herself together and hired a clever lawyer and who knows what would have happened. There was Lohman to reckon with, and the weakness of a jury when a pretty face and a dimpled knee is at stake. I wanted to crack her shell, to break her morale, to make her talk while she was still unstrung. I didn't know she was going to try to poison me until I saw her fumbling with the bottle. Okay, so it was a grandstand play, but it worked."

"It worked," he said blankly. "Why? Because she went in there and knocked herself off?"

I shrugged heavily. "The state has no beef. It would have spent a lot of money to prosecute her. And in the end they could not have done any more to her than she has already done to herself."

His eyes were condemning. "You drove her to it. You made her do it. You had no right, Jordan. Who the hell do you think you are, God?"

I did not say anything.

He moved back and then lunged against the door and it shuddered under the impact. The third shock splintered the latch and the door sprang open. One look was enough for him. I did not look at all. He went over to the telephone and made a call to Headquarters and came back and hinged himself on the edge of the chesterfield. He lit one of his thin, dappled cigars and blew a pale lungful of smoke into the air. When he spoke his voice sounded empty.

"I wouldn't be surprised if you deliberately needled her into it so you wouldn't have to wait around a couple of months as a witness."

I said, "It's a consideration that might have carried weight had I thought of it."

He squinted at me searchingly. "Maybe you didn't want to subject that girl friend of yours to a long-drawn-out family scandal."

I made no comment.

He was lost in thought, then he shrugged. "What's done is done." He waved his cigar. "Arnim did a lot of talking. He's trying to get into the good graces of his parole officer. He admitted ringing you the first night and trying to scare you off. He'd heard about Verna's death and he was afraid she'd gone to see you and given you some hint about what she had on him. Everything he did after that was motivated by his fear of being connected with Ivy and leading to the discovery that he'd broken his parole. A funny thing—he might have gotten permission to leave the state if he had applied, but he was afraid to ask, and he didn't figure on being away more than twenty-four hours. It looked safe. And he was just crazy enough about his ex-wife to take the chance."

"Did you talk to Quimby?"

"Yeah. We hauled him down and he leaked information like a straw roof. You remember that diamond tiepin we found on Verna?"

I nodded.

"She got it from Quimby. She led him a merry dance, always on his neck for money. He found it in Pernot's house."

I said, "She was collecting from everybody. Well, that seems to tie it up, except for Cambreau's friendship with Verna."

"Let's say he picked her up at Dillon's office. She simply never connected him with the divorce when she walked into your apartment to be a corespondent."

It sounded logical and probably as near to the truth as we'd ever get. Outside a police siren keened sharply into the night, gathering intensity and then dying like the wail of a sick cat. John Nola smiled sadly.

I picked up my hat and said, "You don't need me. I'm going home. Tell the boys you trapped her and she raced into the bathroom and swallowed the stuff before you could stop her. You figured most of this out for yourself and you may as well take the credit anyway. Hell, I'm not in the department and it can't do me any good."

He watched me put on my hat, his dark eyes steady and brooding, and he made no move to stop me. I went out and down to the street just as a loaded squad car piled up to the door and disgorged its cargo of technicians. Behind it came the old, dispirited dead wagon. I stood there and watched the boys debark and go around to the rear to slide out the long wicker basket.

I walked through the park. The night was clear again and the pale moon was like an open porthole against an endless black bulkhead. I shook my head as if I could knock the memories out but it wasn't that easy. I seemed to be walking on joints that had been loosely bolted by a careless mechanic. I became aware that my mouth was open and that I was breathing like a middle-aged suburbanite chasing the 7:45 on a full stomach.

On a Friday night two weeks later, I was standing at a window of the St. George in Bermuda. It was only three hours by Pan American Clipper and yet New York seemed worlds away. The fading sun sent a spray of washed gold through the curtains. The air was warm and fragrant and the sky was a purple bruise where it struck against the sea. It was a fabulous sight, but I turned away from it and looked at the large, soft bed. Dulcy moved her head on the pillows.

"Let's get married, darling," she said.

I laughed. "That plane ride must have jolted your memory, baby. We were married this morning."

"Oh! Then come to bed."

I went over and she curled her arms around my neck and pulled me down. "Scott, how many children do you think we ought to have?"

"Two would be just right," I said. "But we'll probably have about fourteen."

She gasped. "So many!"

"It can't be helped, baby. I have insomnia."

She hid her face in my neck, nuzzling there. After a moment, she asked, "What are you thinking about, darling?"

"How everything wound up according to schedule," I said. "Dillon settling the Pernot case with Quimby getting the short end. Leo Arnim sent back to Sing Sing to finish his stretch. Janeiro caught and slated for the chair. Karen Pernot getting herself a job singing at the Moonlight Terrace. And me getting you. And the sound of the surf lapping at the beach below."

A soft breeze fluttered the curtain. The room was growing dark. It was quiet and peaceful.

"Scott?"

"Yes."

"Does it rain much in Bermuda?"

Her hair was like silk between my fingers. "Why, baby?"

"Well, you remember what you said about spending our honeymoon in India during the monsoons because rain always made you so—so ardent——"

I began to laugh.

"I don't care," she whispered passionately. "I hope it rains all week."

I held her very tight.